I won the Lottery...

And then all hell broke loose!

ADAM MERTON

Copyright © 2021 Adam Merton

All rights reserved.

ISBN: 9781910811818

Also available as an e-book ISBN 9781910811801

Published by Hadleigh Books

www.hadleighbooks.co.uk

The rights of Adam Merton to be identified as the Author of the Work have been asserted by him in accordance with the Copyright, Designs and Patents Act 1988. A catalogue record for this book is available from the British Library.

No part of this book may be used or reproduced in any manner whatsoever, nor by way of trade or otherwise be lent, resold, hired out, or otherwise circulated in any form of binding or cover other than that in which it is published, without the publisher's prior written consent.

Whilst some of the people and places mentioned in this book do exist, all events and characters described in this book are purely fictional and any likeness to real events or people is purely coincidental. This book is a work of fiction.

CONTENTS

1	Money, money, money	1
2	In My Life	20
3	Changes	40
4	A New Beginning	59
5	Going up the Country	83
6	Don't you want me	103
7	End of the Beginning	126
8	Crazy City	145
9	The only way is Up	171
10	Moving On	196
11	New Life	216

1 MONEY, MONEY, MONEY

Most people dream of winning the lottery one day. They have all sorts of ideas of what they'd like to do with all the money, such as buying a flashy car or a large house, going on lots of holidays, telling their boss to get stuffed and quitting their job.

The thing is, it is not exactly like that in reality. How do I know? Well, the reason is that I was a lottery winner back in 2012, winning just over £11 million on the European Lottery. I know just what winning the Lottery means in reality. By the way, my name is Gary Whitemore. Not my real name of course but being in my position you make sure that you stay incognito to as many people as possible. Otherwise, you will have every Tom, Dick or Harry knocking at your door asking you for money, not to mention the tabloid press wanting to know every juicy bit of your private life. So, you become a hermit, not wanting to go out in case you are recognised.

Well, that is what some lottery winners who chose to go public have told me. I have tried to lead a quiet life and in the early days of my lottery win I told as few people as possible. It was difficult of course, trying to keep such a big secret and I was at the mercy of those I did tell not to let the cat out of the bag. It made me very paranoid I can tell you.

Since winning the lottery on that fateful day in February 2012, my life has changed considerably. Whilst you may think that it has been one big spending spree and a champagne lifestyle, the reality is that it has not really been like that at all.

Sure, I have spent some of my money on stupid things that I did not really need, but my life did change in many ways, though not necessarily for the better, with many ups and downs. In fact, to be brutally honest it has been both heaven some of the time, and hell at other times. That's because winning the lottery is not as simple as it seems. You may think that it involves being given an obscene amount of money and then your life changes for the better.

That's what I thought before all this happened, but nothing can prepare you for what happens. Like many people I thought winning the lottery would be a piece of cake with all sorts of good things happening to me. The truth is, it's nothing of the sort and that's mainly why I decided to write this book. If you are ever lucky enough to win the lottery, I hope that by reading this book you will not make the mistakes that I have made, and that your life after winning the lottery will be one of bliss and happiness, and not upset and stress. So read on and find out what life is like on the other side of a lottery win.

* * *

The day I found out that I had won the lottery was not the day the actual lottery took place, but in fact a few days later. You see I was busy with my job as a secondary school teacher, and I never ever checked my numbers so soon after the lottery draw had taken place. I usually waited until the weekend when I had some free time to myself.

I suppose like most people in this day and age, winning the lottery was a dream come true, but never in my wildest imaginings did I ever think I would be the lucky one. I had been doing the lottery on and off ever since it began. I had always imagined what I would do with all that money, but it was only me daydreaming and not expecting it to become reality. I honestly thought I would be doing my job teaching English to teenage children in a North of England comprehensive school until the day came when I retired. Yet the day I won the lottery would change all that for ever.

Would I say that it was the happiest day of my life? No. Not really. Perhaps the day I got married? Or the days my two children were born were really happier. I know that may surprise you but winning the lottery didn't all happen in one go with me, unlike many other lottery winners. They get their money then quit their jobs, go on exotic holidays, buy a mansion, splash out on flashy cars, and spend, spend, spend. For me though, it was not like that at all. Well, some of it was, which I will tell you in the course of this book.

The actual lottery life changing event for me was different. It was a gradual process which began with a whole lot of soul searching about whether I should go public or not, then ringing up the lottery people and finding out that I had definitely won, before the money was put into my bank account – a new account I would add. Then I had to go through the process of telling those close to me about it, and then going through all the various life changing things in my life to where I am today.

Whilst there have been some happy times in all of this, there have also been quite a few unhappy times as well. Was it life changing for me? Yes, definitely. Was it a good experience for me and my family? Not particularly. Only for some of the time, I can say with real honesty.

The problem with the lottery is that whilst it guarantees you lots of money, it doesn't necessarily guarantee you happiness. Sure, you don't have money worries ever again, but you do have money "thoughts" all the time, which I shall explain about later. In the meantime, let me go back to the day I found out that I had won the lottery.

* * *

It had been a busy week at school as usual and I had been rushed off my feet. It was February 2012. The week before, it had snowed quite heavily all over the North West of England and most of the schools in the region had been shut for three days from the Wednesday to the Friday. Although that meant no school and plenty of fun in the snow for all the children, for us teachers it meant that all the lessons we had prepared for those three days had to be rescheduled for the following week. As the head of the English Department, it had been my job to sort out this little problem.

Over those three days I had to work hard, rearranging lessons for most of the classes and the staff timetable as well for the following week. This meant three days of lessons had to be added somehow into the next week's lessons. Impossible of course! So, some of the lessons for that week inevitably got moved back a day or two into the following week to accommodate this. Something as insignificant as the lottery (or so I thought!) was the last thing on my mind.

I usually bought my tickets at the weekend; sometimes on the Saturday; sometimes on the Sunday. I preferred to play the European lottery on the Tuesday or the Friday, as opposed to the original lottery on the Wednesday or Saturday. I decided to go do this several years ago as the prize money was that much bigger. I didn't consider the fact that the odds of winning the European lottery are a lot less than the ordinary lottery. The experts reckon it is a 1 in 160 million chance of winning the European lottery. Whilst it is a 1 in 45 million chance for the ordinary lottery. However, I was influenced not only by the size of the potential jackpot, but also the fact that the lesser prizes seemed so much bigger than the ordinary lottery. Mind you I wasn't hankering over the massive European lottery jackpots that seem to be getting larger and larger as each year goes by. No, I would be quite happy with just a million pounds. What would *I* do with a £70 or even £100 million pound win? It seemed obscene to me to be given so much money in one go. I would be quite content with a million pounds, which would pay off the mortgage, as well as all my other debts and give me plenty of spare change to help my immediate family to be set up for the rest of their lives. That was all I ever wanted and hoped for.

By now I had decided that my chances of winning would be far greater if I stuck with the same numbers. I know a lot of people just go into their local shop and ask for a ticket for the next lottery draw, being given random numbers in the hope that these will be their gateway to a win on the lottery. I did that for many years, thinking the same thing. But then I decided my chances would be greater if I stuck with the same numbers. Which numbers did I choose? That's private, but like many people, the numbers I chose were based on things like people's birthdays and favourite numbers, and so on. After a while, when I got fed up with physically filling in a slip each time I went into my local newsagents, I got my newsagent to make up a printed slip with the numbers on. This made things much easier for me each time I wanted to play the lottery. All I had to do was hand over the slip with the numbers on and hand over the cash, and that was it. Well as long as I remembered to check the numbers of course!

Getting back to checking the numbers for the day I won the lottery. It was sometime on the Saturday evening that I finally got round to checking the numbers for both the Friday and the Tuesday draws. In fact, it was a type of ritual that I did sometime over each weekend, when things were a little quieter and I had some spare time. I usually did it upstairs in my bedroom as that is where I kept my wallet – on my bedside table – and inside the wallet was my lottery ticket. I wasn't being secretive as you might think. It was more a case of where my ticket was kept. I had a tablet which I carried round the house with me a lot of the time and that was where I looked up the numbers on.

I began to check the numbers. Straight away the first number drawn was one of mine. I didn't think too much about that. Then when two numbers matched, I thought that I would win a few quid. Then the third number matched, and then the fourth. My heart started racing. That could be a few hundred pounds at least – as long as the bonus balls were the same as mine of course. Slowly I looked at the fifth number and yes it was yet another one of mine. My heart was now pounding and I knew that I had definitely won quite a bit of money. Several thousand I guessed. That would come in really helpful; but not really life changing. All I needed was for the bonus balls to be the same. I knew them off by heart as they were connected to the dates of my birthday – 4 and 6. It was as though everything was going in slow motion as I began to look to see what the two bonus numbers were. Yes! They were a 4 and a 6! I couldn't believe it. Could I really have matched all five balls, plus the two bonus ones as well?

I immediately went through the winning numbers again in disbelief and no they hadn't changed. They were the same as the ones on my ticket. My brain went into overdrive as all the different permutations of what I could do with my life now I was a lottery winner. 'Hold on a minute!' I thought. 'If you have won the lottery, just how much have I won?' I pressed the prize breakdown button and looked. It read, "UK cash prize fund - £11, 286,733.21". My heart began to beat even faster than before. I looked to the left of this where it said, "Prize per winner - £11, 286, 733, 21". Immediately I realised that I must be the only winner in the UK. Finally, I looked to the left of that where it said, "UK Winners" and right underneath this was a single number "1", which confirmed this. I had actually done all this in just a couple of seconds, but like a minute ago, everything seemed to be happening in slow motion.

So here I was a lottery winner, and I just couldn't believe it. I lay back on the bed and looked up at the ceiling. Everything was spinning. So, I sat up again and carefully put my ticket back inside my wallet and tried to think. My first thought was 'I must tell my wife Tracy'. But then I thought, 'Hold on! What if she starts telling everyone; like her brother and his wife, and her friends, and the neighbours?' All hell would break loose, and I definitely didn't want that. I knew I must take all this very slowly and not rush into doing something that I would later regret. Then I opened my mind to all sorts of scenarios about what I was going to do next.

I always knew in my mind that if I ever won the Lottery, I wouldn't want publicity and now I firmly knew that was the course of action that I wanted to take. However, I did feel quite strongly that I wanted to think about all of this first before I told anyone. Plus, it hadn't actually been confirmed yet that I had won the lottery. I still had to ring up the lottery people to check that I really had won.

'I could call them up now, I suppose,' I thought, but then I thought, 'I need to sleep on this, first.' I was one of those people who always tried to think things through, before rushing into something. That was part and parcel of who I happened to be as a person. So, I tried to forget all that had happened in the past few minutes as I went back downstairs to Tracy and the distraction of the evening news on the TV.

I tried to act normally as if nothing had happened, but it was very difficult. Tracy made some casual conversation about something or other and I just answered, 'Yes' or 'No' to her comments, not really listening. All the time my mind was on something else – the lottery and what it meant to me.

'You're not really listening, Gary,' Tracy said after several sentences.

'Yes I am,' I replied. 'You're talking about Susie's new dress.'

At least I had taken in that piece of trivia and it stopped her questioning me. She was about to go on, but the 10 o'clock news started and we both started to concentrate on that.

My yawning at the conclusion of the news was a sign for us to go to bed. So, we both went up soon after that, but I knew I wouldn't sleep.

In fact, that first night after finding out that I had won the lottery, was one of the worst night's sleeps in my life ever. Although Tracy went out like a light, I just could not switch off. My first thought was, 'Is it really true? Could I really have won the lottery? 'Did my numbers really come up?' and 'Why Me? Surely I didn't deserve to win the lottery?' In a way I felt guilty about it, for I was going to be a rich man for the rest of my life - if I was sensible about it. To be honest, having lots of money went against all my working class, socialist upbringing.

The working man was on earth to do just that...work for the rich and get little reward. If he was lucky, he might be able to buy his council house, as my father did in the eighties. But life for most of us was always going to be the 9 to 5, with some respite at the weekends like going down the pub or club or watching the football or horses and possibly winning a little bit of money if you were lucky. What would my dad think of it all if he were here now?

Then there was the question of who I should tell. Obviously, Tracy would be the first person of course, but what about my children, Lesley, and Jon, who were both away at University? Would it upset their studies if they knew, and would they start telling their friends and then it would all over social media? Nightmare!

Next on the list of who to tell was my brother Alan and his wife Sue who I knew I could trust. What about my sister though? Definitely not my sister, Dawn! She was rich enough anyway and didn't need any of my newfound money. Then there was Tracy's brother Barry and his wife, Jill. He had become a good friend over the years, and we often went out socially together. Finally, what about my cousins and my nephews and nieces? Just where would I draw the line? No wonder I couldn't sleep!

I next had the thought that if I did tell all of them, would they keep it a secret? I suppose the more people you told, the greater the likelihood of other people finding out. Then would you get people knocking on my front door saying they'd heard I had won the lottery, and could they have a piece of my newfound wealth? I really didn't want that to happen. What should I do? I tossed and turned even more.

I was tempted to get up after about half an hour of tossing and turning and go and check the numbers once more. I still couldn't believe it and kept thinking that I might have made a mistake. I knew if I got up that this would disturb Tracy. If she woke up and saw that I wasn't in bed, she would want to know why I had got out of bed and gone downstairs to go on the computer.

I really wasn't ready to tell her just yet, I suppose. As usual I was putting off the fateful moment. I knew I would have to tell her sooner or later, but the question was "when?" I guess I was afraid that when and if I told her, she would no doubt scream and then start telling the whole world. That was my biggest fear - other people knowing.

As I struggled to settle down to sleep, I affirmed in my mind that I was quite sure and quite determined that I wanted as few people as possible to know about it. I also was sure in my mind that I did not want to go public with the lottery people. I had heard lots of horror stories about lottery winners who had gone public. Not only had they been pestered to death by the media, especially the tabloids, but also the general public had inundated them with begging letters. Then there were members of their own family and their friends who no doubt would be asking them for handouts. That was just one the many thoughts that was going through my mind. Just who was I going to tell?

Next thing in my thoughts was the question of just who of my family and friends I would give a portion of my newfound winnings to? And 'how much' should I give them? The question, 'How much?' would come to haunt me for the next few years as you shall see. I knew that the amount that it said I had won was just over £22 million, shared with one other winner. But would I have to pay tax on that? They did in the USA. Would it be the same in the UK? I really didn't know.

Apart from the question of how much should I keep and how much I should distribute to friends and family, there was also the question of whether I should give some of it to charity, seeing as there was much more than I would ever need? Maybe the lottery people would be able to advise me of all these questions? But as I hadn't made the phone call to claim my half of the jackpot, I would have to wait for the answer to that. 'When would I make that call?' was another question that went round in my mind. Should I do it before I'd told Tracy? Or wait until after? Perhaps it might be better to wait until I'd spoken to them, so I had a better picture of how things stood?

I tossed and turned some more. If only there was someone who I could speak to about this. Someone who wouldn't blurt out the news or ask me to give them some of the winnings? The obvious choice was Tracy, but I did feel that I should see what the lottery people said before I told her. Then a thought suddenly came into my head. There was one person who fitted all these criteria and that was my mum. She was the one person who I always went to or rang up when I had I problem that I couldn't sort out with Tracy. She would be the perfect person to speak to. I resolved to go and see her the next day. It would be quite easy to do without raising any suspicions, seeing as Tracy was going round to her friend Jane's for a natter. With this comforting thought in my head, I then went to sleep.

When I finally woke up the next morning Tracy had already got up. When I looked at the clock it was after 10 o'clock, which was pretty late for me. Then it all came back to me. I had won the lottery! I was first jubilant and then depressed all within the space of a few seconds. All the questions and fears about it all suddenly came rushing back into my thoughts. Then I remembered my plan to go and see my mum. But first I went downstairs, and Tracy's first words were, 'You had a bad night last night? I've been up for nearly an hour. You were dead to the world when I got up. Is there something on your mind?'

'I just couldn't get to sleep last night. Too much thinking about school I think,' I replied. That seemed to answer her questions and then she went on about something on the news, before reminding me about going round to her friend Jane's that afternoon. I threw in my notion of going round to mums and she didn't blink an eyelid. So that was sorted. I knew mum would be happy to see me and after a quick phone call after breakfast to her, it all was sorted.

All morning I still kept thinking about everything to do with the lottery. I even started thinking that it would be OK to go public. Then I wouldn't have this burden of keeping secrets from other people. Certainly, I wouldn't have to worry about who to tell or who not to tell, but I knew deep down that it was a silly thing to do. Did I really want the world and his wife to know my business? Plus being a schoolteacher, going public would be a stupid thing to do with hundreds of pupils all knowing that a lottery winner was teaching them!

That was another thought on my mind – handing in my notice at school. I could quit my job just like that of course, but it would make one hell of a mess at school, with pupils not being able to have their lessons and teachers having to cover for me until a replacement could be found. I would end up with a lot of enemies at school if I did that. No. That was not the best course of action. I knew I definitely would quit my job, but I would give the proper length of notice, which at my school was a full term.

Then again, what would be my reason for leaving? Would I tell the head in my letter of resignation that I had won the lottery? Not in a million years. So, I started thinking about what I would say and began to think up stories that would sound both believable and convincing.

* **

Tracy went out soon after 2.00pm to visit her friend Jane. I left home about ten minutes later and within the hour I was pulling up outside the residential home in Leigh, where mum was a resident. She had been living there for over a year now after having a bad fall in her house. Although none of the family didn't like doing it, we knew that this was the best place for seeing as her balance was not that good and she was lonely all by herself in the house. I hoped to God that there was no one else visiting her, otherwise I would be even more on edge playing a waiting game, waiting for them to go. Usually, my sister and brother visited her during the week, but sometimes an old neighbour or friend might visit her on a Sunday.

When I got to her room, it was empty, so presumably she was in the residents' lounge. I walked along the corridor and found her there, chatting to some other residents. When she saw me, her face lit up and luckily, she made her excuses and we walked slowly back to her room. I got her into her bedside chair, and I sat on a smaller upright chair and started to talk to her. I was about to start to tell all about my lottery win when there was a knock on the door. It was one of the staff asking if I would like a cup of tea. I was about to say, 'No', but then thought better of it. It might sound rude, so I said, 'Yes. That'll be very nice'.

I continued to talk about minor things like Tracy, school and who had been to see her recently until the cup of tea arrived. Then I got down to business.

'Mum. I've got some important news to tell you. Only I would appreciate if you can keep it to yourself and keep it a secret.'

'Ah, a secret. That sounds interesting!' she said, sounding like it was game.

'Mum, I'm being serious here. It is very important that you do not tell a soul. Do you understand?' I was sounding like a schoolteacher almost!

'What's so important about it that you don't want me to tell anyone about it?' she enquired.

'Well, it's so important that even Tracy doesn't know yet.'

'You mean to tell me that you haven't even told your wife about this secret? I hope you're not having an affair, Gary?' she replied suspiciously.

Trust her to see something seedy in it all!

'No, I am definitely not having an affair, Mum. I'm much too busy at school for one', I half joked.

'Well, what is it that you put me first before your wife?'

'You will promise to keep it a secret?' I pushed her once more.

'Yes. I do promise', she replied getting exasperated.

I decided it was time to stop dithering and get on with it.

'Mum, strange as it seems, I found out yesterday that I won some money on the Lottery,' I admitted.

'You won some money on the Lottery? How much?' she questioned me.

She would be the first of many people to ask that question.

'A lot of money, mum' I paused to let it sink in.

'Several millions......'

'You mean you're a millionaire?'

'Yes mum. I am. Or at least I will be when I've got the money,

'Well, you can get me out of this place, then!' she replied.

I wasn't sure if she was joking or telling the truth.

'Of course, I will, mum,' I promised, though inwardly I knew this wouldn't be an option, as Dawn would never agree to it, and she'd find out about my lottery win.

'I came to you first as I'm really not sure what to do about it.' I confessed.

'Not sure what to do about it?' she half mocked me. 'Well, you were always one for dithering and not making your mind up'.

That was true. I had always been one for sitting on the fence and not making decisions.

'You take after your father, you do Gary. In fact, you're so like him in many ways.'

She still hadn't answered my question yet, so I pushed her slightly.

'Mum I'm being serious here. Do you think I should go public or try and keep it a secret as much as possible?'

'Go public? Not on your Nelly!' She always sounded so authoritative when she had an axe to grind.

'If you went public Gary, you'd have a hard time with no end of people pestering you for money. I've read about it happening so many times. No. Keep it quiet as much as you can. You deserve an easy life after all that hard work you've done over the years; what with all that studying and having a hard time teaching all those naughty teenagers over the years.'

I was instantly relieved as she had backed up what I had been thinking all along with her own outspoken viewpoint.

She continued, 'I take it you have rung the lottery people to check it's all true?'

'No mum. Not yet,' I confessed like a little boy.

'Well don't you think it's about time you made that phone call?'

'Yes mum. I'll do it now,' I said obediently.

I was more than a little worried that we could be interrupted again, so I went into her bedroom toilet and did the dirty deed. Well not in that sense! I was very nervous and made sure the toilet seat was firmly down and then sat down on it. Next, I got out that very important lottery ticket. Then I pressed the claims phone number into my mobile and waited....

* * *

So here I was, making that all important phone call to the lottery people. It made me more nervous than I had ever been in my life. I only had to wait seconds before someone picked up the call and asked me what I wanted. I nervously explained that I believed that I had won the European lottery for the previous Tuesday and waited for the lady's answer. After asking me for my name, address, and contact telephone number the receptionist asked me to say the numbers on my ticket and where I had bought it from. I spoke the numbers slowly and clearly so there would be no misunderstandings. She asked me to repeat them which made me doubt that it was all in vain, but this was to be doubly sure that I had got the correct numbers for that particular draw.

Finally, after all that agonising and lack of sleep and worry it was actually confirmed that I had won just over £11 million. To hear the words from the lottery representative over the phone was quite mind blowing.

'Congratulations Mr. Whitemore', she said. 'I can confirm that you have won a half share in last week's European Lottery jackpot of twenty two million, five hundred and seventy three thousand, four hundred and sixty six pounds.'

My heart suddenly started beating fast and I suddenly felt faint. I just could not take in what she had just told me. She proceeded.

'There were just two winners, a person from Italy and yourself. Your winnings come out as eleven million, two hundred and eighty-six thousand, seven hundred and thirty three pounds and twenty one pence'.

I still could not take it in. My head was spinning as a thousand different thoughts went through my mind. It was quite unbelievable, as I simply didn't comprehend the enormity of it all. I had all these questions going through my head, all at the same time. 'When will I get the money?' 'How will I get paid?' 'Will it be by cheque, like you see on the TV?' 'Or will it be transferred into my bank account or building society account?' Even the two hundred and eighty-six thousand pounds would have done me, but to get another £11 million on top of that, was way beyond anything that I could comprehend.

'I don't want publicity!' I suddenly blurted out, being very wary of letting the whole world know that I had won the lottery. This was something that had been going over in my mind over the previous few days and now I was quite sure about it.

'Certainly, Mr Whitemore,' she answered. 'You can be assured that we will carry out your wishes exactly as you want. If you are quite sure that you do not want publicity, I will make sure that is put into your claim details.'

'I'm quite sure,' I reiterated, my heartbeat going up a notch. That was the thing that scared me the most about winning the lottery – being pestered by all and sundry; all of them wanting their pound of flesh.

When I had composed myself, she told me that the next step would be to meet up with a representative from the lottery company to go over a few things. This would include learning about how I was actually going to be receiving all that money, and just bits of advice about coming to terms with having all that money in our lives.

Hearing this made me relax a little. I had often thought that you had to go and see them with your lottery ticket at their headquarters, but now I found out that they actually send someone round to your house to sort it all out. If you are worried about nosey neighbours wondering who that strange person coming round to your house is, you can meet up in neutral place like a local hotel, if you want. I wasn't too worried about the neighbours though, so I arranged for someone to come round to my house in person. As both Lesley and Jon were away at uni at that time, I knew that we shouldn't be disturbed in the house.

My only worry was that a friend or a relative might suddenly turn up on the doorstep unannounced. In the end I tried not to worry about that and just got on with it. The only problem for me was fitting it in. As it would take an hour or so and I couldn't really have time off work, it had to be the following weekend. Saturday was out though, seeing as I was going to see my team, Manchester City play at home on that day. So that left the coming Sunday as being the only time free that weekend. I told the receptionist my choice and she put that down in her notes. So, everything was now sorted, or rather the wheels had been put in motion at least. In the meantime, I had to tell Tracy…..

* * *

I put my lottery ticket carefully back into my wallet, got up and walked back into mum's room.

'Well?' she asked.

'Yes, I've done it Mum,' I answered.

'It's all confirmed. I *have* won the lottery. Eleven million and several hundred thousand pounds.' I had immediately forgotten the rest of the amount that I had won. What with all that there was to take in, it was hard to remember.

It didn't matter of course. The eleven million pounds was the important part.

'Well, I never!' said mum. 'To think that one of my children has become a millionaire! It doesn't sound right.'

'Mum!' I scolded her, but she didn't mean that I shouldn't be a lottery winner. Just that it was hard to take in.

'Please can you keep this to yourself?' I asked her again.

'There's one or two people that I have to tell like Tracy and the children, but the less people know the better.'

'Of course, I'll keep this a secret, Gary,' she promised.

'But please don't go silly and all posh on me, will you?' she half pleaded.

'No mum, I won't,' I promised. 'I'm going to try and stay as normal as possible.'

We talked some more, but as it was getting on and Tracy would be home soon; I said I had to go. Mum asked me to visit her again in the near future and I promised I would. Then I was off, back into the car and driving home in the darkness that had appeared whilst I was in the Home.

As I drove home, I still had the burden on my mind of who to give money to and who not to give money to. I was in no doubt that whichever way I went, some of my friends and wider family would be offended and might never speak to me again. I tried to put myself in their shoes. If I heard that a cousin of mine had won £11 million on the lottery, would I be pleased for them, or jealous of them? Would I expect them to give me some of their money? Or would I just shrug my shoulders and think, if they do, fine; if they don't, fine again!

'Perhaps the advisor from the lottery might have some advice on that front' I thought.

Then I started to think, 'What if I did give some of my money to a cousin or a nephew for example and then they decide to put it out on Facebook or Twitter. The whole world would know about me in seconds! Maybe I shouldn't give them any money at all?' It was difficult. I knew I would be at their mercy and in the end, it came down to a question of trust. I just wasn't sure what to do.

I knew that the minute you tell someone that you've won the lottery; it is like the Bush Telegraph. It's virtually impossible to stop your friends and family from keeping such a big secret to themselves, no matter how much you tell them not to tell anyone about where they suddenly got this large amount of money from. I decided that the best tack for the time being would be to say I had received a legacy in a will from a rich uncle. Whether they would go with that story was up to them, but I knew deep down inside that someone somewhere would let the cat out of the bag. I couldn't stop them of course and once I'd given them the money, there was no way I could get it back. Plus, I had no control as to how they spent that money that I gave them. But surely, that was up to them.

All of a sudden, I started to realise that winning the lottery seemed such a huge responsibility. I now had all this power from the money I was soon to receive. Not only would it change my life, but also the lives of quite a few people connected to me. I tried to put this thought aside as I got nearer home. The more pressing question though was, 'When was I going to tell Tracy?'

2 IN MY LIFE

Before I continue with what happened next after I had spoken to the lottery people, let me go back in time to explain how I came to be where I was when I won the lottery and how I had got there. How had things worked out in life for me and what sort of person was I?

I was born in Manchester in the summer of 1967, "The Summer of Love" according to those who remember it. There was always plenty of love in my home, where my parents did their best to provide for myself and my brother and sister. I was born into a typical Northern working class family, where the father went out to work and the mother stayed at home to bring up the children. My sister had been born three years before me in 1964 during the height of "Beatlemania", where news of the Beatles was everywhere. Then my brother came into the world two years after me in 1969, when the Vietnam War was dominating the news. The world was changing rapidly at the time and the Seventies was just starting with males having long hair and the Women's Liberation movement taking hold.

My father Roy, worked on the railways as a train driver on many of the routes around Manchester. He was born in Wigan in 1937 and lived through the War - the Second World War that is. Although he was a child during it, he still told us tales of what it was like, with rationing, evacuation and enemy planes flying overhead after raids on Liverpool and Manchester. He had a hard life as a child, with his father working as a miner in one of the many mines near Wigan, barely earning enough to support him and his three siblings, as well as his mother. He was quite a gentle person with jet black hair and quite thin until he met my mum, who fattened him up!

When he was sixteen, my dad started work with British Railways as a clerk in the ticket office at Wigan Wallgate station. He chose the railways as he really did not want to follow in his father's footsteps and end up working down the pit. Back then when you got a job "it was for life" as they say. He worked there for a few years until he was called up to serve his National Service, which interrupted his railway work.

He couldn't really get out of it and was sent to an army training camp on the South Coast, before being posted to Catterick. He hated his army days and used to tell us in later years that it was the worst time in his life. When he eventually came out of the army, he applied to become a train driver on the new diesel trains that were being introduced at the time, replacing the much loved steam locomotives. I suppose he liked the idea of being by himself in the driver's compartment, free of interruptions and in his own little bubble.

After completing his training, he started work as a fully qualified train driver of diesel multiple unit trains, being based at Newton Heath depot to the east of Manchester Victoria. He enjoyed all the travelling which his job involved, going to places like Leeds, York, Liverpool, and

Blackpool, as well as having the responsibility of making sure the passengers got to their destinations safely and on time.

It was when he came home on leave from the army one weekend that he first met my mum June, at a local dance hall. It was the time of Rock and Roll music dominating the charts and although he wasn't a Teddy Boy, he loved the music of the time and enjoyed dancing and meeting girls. My mother was five years younger than him and was from Bolton. She was quite petite with long brown hair and had a nasty temper if she was pushed, so no one messed with my mum! She worked in the local branch of Woolworth's.

If you can't remember Woolworth's, it was a type of general store selling everything from sweets to records, and clothes to household goods. They were everywhere in Britain in both the big towns and the smaller ones. Sadly, it all came to an abrupt end in 2008 when their eight hundred stores were closed, and the company went bust.

After three years of courting, my parents married in 1963 and lived in rented accommodation for a year before buying their first house, a two up, two down terraced house in Manchester, near to my dad's workplace. Life was tough with just one income coming in and as the years progressed there were more and more mouths to feed, but we didn't ever go short. My dad was always doing overtime to help make ends meet.

My sister was the first to be born out of us three children. She was born in 1964 when the songs of the Beatles could be heard everywhere, and she was my closest companion until my brother came along. As I was younger than her, she dominated me in the games we used to play. I was the patient whilst she was the nurse. I was the Indian, whilst she was the Cowboy. This was a trait she carried on in adulthood until it all came to a head one day, which I will go into later.

When my brother came along, I was quite jealous of him at first, as he was getting all that attention, whilst I felt I was being neglected, as I was no longer the youngest. After a few years though when he could walk and talk, we become inseparable companions and would play out together. This was usually in the street as cars were still quite rare in the streets where we lived, and later when we were older, we would venture into the fields and woods that were a short bike ride away from our house.

* * *

For the first seven years of my life, we lived in a traditional two up two down red brick terraced house, many of which can still be found all over the north of England. It was only when my brother started to grow from a baby into a toddler and could no longer sleep in my parent's bedroom that a move to a bigger three bed roomed house happened. This was in the Newton Heath area of Manchester, near to where my father's train depot was. It meant that my sister got her own bedroom and me and my brother had to share a room with bunk beds.

We had great fun when we were younger attacking each other from above and below. When my mother heard us shouting and arguing, she would charge upstairs, shouting,

'You two. Stop this nonsense at once!' and we would meekly obey; only to go back to our playful fighting, albeit in silence so as not to stir up my mother again!

My Dad had to work most Saturdays, but occasionally he did get Saturdays off and would take me, and later on my brother, to Maine Road to see Manchester City play their matches there. It was when I was eight years old, that my father took me and my sister to Maine Road for the first time.

It was a match between Man City and Leeds United on Boxing Day 1975. That first visit has stayed with me ever since. The large crowds, the smell of cigarette smoke, the street vendors shouting out and of course the excitement of an English 1st division football match. City lost 1-0, but I wasn't worried about the score. I was just overawed with all that excitement and action and became hooked for life. Although most of my friends at school were fans of Man Utd, I became a City fan for life that day.

As we were still quite young and wouldn't be able to see much standing up, my dad had forked out for seats, which looking back was a wise move. As I looked towards the Kippax stand opposite, I could see a swirling mass of humans being pushed too and fro, like the currents in a raging river. That was hardly a place for two children, so my dad had made a wise decision. I don't think it had that much of an impact on my sister though, as she never went to a football match again as far as I know, but I was hooked for life and continue to watch City to this day. In fact, I have been a season ticket for almost twenty years now.

Another experience that I can thank my father for was my love of going out into the countryside. As he was a train driver, he was allowed free train travel along with members of his family. So, he would take us out on day trips by train to either the seaside or out into the countryside. We loved a day by the seaside in places like Blackpool and Southport, but we also liked a day out in the country just as much.

If we were going for a day out in the countryside, we would take a picnic lunch with us and usually take a train from Manchester Victoria and then head east. My favourite destination was the village of Greenfield on the way to Huddersfield. We would get off the train at the quaint station there; walk through the village, often stopping off in the park to play on the swings. Then we would walk up onto Saddleworth Moor, stopping at the monument up the hill called "Pots and Pans". Up there we had fantastic views in all directions over the endless moors. We would continue on to the reservoirs at the top and play skimming stones and then stop to have our picnic.

When I was a teenager, I would often come back to this area, but this time I was on a bike as that was one of my hobbies. I joined a local cycling club when I was fourteen and would ride with them up into the moors, which helped to make me pretty fit back then. Like my father I loved the freedom of being out in the fresh air, away from the towns.

As for my education, I enjoyed my primary school and shone academically there. I did not feel the same way at secondary school though. It was quite a shock to the system making the change from being top of the tree in the juniors to becoming bottom of the pile in the seniors. Although I wasn't bullied like some of the children, as I was in my year group football team and was one of the boys, I did find it hard making close friends.

It wasn't until the third year that I got to know Jim McKeith who was new to the school back then. He and his family had moved down from Glasgow due to his father's work and like me, he found it hard at first settling in and being accepted. He was a big Celtic fan and although he wouldn't be seeing them play that much anymore, I soon introduced him to the delights of Manchester City. By now I was allowed to go to see City play at home as long as I went with a friend.

When I first invited him to come with me to Maine Road he jumped at the chance. Although he had a strong Glaswegian accent at first, he gradually picked up a Mancunian twang. Perhaps it was his way of trying to become accepted, but he seemed to pick up accents quite easily and was soon known as the class clown with his imitations of some of the teachers.

Jim and I went through our teenage years together, going through the transition from boys to men. We started going out to discos from aged fifteen onwards and at the discos were plenty of pretty girls, many of whom we started dating. He was definitely my best friend during that period of my life, but there have been plenty of other friends along the way.

When I got to the age of sixteen as there was no sixth form at my school, we either left to go out into the big wide world or went on to sixth form college. I chose the latter on the advice of the teachers at my school, whilst Jim left and went to work in a factory for a little while. One day he came round to see me to tell me that he wouldn't be around for much longer as he had signed up to join the army. I was naturally shocked and saddened by this piece of news, as it meant my best friend was going out of my life and maybe might never come back in. At the time there was the war going on in Bosnia, soon to be followed by the first Iraq war. Inevitably we lost contact with each other and it was several years later that we were unexpectedly reunited.

At school when I was about thirteen, I developed a thirst for books and would read avidly in my bedroom late into the night. Luckily, there was a public library nearby, so I was spoilt for choice most of the time. I liked authors like George Orwell, Graham Greene, and Alan Bennett. I also got into poetry, liking poets, especially the northern ones such as Adrian Henri, Ted Hughes, and Eric Mottram. The outcome of all this was that I shone in English at school and decided that I would like to go on to study English at University.

Firstly, though I had to get good enough grades in my GCSEs to get me in at the local Sixth Form College. I worked as hard as I could and was rewarded with mostly A's, which was easily good enough to be accepted. Once I was in at the sixth form college, I made sure that I worked doubly hard to get the required grades for university. Although not many people from the college went onto University, I knew that if I worked hard, I could do it. You see, once I get a bee in my bonnet, I am quite determined to achieve it. So, in 1985 I worked extra hard to achieve the grades I needed for Uni.

I wasn't too bothered where I went, but did look at Birmingham, Southampton, and Lancaster before opting for York. I liked the idea of being away from home, but not too far away and as York is only about an hour and a half away from Manchester by train, that was the one I chose for my first choice.

When the results came out in August that year, I was pleased to see that I had got the grades I needed to get into York University, and so I started to get ready to leave home for the first time. Me leaving home was a big wrench for mum as I was the last to fly the nest, as both Alan and Dawn had already moved out. Mum and dad also made sacrifices with their savings to provide me with some financial security, which was really kind of them.

I had finally made it to university, being the first on both sides of the family to do so, I must confess that I was a little homesick at first, and even thought of dropping out and coming back home. I did eventually settle down into student life though and must say that I enjoyed it all in the end. It was good for me to mix with a wide variety of people from different backgrounds and from different countries as well. It certainly widened my view on life and helped me to become more tolerant of other people.

Whilst at York I made many friends and although I did have one or two girlfriends, none of them was the one for me. I did make a lifelong friend in Tom Webster who was from Sheffield and a Wednesday fan. We both liked sport and the music of the time in such artists as Def Leopard, the Housemartins, Simply Red and U2. We also had some great discussions about life and love well into the night lots of times.

I also enjoyed living in the city of York with all its history. It was great to walk down those ancient, cobbled streets full of quaint shops - and the inevitable tourists! I never ceased to marvel at the structure that is York Minster, and enjoyed sampling the city's many pubs. I also liked the fact that York was a major railway centre with its railway museum and a big interchange for several important routes.

I soon cottoned on to the fact that London was just two hours away by train and so I, along with my uni friends would often take a train down to the "Big Smoke" for the day and sometimes for the weekend. Once or twice, I went to see Man City play some of the London teams like Arsenal, Tottenham, or Chelsea. At other times I would go to a play or a musical or a big gig by one of my favourite groups.

Gradually, I got to like London as a place to be in with its many attractions and so I decided that I would perhaps like to live there one day. By the time of my final year at York I had decided that I would like to go into teaching for a career and go to train as a teacher somewhere in London. As there were several teacher training colleges in and around London I was spoilt for choice, but in the end, I chose St Mary's College in Twickenham.

The reason I chose Twickenham was not because of the rugby, but rather because of its situation by the river Thames and the fact that it had good train services into Central London. The idea of being able to go to watch football matches and shows in London more easily than if I was at college in the North was also a factor.

Plus, I felt that training at a London college would give me a better chance of finding a job in the London area, than if I had been up North. By now life for many Northerners was much harder under the leadership of Margaret Thatcher, what with the Miner's Strike and riots happening. So many people were moving from the North to the South where the work was and that was also part of my thinking.

I did come down to earth with a large bump when I did my first teaching practice in Hounslow, next to Heathrow Airport. Some, though not all of the pupils found my Northern accent funny and some even imitated me to my face when answering questions, much to the amusement of the rest of the class.

I quickly put it behind me and gradually won then over with my tales of football matches and the lovely green hills of the north of England. I found it hard to believe, but most of them had never been out of London, or if they had, it was only as far as the South Coast. In a way, I was like a foreigner to some of them. Yet the class I taught was made up of several different nationalities, many whose parents worked at Heathrow. It was a good experience to see all these children from around the world, all living and getting on with each other.... most of the time at least.

My second teaching practice in the summer term was a lot easier in terms of the children that I was teaching. This time the school was in Kingston-upon-Thames where the children were more middle class, and I must admit that I did enjoy this second practice more. Also, I got an "excellent" grade for my teaching practice. This would be very useful when I started to apply for jobs.

* * *

It was whilst I was at Teachers training college that I first met Tracy, who would become my wife. The college had a disco every Friday night which was open not just for the students but also local people - provided they behaved themselves. There had been quite a bit of fraternisation over the years between the students and the locals, so it was all quite normal by the time I went there.

I remember the first time I set eyes on her. She was wearing a white blouse with a black skirt. Her hair was blonde in colour and she had sparkly blue eyes. As soon as I saw her, I had the thought that I would like to get to know her, so when her mates had gone off to the ladies, I went over to her and asked her for a dance. I can't quite remember what the music was that was playing, possibly *Ride on Time* by Black Box, but anyway she accepted, and we had a dance. During the dance I introduced myself and asked her what her name was, and she told me it was Tracy. As the music was quite loud, it was quite hard having a conversation, so when it finished, I offered to buy her a drink. She asked for a Pinot Colada.

When I got back, I said, 'Let's go somewhere quieter where we can hear ourselves think.'

So, we went out into a corridor next to the hall. It was cold but quiet and we could actually carry on a conversation without being drowned out by the noise.

It turned out that Tracy was a local girl who lived about half a mile away in Twickenham. She had come with a couple of her friends, Julie, and Dee. She worked in an office in Central London as an admin assistant and enjoyed her work, though not the travelling.

Although she knew a little of Manchester, she had never been there. In fact, she hadn't been further north than Birmingham! I could tell that she was intrigued with me and liked my northern accent. I in turn quite fancied her and after talking for twenty minutes we went back into the hall for a couple of dances. When it was time to go, we exchanged phone numbers and said we'd meet up for a walk along the Thames on the following Sunday.

So, two days later, I was there by the bridge that goes onto Eel Pie Island, well before the allotted time. I was half expecting to be stood up, but as promised she arrived right on time. This time it was more relaxed with the sun reflecting on the Thames making a mirror effect on the water.

We got to know each other even more and at the end agreed to meet each other at the college disco the following Friday night. We soon became boyfriend and girlfriend and grew very close but didn't sleep together for several months. Eventually we did become lovers and little by little we fell madly in love with each other.

Towards the beginning of the final term of my teachers training course we all began to look for jobs to start the following September. I had always thought that when I graduated, I would like to stay near London with all its attractions of both sport and music and theatre. The added attraction now was that Tracy lived nearby and as we were in love and couldn't bear to be separated, I started looking for jobs in the west London area.

I applied for as many jobs as I could in places like Shepherds Bush, Watford, Harrow, and Ealing. I soon got offered two interviews: one in Ealing and one in Watford. The one in Ealing came first and was at a comprehensive. To say I was nervous was an understatement. I was so nervous in fact that I fluffed it. They offered it to a girl who had gone to Cambridge University and was very self-confident – "Good luck to her!" I thought.

The second interview was at a boy's grammar school in Watford and although I wasn't too sure about teaching both in a grammar school and just to boys, the fact that it wasn't too far from the M1 and the West Coast mainline for getting back to Manchester had its advantages. This time I was less nervous and more confident and knew what to say to the similar types of questions that they asked. The other two candidates must have messed up as they offered the job to me. Mind you it was on a year's probation just in case I wasn't up to it.

After going out for a year, Tracy and I moved into my flat, which was in Kenton, near Wembley. It was handy for getting the train to school in Watford and for going back up north to Manchester.

As we were madly in love and just couldn't bear to be apart living together would either make or break us. A good friend of mine once suggested to me that if you are thinking of getting married, it is a good idea to live together for a year first and see how you get on. If at the end of that year you are still together and haven't killed each other, then you can make a go of marriage. Sound advice I reckon. We thankfully survived our first year of living together and although we did have the occasional spat, our love for each other became even stronger I believe.

I proposed to her on Valentine's Day 1990, and she accepted straight away, just as I hoped she would. Straight away we were making wedding plans and as we couldn't wait, arranged the wedding for December that year. Naturally in December it was cold, but what we didn't bargain for was heavy snow the day before! Luckily, everyone who was invited showed up, including mum and dad, Dawn and her husband Nick, Alan and Sue and various friends on my side. Sadly, on Tracy's side, her parents had died a few years earlier in a car crash, so her brother Barry gave her away.

Still, it was a lovely day and was followed by a honeymoon in Paris, where the weather was just as dire, but we still enjoyed ourselves. Then it was Christmas, and we went up to Manchester staying at Mum and dads who showed Tracy some good old Northern hospitality.

When Tracy became pregnant in the Spring of 1991, we both couldn't believe it. Although it was a little earlier than we wanted, we were both overjoyed. The idea that we had created another human being was a wonderful feeling. She worked for as long as she could, but actually went into labour two weeks early in November. It was a Sunday and City were on the box, but it was ok as it was an away match, so I was at home. We were able to get to the maternity hospital pretty quickly and then it was a ten hour labour, with it being touch and go as to whether she would need a Caesarean. Luckily, baby Lesley came out in the nick of time and we were overjoyed.

After living in a cramped flat for nearly two years we had started to think about buying our first home together. Buying even a small flat was not an option as house prices in London and the Home Counties were beyond our combined salary, so I started to think about moving back up North. Although I was fairly settled in the grammar school, I knew that if was to get on in teaching, I would have to make a move sooner or later.

When I put the idea of moving up North to Tracy, she naturally had her reservations, citing the fact that she would be moving away from her workmates and her friends from school, who she had known for years. However, one event seemed to swing it for Tracy and that was the fact that her brother had recently moved up to Liverpool. His job led to him being relocated there and whenever we made the journey up to Manchester, we would pay a visit to him and his wife Jill.

The fly in the ointment was getting a job. Would I be able to get a teaching job in the North West, seeing as there was so much unemployment up there at the time? On my side were two years' experience and hopefully a glowing reference from my head. Also, I did like the idea of any future children of mine, being born in the North West.

There was one more thing that happened which confirmed that moving back up north was a good thing and that was my father being told that he had terminal cancer. It wasn't long after my father retired that the diagnosis of cancer first came to light. He had been feeling tired and lethargic for a few weeks and had lost his appetite. Plus, he had always had this irritating cough which never seemed to clear up. Mind you he had smoked ever since he had been in the army. So, I wasn't surprised when I heard the news.

Mum was naturally worried about this and eventually persuaded him to go and see the doctor. He said it might be his age catching up on him but arranged for him to have a blood test as well as a chest X ray. It was the latter which showed up a dark patch above his right lung. When I heard about this, I knew straight away that this was his chips.

He went into hospital for "investigations" and when he came out, they said he had possibly up to six months to live. Mum was devastated of course and became ill herself with even more worry. I tried to tell her that she needed to be strong for dad, but she wouldn't listen. She always feared the worst and looked on the worst side of things.

In all of this I was driving up the M1 and M6 at weekends making the long journey home just to spend some time with him. Of course, my sister had taken over at this point and was ordering everyone about with her usual gusto. Alan had also taken the news badly and didn't seem to accept it, thinking that he would make a full recovery. Dad did have a course of chemotherapy, but most of the time he seemed worse. Looking back, I sometimes wonder if all those drugs being pumped into his ailing body hastened the end.

I applied for every job that came up in the *Times Educational Supplement* and was invited for an interview for a school in Walkden to the west of Manchester. It was a co-educational comprehensive so would be a bit harder teaching wise, but as I had the experience there was a chance of promotion after a year. I gladly accepted it when they offered me the job. Now we just had to find somewhere to live.

We eventually found a two bed roomed flat in Swinton not far from Walkden, but out of the school's catchment area, as I didn't want to live too near the school. As it was in the north we could easily get a mortgage on my salary alone to buy the flat. So, we moved up to the North West in the summer of 1992. Although it meant a struggle for us at first, it meant that we were able to get a foot up on the property ladder.

At least I could be near Dad for the last few months of his life. I was so glad when Tracy became pregnant for the second time soon after we moved up to Swinton. Our next child, Jonathon was born in the summer of 1993. Compared to Lesley's birth, things were much different. Tracy was in labour for only two hours, and we'd barely got to the hospital before he popped out! Thankfully both our children were blessed with good health and have grown up to be confident, carefree, and loving young adults.

* * *

Dad finally died in the Autumn of 1994, after hanging on for so long. He was in such a lot of pain in the final months, and I was glad that I was by his bedside when he finally went, as was my mum, brother, and sister. It was an emotional time for us all, but we gave him a good send off three weeks later, with many of his railway colleagues at the funeral.

After my father died, I hid a lot of my grief inside and concentrated on my work. As the years passed, I did manage to gain a promotion, but it was only by moving to another school in the south of the Manchester, which meant a lot of travelling. So, with promotion and a new school to go to we started to think about moving to a bigger house and one which was within easy travelling distance of my new school. In the end we settled on a three bedroom semi in Chorlton-Cum-Hardy, to the South West of Manchester city centre.

We were also attracted by the better schools than where we had been living before and so we moved there in 1998. After a few years we had decided that it was slightly too small for us, but in the end rather than moving again, we re-mortgaged and paid for the house to be extended at the back. The bathroom at the back was moved to the front where Jon had his bedroom. As we moved outwards both Jon and Lesley were able to have bigger bedrooms. Downstairs we had a bigger kitchen and a conservatory added to the back which was really a whole extra room.

Mind you, re-mortgaging didn't come cheap and our mortgage almost doubled, but with Tracy now back at work full time, we reckoned that we could manage. This was helped a couple of years later when I was promoted within my school to head of the English department.

* * *

I mentioned earlier about me falling out with my sister. It happened like this. She had always tried to dominate me and boss me about I suppose. It was the same with Alan, even more so, being the youngest. With her being the eldest I suppose that's natural, but she didn't like it when both Alan and me stood up to her.

She liked organising things and often had family get togethers at the slightest excuse such as birthdays, Christenings, housewarming dos, Christmas parties. You name it; she would have these dos where she went to town with the food and the decorations.

So, in a way Alan and I felt we had to do the same, not so much as competing with her, but more from the point of view of thinking that was what was expected of us. Poor Tracy and Alan's wife Sue would be tearing their hair out trying to put on a feast as good if not better than my sister's. This was especially true when our children were young and liked going to get-togethers like this. But as they got into their teenager years it all become a bore for them and they didn't want to go anymore. This offended my sister when one or both of my kids decided they didn't want to go and so they made their excuses.

She also tried to dominate both Mum and Dad and once Dad had died, she tried and tried to get Mum into a home, even though Mum didn't want to go into one. Mum still wanted her independence, and her house had all those memories of Dad in it, so no way did she want to go without a fight.

But with all the pressure from Dawn, my mum eventually agreed to go into sheltered accommodation, or so we all thought. It was actually an Old People's home and both Alan and I found out too late to stop it. All the talk about potential falls and forgetting to take her tablets swung it. But no sooner had Mum gone into the home than Dawn and her husband Nick were busy clearing out her home, a place she had lived with dad since the 60's.

By the time I got there she had taken the decent stuff and left the scraps for Alan and me. One thing which I'd always wanted, which she took without our knowledge was Dad's signed photo of the Man City team that won the League Championship in 1968. It had all the City greats on it like Mike Summerbee, Frannie Lee, Alan Oakes and Colin Bell. I distinctly remember Dad saying to me that when he died that photo would be mine. Although he never made a will, so I could prove it, my sister had removed it without checking if either Alan or I wanted it.

After that, I became cold towards her and whenever she invited us to one of her 'dos', we always had an excuse as to why we could not attend. Although I could never tell her to her face, I do believe that Alan did tell her the reason why I hardly ever saw her. Over the years this distance between us grew to such an extent that we basically lost contact with each other. It was only through Alan, who became the go-between that we knew of each other's news. We do still exchange Christmas and birthday cards, but that is the limit of our relationship. Looking back, it was all quite childish, but the loss of that signed photo was the straw that broke the camel's back.

* * *

Our children both did well at school, and both stayed on for the sixth form. This meant that the likelihood of them going onto university became more likely. So eventually Lesley went up to Bath University in 2009 to read Chemistry with a view to becoming a pharmacist. Two years later, Jon went to Lincoln University to read Mathematics with a view to becoming.... Well, he was never quite as focussed and motivated as his sister who knows!

Long before they applied for university, Tracy and I had already discussed the options of helping them out. I really didn't want them to be struggling with debt before they had gone out into the wide world, so we said that we would pay their student fees and half of their accommodation costs, even though it meant taking out another re-mortgage. But as my parents had struggled to help me, I too felt it right that my children should have a good start in life.

That is why Tracy and I were still working very hard in our jobs to help support our children when the lottery win happened. Mind you, we made it very clear to them that once they graduated, it was up to them to go out and earn a living in the world. No handouts anymore.

That brings you up to date with all that has happened in my life. Here we are now back in 2012 with the London Olympics coming up and me working every hour God sends in a North West of England comprehensive. Life is OK. It's certainly not as hard as my mother and father had it, but I have to admit it is still hard in some respects. My job doesn't get any easier. What with all the Government demands on our time, telling us what to teach and what not to teach, lack of funding and so on. I could go on, but it is time for me to tell you what happened next in my life. Winning the lottery was about to change everything in my life and not necessarily for the better……

3 CHANGES

As mentioned earlier, I have always been a procrastinator, being pretty poor at making decisions. I would always sit on the fence when it came to making an important decision and now with winning the lottery, there were lots of important decisions to make. I knew telling Tracy was the number one priority; so telling the person closest to you that you have won the lottery in theory should be a piece of cake. On the other hand, it could be quite difficult. For me it was the latter.

Looking back, I should have just told her there and then on that Saturday night when I found out that I had won. The trouble was I knew what Tracy was like and would go berserk and then start telling all and sundry. I really didn't want that to happen, so I kept waiting for the best moment to tell her; but the problem is that there is never a best moment.

When I got back from seeing my mother on the Sunday evening, after speaking to the lottery people, I should have told her the minute I walked through the door, but something in my mind said, "Hold fire!" I knew if I told her on the Sunday night, it would be another sleepless night, as she would be asking question after question, and going on and on about it, when all I wanted to do was sleep.

Then the next evening, I had a parent's evening at school and when I eventually got home, she probably would have gone to bed. Can you imagine what it would be like if I woke her up and told her then? It would be yet another sleepless night. So, I made my mind up that I would tell her on the Tuesday evening, after *Eastenders* had finished and she wouldn't be watching TV.

In the meantime, I began to worry that the lottery people might ring up. What if she answered the phone? That would surely freak her out! Mind you, she would probably think that it was someone winding her up. So, I put this thought out of my mind and tried to concentrate on school and all the problems that it brings.

I did have two better night's sleeps, though the lottery win was always on my mind. At the parent's evening I found it difficult to concentrate on what I was doing, speaking to this parent or that parent and trying to be positive about their darling son or daughter.

At long last on the Tuesday evening the appointed time in my mind came round and just as I was about to start up the conversation, the phone ring. I rushed to answer it, but it was Tracy's friend, Jane and so after an interruption of half an hour I was finally ready to spill the beans…..

'Tracy,' I said. 'There's something important that I need to talk to you about.'

She looked all concerned. "Was I in trouble at school?" she thought. "Had I got a serious illness?"

'No, it's not bad news,' I said reassuringly. 'It's really the opposite.'

Her face looked puzzled.

'Go on then,' she beckoned.

'You know I do the lottery,' I went on, trying to slow things down. 'Well, I have actually won the lottery!'

'You're having me on!' was her instant reaction. 'I don't believe you!'

'OK. Here's my ticket, then.'

I took the ticket out of my wallet and showed her it. Then I showed her the results for a week ago on my tablet.

She gingerly looked at the ticket and then the results. All the time I kept hold of the ticket as I didn't want here tearing it in her excitement.

'So, you're not telling fibs then,' was all she could say and as she sat down in shocked disbelief and looked gob smacked as they say.

After a few seconds she came out with, 'How much?'

'You're not going to believe this,' I warned her. 'Eleven million pounds!'

With that she reacted just like a Jack in the Box being freed from his box. She jumped up in the air and screamed. I hoped the next-door neighbours didn't hear.

'Oh my God!' she shouted. 'Our lives are going to be changed forever! I'll be able to give up work! I can go out and buy an MX5! I've always wanted one of those. We can move to a bigger house! We can go to Australia!'

It was all the usual things coming out of her that most people decide they must have whenever they win the lottery.

Then she became more rational.

'Have you rung the lottery people yet?'

'Yes. It's all been confirmed. There's someone going to come over on Sunday to discuss things.'

For some reason she didn't ask when I rang them, much to my relief. Clearly that wasn't a concern.

'Have you told anyone yet?' she asked.

'No,' I lied. I knew if I said I'd told my mother she would have gone ballistic.

'You're the first to know,' I lied.

'Oh, I must ring Lesley and Jon and let them know. And my brother....'

'Hold on a minute!' I interrupted. 'No one's going to know about it at this stage.

That's what the lottery people said was the best thing to do when I rang them,' I lied again.

'Why? Are you telling me you don't want publicity?'

'Of course, I don't want publicity!' I countered.

I WON THE LOTTERY...

'Can you imagine what it would be like if people found out? There'd be people ringing our door bell every five minutes asking for money. And don't forget Lesley's got her finals coming up soon. That would be bound to screw her up if we told her now and ruin her chances of getting a good degree.'

She thought about it for a few seconds and then nodded her head.

Little by little, Tracy was taking in the enormity of it all and the responsibility that winning the lottery brings.

Like me the week before, all sorts of thoughts and questions were rushing around inside her brain. More questions started coming out.

'Maybe I could hand in my resignation from work?' she suggested. Then almost immediately she thought about the consequences.

'But then again what reason am I going to give them? Can you imagine their faces if I said it was because I had won the lottery? Perhaps we need to think a little more about that?'

'*You've* won the Lottery?' I questioned. She blushed as she realised what she had just said.

'The lottery people said for the time being the best course of action would be to continue as normal, as if nothing had happened,' I lied once more, trying to make sure that Tracy would behave in the way that I wanted her to.

'I suppose they know what they're talking about,' she replied, agreeing with me at long last. 'Phew! It's such a lot to take in at once!' she admitted.

For the next hour we talked about every little thing we could think of to do with the lottery and then I put the TV on for the 10 O' Clock News to try and settle the both of us down. It was no use of course, as when we went up to bed, we both tossed and turned. Eventually we began to make love. I suppose that was the best way of letting off all the steam that had been building up!

* * *

Over the next few days, the lottery win was all that we talked about each morning when we got up and each evening when we got home from work. We talked about not only what we would spend the money on, but also about who in our family and amongst our friends would be given some of the winnings. We did not really say just how much each relative and friend would get at this stage, but I knew it could be a bone of contention and was really a minefield when we began to go into it.

I was still quite adamant about making sure as few people as possible were aware of my lottery win. In fact, it became a sort of obsession with me to the verge of paranoia even. Tracy on the other hand didn't see it as a problem or wasn't aware of the possible dangers such a course of action would bring. So, I showed her a couple of news stories on the Internet about lottery winners going public with their win. She couldn't believe what she read, so I emphasised how important it was for us to stay living as normal lives as possible, otherwise our lives could become hell.

Gradually, Tracy came round to my way of thinking. She even started to think up various stories of how we had got a lot of money in such a short space of time. One story that we thought of was that either her or me had done a business deal which had involved investing all of our savings in an overseas investment scheme. It had worked out and as a result we were several hundred thousand pounds richer.

Another one was that I had been betting in secret for several years and had eventually built up a small fortune from my winnings. We both laughed at the ridiculousness of it!

I WON THE LOTTERY...

The final story we thought of and the one which we would eventually use was this one. I had a rich uncle; an Uncle Philip who lived overseas, who I hadn't seen since I was a teenager. He didn't have any children or any brothers or sisters who were still alive. Then last year he died, leaving a substantial amount of money to me and my brother, which meant that we could give up our jobs and live on the money we received. Just who we would tell that story to amongst the family and our friends would soon become a bone of contention.

The following Sunday couldn't come sooner enough. The man from the lottery arrived at our house at 2.30 pm sharp. Tracy and I were both quite nervous as it was all a big unknown to us, but in the end there wasn't any need. He was a genuinely nice man and soon put us at our ease.

The first thing he did was to actually look at my ticket; not so much to check my numbers, but to check that it was a genuine ticket and not a forgery. He scanned it in a portable scanner he took out of his brief case and asked if I could remember where I had bought it from. That was easy, as it was the same newsagents on Manchester Road that I always bought it from - usually at the weekend, but occasionally during the week when I was on my way back from work. He told us that he had to do this as there were always people out there who try and con the lottery people into believing they have won, when clearly, they haven't.

'You would be surprised at the lengths some people go to, to try and get hold of lottery money,' he said. 'Such as gluing numbers onto their ticket or, saying they've lost their ticket, but they bought it at a newsagent in a town where there was an unclaimed prize. Some even put their ticket inside a pair of trousers and put it into a washing machine in the hope that the numbers would look illegible! As if we would fall for that' he chuckled. 'They don't seem to realise that all lottery tickets have a bar code with security details on.'

After checking my ticket, Dave (as I shall call him) then looked at the two proofs of identity that were needed – my driving licence and passport to confirm that it was me and not someone else. Once that was all confirmed he explained about how they suggest you receive the money from them. You can of course just have it transferred straight into your current bank account, but he advised us against this. You see, any person working in the local branch of your bank or building society could easily see that an exceptionally large amount of money has been transferred into your account and could easily start gossiping to their other colleagues or their family or friends. Then the next thing you know the whole world knows.

Instead, Dave said that the best thing to do was to open a special account with a bank of my choice that would be kept secret from anyone apart from the bank's specially trained staff in their headquarters. Apparently, all the big banks have special accounts for the very wealthy who have got millions of pounds to deposit, and this includes lottery winners. I would of course have full access to it as and when I needed it. This seemed to make sense to us, so we said, 'Yes. Go ahead'.

He also said that having the services of a financial advisor was a must as there was all that money sitting in an account that would soon be accruing interest and although you are not taxed on your winnings, you will be taxed on the interest that you receive. He did say I could of course use my own financial advisor, but straight away he would know that I had won all this money on the lottery and once again my secret would be out. They had a list of specially vetted financial advisors who I could choose from; several of them were based in the North West.

Although I was nervous about having a financial advisor sticking his nose into my finances, I could see Dave's point. Tracy agreed and after we had chosen one from his list, he arranged for this financial advisor to get in touch soon to help us get the best out of my winnings.

All the time that he was saying 'you' to me, I could see Tracy wincing a little. I hadn't actually discussed sharing the money with Tracy, but I got the vibes that she felt that the money was hers as well. It was in a way, though she wasn't the person who had won. I had; and as such the meeting was directed at me, no matter how much Tracy believed it was about "us".

He also mentioned that we should get a solicitor if we didn't already have one. Not only would he or she be needed to check through any legal documents that we signed, but getting new wills drawn up so that our children were guaranteed the money should either or both of us die, was a priority. Plus, if we decided to move to a new house in the future, a solicitor would also be needed.

We had used a local solicitor who I liked, when we moved to our present house and when we made our wills a few years ago. So, I said there and then that I would be happy to use the same one, as long as he could be discrete about the money. When I mentioned this to Dave, he soon allayed my fears by saying that all solicitors, like doctors have to show complete secrecy when dealing with their client's affairs; as do their secretaries, of course.

Finally, he said that I would also need an accountant, as with the interest accruing on the millionaire account; the taxman would want yearly accounts from me. I found this hard to swallow, seeing as I had always paid my taxes through school with the "Pay As You Earn" system. Clearly this way of paying my taxes was no longer going to be relevant to me.

We talked about our present jobs and how it would be foolish to walk away from them tomorrow. He knew about teachers having to give a term's notice and said that I wasn't the first teacher to have won a jackpot on the lottery and no doubt I wouldn't be the last.

His advice was to take things slowly. Let it all sink in and be careful of who you told, as even if you didn't choose publicity, people still found out. He also said that it would be unwise to start splashing out on things straight away.

'You need to gradually ease yourself into the role,' he warned. 'Buying flashy cars or a new house straight after you have won the lottery is not the best way forward.

You need to think carefully about what you would like to spend your money on.'

One suggestion he made was about writing things down in the form of lists.

'It might be a good idea for you to make two lists. The first one is for what you need to spend some of your money on straight away, such as repairs around the house, or paying off your credit card bills, or even the mortgage. The second one is for major spending, such as a new car for each of you or a new house. In either case make sure you keep all your receipts as your accountant will need these for your tax return.' It all made good sense to me.

'The financial advisor is a much better person than me to advise you on this,' he went on. 'It is all too easy to spend, spend, spend, as some previous lottery winners have done so. Now they have nothing left and have been forced to return to work to make ends meet.'

A shiver went down my spine; thinking that all that money might all eventually go. A crazy thought when I hadn't actually received a penny of it! He was right about getting financial advice, though. You couldn't be careless with all that money in your hands. You had to spend it wisely.

Dave also gave us the phone number of a previous lottery winner called Stuart, who was happy to speak to me, to help me avoid some of the pitfalls that can happen to lottery winners in the early days. I was to find this man's advice and counsel invaluable, as you will see.

When I asked him about just who we should and shouldn't tell, his advice was mixed.

'That is really down to you', he replied. 'If you want to try and keep it a secret, only tell those who you know you can really trust. If just one person tells someone else about you winning the lottery, then inevitably lots of people can find out. Only you know who you can trust. I did come across one jackpot winner, who made every person he told sign a document to say they would not tell anyone else. A bit extreme, I know. But in the end, he was only trying to protect what was his.'

He answered some more questions, and then let us know that the money would be transferred into my new bank account within forty eight hours, and that he would ring me just as soon as this had happened. I asked him to ring me at home in the evening, rather than during the day when I was at school - just in case someone overhead.

'Of course, I will, Gary,' he promised. 'I will also ring you a few days after that in case you have any more questions and to check everything is going OK.'

With that, he left us to let everything sink in. My head was spinning with facts, figures, and questions, even more than last week. Of course, no sooner had he gone, than I began to think of a question that I wished I had asked him. So, I got myself a spare notebook from upstairs and vowed that I would write down anything that I wasn't sure about or something that I needed clarification on. This way I wouldn't be repeating myself when I next spoke to him. It was also useful as a source of questions that I could ask the lottery winner that Dave had put me in touch with. I'm sure he would be able to point me in the right direction when it came to living a new life as a lottery winner.

* * *

That night I had another bad night's sleep, as all the things that Dave had said played on my mind. The first of these was who should we tell about the lottery win and the next was how much money we should give to our friends and relatives. Then there was the question of having a financial advisor and accountant to deal with all that money. "How much was all this going to cost me?" I thought as I was still thinking in terms of my financial situation pre lottery situation, rather than post lottery win. Tracy was just as bad; tossing and turning for ages until she finally went off to sleep, exhausted by it all.

Although work was hectic for the both of us over the next couple of days it did take our minds off the lottery win. Though when Dave rang on Tuesday evening, to let me know that the winnings had been transferred into my new bank account, as he had promised, both our minds were stirred up once more.

Dave had arranged for the bank account to be opened at a major branch of a well-known bank in the centre of Manchester. This was what I had chosen as it was not too far away from where I lived, yet still unknown to the bank staff of my own local bank. He gave me the name of my contact at the bank, a Mr Jameson, who he said would ring me tomorrow evening to arrange an appointment for me (and Tracy) to go in and meet him to discuss things, including how to access the account.

Mr Jameson duly rang the next evening and introduced himself. We made an appointment to go into the bank on the next Monday morning as it would be half term, so it worked out fine time wise.

I also managed to speak to Mr. Garner, our new financial advisor, the next morning at school when I had a free period. He sounded quite OK on the phone and an appointment was made to see him on the Monday afternoon in Manchester to discuss how he could help us and what his terms would be. It made sense to kill two birds with one stone.

Finally, I spoke to our solicitor, Tim Watson, to make an appointment to see him, on the Tuesday afternoon, once we had seen the two other "advisors" in Manchester, to explain things and see about doing news wills. I was tempted to say that it was about some money that had come into my possession, but I held back from telling him over the phone but did say it was about changing our wills.

I hadn't had time to sort out an accountant yet, but I thought that either the financial advisor or the solicitor would be able to help here. It was going to be a busy week. Winning the lottery seemed to be one round of meetings at the moment!

Tracy and I were glad when it was Friday evening, as for me at least it was now half term and it meant that we could really focus on all the red tape and admin stuff surrounding being a lottery winner. Tracy had taken some of her annual leave for the half term week so we could spend some time together. We had decided well before the lottery win that we might go away for a few days at this time but plans for that had gone out of the window with all that had been going on. Once we had completed our business meetings, we agreed that we would go away in the second half of that half term week. But first business called.

After deciding to write down any questions I had down in my little notebook, I had by the end of the week made quite a substantial list. I decided it was time for me to make that phone call to the lottery winner, Stuart, whose phone number Dave had given me. I was going to ring him soon after Dave had been but decided to wait until the first Saturday of half term, once school was out of the way. Also, as it was so soon after the money had gone into my new bank account and I had yet to see the financial advisor, it gave me a chance about what to expect. So, I rang him on the afternoon of the first Saturday of half term.

I knew from Dave that he lived somewhere near London, possibly Essex. I didn't know how much he had actually won and whether he had gone public or not, but as soon as I got through to him it was like talking to a long lost friend.

'Hello Garry, mate. I've been expecting you to ring. What took you so long?!!!' He obviously had a sense of humour which put me at ease.

When I told him that I had a few questions to ask him, he was fine.

'Go on mate!' he said. 'Fire away!'

I proceeded to ask him the various questions that I had written down in that notebook and he duly answered each of them in his own inimitable way.

He told me about how the money was going to be paid into my new account and not to be tempted to go wild, but to hold back for a few weeks or even months at first. When I told him that I was a teacher and wouldn't be quitting my job until the summer, he said 'Perfect!' By that he meant that I wouldn't make the leap into the millionaire lifestyle in one go, but would do it gradually, thus giving me time to make decisions more easily.

Regarding the question of who I should tell about the lottery he had this to say.

'Try and keep it as quiet as possible, mate. I know you've got children and brothers and sisters you're probably going to tell, but my advice is the less people who know the better!'

That seemed to fit into my way of thinking and eased my fears straight away. To know from someone who had gone through all this was kind of soothing.

When I asked him about giving money to family and friends, he had this to say.

'I know you will want to give some of your money to your best mates and to your family, but don't give them too much mate. Best to drip feed it to them, mate and then they'll appreciate it more and won't go and spend it all in one go.'

He told me about some of the mistakes he'd made by telling too many people about his lottery win and the inevitable scroungers and the pesterers. Once he'd moved to a new house in a different town, it all became a lot easier, he reckoned. This gave me food for thought. I was quite happy where I lived but moving somewhere else might be a good way of protecting my privacy.

Finally, he wished me luck and said, 'If you ever need to talk, you're very welcome to give me a call. Now I've got your number on my phone, I'll know who it is. All the best mate!'

And with that the call was finished and I was ready to start the lottery winner's journey…. wherever that may take me.

* * *

On the Monday morning of half term, we both woke up early in anticipation of meeting our new "bank manager". I called him that as I wasn't really sure what his exact title was. We both wore suits as we felt that was the best attire to wear meeting two very important people who would now be part of our lives. When we went into the bank and said who we were, a security guard took us into a small room where our ID's were checked and then we were told to wait. After a few minutes, a man in his forties with short grey hair came into to the room.

'Gary!' he boomed. 'And you must be Tracy?' he went on, shaking our hands profusely. 'Welcome to our bank. You are both very welcome!'

I thought he was overdoing it a little, but with all that money from me in his bank's hands, I suppose it was expected.

I was quite excited in a way; being treated like a VIP - just because I had all this money.

We went in a lift down into the bowels of the building and had to go through an airport style security screening device, before walking along a long corridor and then going into his office.

'Please sit down!' he said, holding out his hand.

'Would you like some tea? Or a coffee maybe? I'll get my secretary to make it.'

I chose a tea, whilst Tracy chose a coffee.

He then looked at the proofs of identity that we had taken in with us, including our passports and two utility bills with our names and addresses on them. These were then photocopied.

After some small talk until the beverages arrived, he finally got down to business. As soon as his secretary had left the room, he shut the door and started our meeting.

'Congratulations Gary!' he boomed once more.

'I expect it's all a little overwhelming for the both of you. Please if you have any questions, don't be afraid to interrupt me.'

He then explained how the bank account worked, which was in my name only as I expected. When he showed us the details on his computer screen, with all that money underneath my name, my heart started beating rapidly. It seemed such a lot of money and such a big responsibility as well.

The important thing as far as I was concerned was how and when I could access this money.

'The account works like this,' he explained and then went onto explain in minute detail how it all worked in practice. If ever I wanted to take some money out of the account, I could ring him direct to let him know how much I wanted. He would then send me a special security code direct to my mobile. I then would go online to put in the withdrawal request, and he would approve it first.

If I ever wanted cash, that too could easily be arranged, though I would be expected to collect that in person from the bank. This really didn't appeal to me; carrying a large amount of cash on the streets was asking for trouble, as far as I was concerned.

So, I said that I didn't think I would be using that option – just yet.

He did say that it might be good idea to transfer some of the money into my everyday current account which was based at my local building society. We agreed that £20,000 would be a reasonable amount and he made it happen with just a few clicks on his computer. I would use this for paying off a few debts and buying a few things for the house. This amount he said shouldn't draw too much attention to my account, but if I wanted to take out larger amounts in the future, it might be worth opening another more flexible "every day" account with them. I told him I'd think about it.

With that sorted and all our questions answered, Tracy and I left the bank with our hearts lifted. Although I wasn't a free man yet in terms of work, I now had as much money as I wanted to buy things and pay off all my debts. To celebrate we had a nice lunch in one of the best restaurants in Manchester, talking in low voices about what he had said and what we might do next.

After a lovely lunch which was washed down with a classy red wine, we walked round a few blocks to have our meeting with our designated financial advisor. His office was in central Manchester, near to where the tram for Altringham went past. It was certainly convenient for us being near to my new bank and away from the prying eyes of our neighbours. He could have come round to our house, but I felt a man in a suit with a briefcase would arouse the suspicions of nosy neighbours.

His name was Adam Garner. He was an erudite man in his fifties who I took to straight away. He tried to break the ice by asking how we were and had we bought anything yet? He explained how he worked and what his terms were, which I was happy with, though I could tell by the look on her face that Tracy was of the opposite view to me. But as it was me who had the money, the final decision was mine.

At that first meeting we looked at the best way of investing all that money, or at least some of it. I really wasn't sure about letting someone loose on my money, even if it was fraction of the total, yet I knew that I couldn't just let it sit there gathering dust, so to speak.

He did say that how I used the money was completely up to me. His role would be to advise me of the best investments and tax breaks, as any amount of money gaining interest would be liable to tax, such is the system in this country. I was keen to try some of the ethical investments that I'd read about but wasn't sure how to go about this.

I agreed to let him invest £500,000 to start with and see how things went. It wasn't a massive amount when the whole amount of lottery winnings was taken into consideration, but it was when you talked of it by itself. Adam also advised us to invest in property if we possibly could, as that always guaranteed a good return over the years. I really wasn't sure about becoming a property investor with a portfolio of houses spread all over the North West to be honest.

However, he did plant the seed in our minds that buying a larger house would be a good investment to start with. The more I thought about it, the more the idea grew in my mind, especially as our present three bedroom semi always seemed a little cramped when the children were home. Tracy was certainly up for this, and it became her personal crusade over the next few months.

One thing he did advise me about giving money away to friends and family was not to give it to as many relatives as possible, but perhaps give it to the main close relatives like brothers and sisters, who then could redistribute it as they saw fit amongst their children. Although I wouldn't have a say as to how much each cousin or nephew/niece received, it did seem like a good idea to me. How they were going to explain where this money came from would be up to them – just as long as they didn't say it came from me!

By the time we came home from meeting the bank manager and the financial advisor, our heads were spinning with money facts and figures. Yet we still had the solicitor and an accountant to see.

Tracy and I both decided that now was the best time for us to get away from it all and think things through together. We decided on York as the place we would go to. Actually, it was me who came up with the idea as I really loved the energy of the city, and I had so many good memories of the place from my student days.

We decided to go by train, rather than drive, especially as York is so busy to drive around, being such an old city with many roads closed to traffic. As I now had some of the lottery money in my current account, I decided to treat us by travelling first class on the train and staying at one of the best hotels in the city centre. After all, we could afford it and we both needed a break from all the pressure.

On the Thursday morning, after having a day to pack and book a nice hotel, a taxi came and picked us up and took us to our nearest railway station. That was an experience in itself and as I hardly ever used taxis, nor could I really afford them in the past. We then caught a train from the station into Manchester Victoria and changed trains there for one which went direct to York.

Again, I was quite excited to be doing something different which the lottery money allowed us to do. A break away from our usual surroundings was just what we needed. It would give us a chance to plan our future without any interruptions, I hoped.

After arriving at York station, we got a taxi to our hotel, checked in and then went straight down to the hotel restaurant for a late lunch. It was just after 2 o'clock, but they were still able to fit us in.

We then went for a stroll around York, walking down the Shambles, visiting several shops, and buying some chocolate gifts for Lesley and Jon. We had afternoon tea in a lovely old tea rooms, just down the road from the Minster and discussed what we would like to do tomorrow.

Eventually we came back to the hotel and went into our bedroom. There on the bedroom table was a bottle of champagne, two glasses, a box of chocolates and two red roses. I had secretly ordered these when I booked the room yesterday.

Tracy let out a half scream and said, 'Oh Darling. How nice of them to think of us!' forgetting that we were just a normal couple away on a mini-break for a few days, and not some honeymoon couple.

'Actually Tracy. It was me who ordered the champagne,' I said. 'I thought it was about time we celebrated winning the lottery properly!'

She laughed and picked up the bottle, easing the cork off with a slight "pop" and filled up the two glasses with the bubbly.

'Here's to us!' I proclaimed. 'To a happy future!'

'Here's to us!' she replied and then proceeded to swallow a large mouthful of the champagne.

'I could get used to this,' she joked.

'Me too,' I replied. 'But first we've got a lot to sort out.

She didn't seem too bothered as she took my glass from my hand and placed it on the table. She then kissed me passionately and within a few minutes we were inside the king sized bed making love.

'Ah this is the life!' I thought.

4 A NEW BEGINNING

When we finally got back home from York, we both came back down to earth with a bump, seeing as we both had to go back to work after such a lovely time away. We were going to come back on the Saturday, but as we were enjoying things so much, we decided to stay on until the Sunday. Also, there was a show on at the Barbican Theatre on the Saturday night which convinced us to stay on for another day. The hotel didn't mind, seeing as they weren't full, and our room hadn't been booked by anyone else.

We continued to live the life of Riley in York, visiting the Railway Museum, going on a cruise on the River Ouse and visiting some of the many other tourist attractions that York has to offer. Plus, we had a great evening's entertainment on the Saturday night at the Barbican.

One result of all this relaxation was that we became closer together and both more relaxed. Whilst in York, we did discuss our next moves of course, including what we might like to buy with our newfound money; when we were going to stop work; and just who we should tell about the lottery.... and when.

These last two questions were two of the biggest problems I found with winning the lottery. I just didn't like lying, but we were both sure that a little white lie in this case was justified. By now, Tracy was of the same opinion as me regarding keeping the lottery win a secret from as many people as possible, so she was game just like me.

The question though was "just who should we tell and who should we not tell?" Obviously, I was going to tell our two children first of all, but when should I tell them and just how much should I give them?

Next on my list were my brother and sister. Yes, I could easily tell my brother, as I wanted to give him quite a large amount of money to either help him in his business or help him to take early retirement like me. My sister on the other hand did not need my money. Although she did not have a fraction of the amount of money that I had, she was still "well off" by most people's standards. This was because she had received some large pay outs when her husband's father and mother had died leaving it all to him as sole heir. If I did tell her, would she tell all her friends? Very likely, and I did not want them knowing, so I decided to keep this information from her and would ask my brother Alan to promise to do the same.

On Tracy's side were her brother and his wife. I agreed with Tracy that they should know and be given some of the money; how much though was a bone of contention between the two of us.

The same question applied to our cousins, and nephews and nieces? Should they get some money from me? And if so, how much? If I did go ahead and give them some of the money, what story would I tell them? Also, could they be trusted to keep a secret?

Finally, there were my friends and Tracy's friends to consider. Some of them would be very grateful to receive even a £1,000, but if I told them about winning the lottery, would they be trusted to keep it a secret and would they keep asking for more?

This sure was the hardest part of winning the lottery. It was such a large responsibility. If only I could have transferred a certain amount of money secretly into all my friends and family member's bank accounts, that would have been that. But in reality, you just couldn't do that. So,

Tracy and I had some long and difficult conversations about just who in our families should we give money to.

When I did discuss this with the financial advisor, he gave me a bombshell. Apparently, if you receive a large sum of money as a gift from someone, you will have to pay inheritance tax on that - if the donor dies within seven years of giving that money. If I died after I had given £100,000 to my brother, once the taxman had taken his 40% share, he would only receive £60,000. I was shocked to hear this as surely a gift is a gift and as I pay tax, why should the taxman get a cut of this? So, this scenario also played on my mind.

With all these questions going round in my mind, I reluctantly went back to school the next day. My job and its demands soon took over most of my thoughts, though the question of whether I should hand in my resignation sooner than later was also on my mind. I had until the first day of next term to do it, so there were six weeks between then and now. In the meantime, I still had to meet up with my solicitor and find an accountant. It was all so time consuming, but a necessary part of winning the lottery.

Next, I contacted my solicitor, Tim Watkins, in another free period during that first week back and arranged to meet him after school one afternoon. Tracy didn't come to the first meeting, as she couldn't get off work in time, though I did come clean with him about the lottery win. As Dave had remarked, Tim said that anything I told him would remain within the four walls of his office.

I had no reason to doubt his sincerity and trusted him to keep it a secret. Mind you, I think we gave him more business in that first year after winning the lottery than in a lifetime if we hadn't! He had to arrange paperwork on the various gifts to our friends and relatives; set up new wills for Tracy and me and sign off the various investments I had made with my newfound wealth. He also had to sort out the conveyance on the new house that we had decided to buy. But more of that later.

I also set the ball rolling with finding an accountant during that second half of the spring term. Our financial advisor, Adam Garner had written to me within a few days of us meeting with him and the letter was waiting for me when we got back from York.

In it he set out his terms of business and told me about the investments he had put that first half a million pounds into. He also said that we would need to meet every three months at first for progress reports and to check that I was happy with the way things were going, and no doubt see if I would let him invest some more of my money with him.

He did give me the name and contact details of an accountant that he recommended, Simon Paige, who was also based in central Manchester. Being busy at work, I decided to give him a go, rather than spend more time and effort trying to find an accountant myself, especially as I really wasn't bothered with that side of things.

I knew that having won the lottery, the services of an accountant was a must as they are the ones who act as go between you and the taxman. If they are any good, they should be able to sort all the various assets you have and 5put together a tax return that keeps as much money as possible for you and stops the taxman from taking more than he should do. Obviously now, the fact that I would be paying more tax per year than the whole of my teacher's salary was shocking in a way, but it was all part and parcel of my new life.

He was another person who I definitely needed to see, but as he didn't work at weekends, seeing him had to wait until the Easter holidays, which was the earliest that I would be able to fit him into my busy life.

I WON THE LOTTERY...

* * *

During our weekend away in York, Tracy, and I (after some disagreements), decided on the cover story that we would use to tell both our colleagues and not so close relatives and friends. We chose the one about my Uncle Philip, a distant relative, who had recently died. We had added a little more since Tracy first thought of it. He had been quite rich and had lived abroad for many years, which is why I hadn't seen him recently. He had left me a generous legacy which was going to enable us to go and buy a house in the Peak District, where we'd always wanted to live. We intended to start living the "Good Life", which for those who don't remember the TV sitcom, means giving up the day job to start living off the land. We didn't intend to keep pigs or other livestock of course - well maybe some chickens perhaps.

The bit about wanting to move to a bigger house in the countryside and maybe grow a few crops was actually true. The fact that we had been given enough money to do this in his legacy made our dream now possible. It may sound dishonest to some people but put yourself in my shoes. Would you like the whole world to know that you had won the lottery? Or would you prefer to keep it quiet and not be pestered by all and sundry? That was my aim, especially in the early days, though eventually I would change this story as you shall see.

We also took on board what Dave from the lottery had told us about taking things slowly and not rushing into things. This was fairly easy for me, seeing as I couldn't just quit my job like that. I had to work my notice and besides, I didn't want to let a lot of people – both colleagues and students down; what with all the exams to get through, followed by the results. I just couldn't walk away from my job as other lottery winners might have done. After I'd left school, I even went back there on GCSE results day to help out and advise some of the pupils on what to do next. After all, my contract didn't officially end until 31st August, so I felt a moral duty to be there.

With Tracy however, things were different. She only needed a month's notice before she could leave and although I advised her not to be too hasty, being an Aires, she jumped ship at the earliest opportunity. She decided to go at the end of May, once she had completed ten years there and so would be entitled to a higher pension; not that it really mattered.

Most of her colleagues were surprised to see her go, but they seemed to accept her story of coming into all this money when Uncle Philip died. Of course, I had to rein her in at times, as she was like a greyhound trying to get out of the traps, desperate to spend that money. At least the advice from the lottery people to spend it slowly on things that needed doing round the house kept her busy, along with going for beauty treatments and seeing her girlfriends who didn't work. She did become a regular visited to the Trafford Centre though, treating herself to new clothes, shoes and jewellery.

At first, we followed Dave's advice about taking things slowly and not going silly, though later we did get a little carried away in our spending. As he had advised, we made two lists of things that we wanted to spend our money on. The first list was made up of the small things that needed repairing or updating. It also included paying off all the debts that we owed. The biggest debt of all was the mortgage, but there were also things like credit cards and university fees to pay off. The second list was of buying luxury things like new cars and a house, as well as holidays to places that we could only dream of going to prior to the lottery win.

We began by looking around the house and the garden to see what needed mending or upgrading. The first thing we spent our money on was getting a new bathroom suite. For well over a year now the shower had been dripping and had been losing power, so we had put it on the list for replacing - when we could afford it. It was great going round to the bathroom centre and choosing whatever we wanted; not having to worry about our budget.

I was cautious however not to get any Tom, Dick, or Harry cowboy to do the job, but someone who had been recommended by a friend or a neighbour. The only problem was that if they were any good you had to wait a while for them to come and do the job. In fact, it was a few months before the plumber that we had chosen was free to come round, which tied in nicely with Tracy finishing work and being around the house when he was working.

In the garden with spring on the way, we decided to get a new garden bench and chairs, followed by a new garden shed. The new shed was erected straight away by the men from the garden centre who delivered it. In the past it would be lying in bits next to the old shed for a few weeks, waiting for me to get round to it. It was a nice feeling to know that I didn't have to struggle with putting something together like that anymore.

One of the best things that I enjoyed in the early days of winning the lottery was the day I found out that I had actually paid off my mortgage. It wasn't that much by some people's standards - £85,000 - but the satisfaction I felt, knowing that I now owned my house outright was one of the positives from the lottery winning experience. Adam helped sort that out for me, so when I opened the letter from the mortgage people and read it, I actually screamed out, 'Yes!!' Heaven knows what our next door neighbours thought.

Also, before that, I had easily paid off my credit card bill. The satisfaction wasn't as much, but with nearly £5,000 in debt on that, I was paying over £50 interest a month and finding it hard to bring the total I owed down. Guess what though? As soon as I paid it off, the credit card company wrote to me to say that they were increasing the credit limit by another £5,000! Talk about trying to get more money out of you!

In a way it was useful to me, as I was now starting to use a credit card more than I ever did in the past, what with paying for the new bathroom suite and the garden furniture. Plus, I was using it again to buy "smaller" things that I wanted such as a new computer and a new TV. But now I was now able to pay it off in full each month before any interest was added and it naturally made my credit score go right up.

* * *

Winning the lottery had another side of the coin that I never thought about before. I was now starting to employ people. Yes, they were there to look after my money, such as financial advisors, accountants, and solicitors. They all had my best interests at heart - allegedly - and so they had to be paid for their services, which if you don't look around can be rather expensive.

Apart from all the distant members of your family and your so called friends all wanting your money, there was also the Tax Man to look out for. As my financial advisor said, 'Unless you are one step of the Tax Man, he will squeeze you 'til you scream!' So, these three "employees" were essential and quite useful for me, especially in the early days.

Although it was very tempting for me to quit my job the day after receiving my money, I chose not to, and I wouldn't recommend it to anyone who becomes a lottery winner. The lottery people also said this to me and Tracy.

Besides, in teaching I just could not do this, as most contracts say you need to give at least half a term's notice or in some cases a whole terms notice.

No matter how much you hate your job, it is not a good idea to just up sticks and walk away. You see you never know if you might need the help or connections of your boss or colleagues sometime in the future. Plus, I would say that it is always best to keep friends rather than make enemies. Obviously if they know you are leaving your job because you have just become a millionaire, there is bound to be some jealousy and so the friendship that you had might break down as a result. If they didn't know about your lottery win, then ask yourself, would you like to keep them as a friend? I chose to keep them as a friend as friendship is precious and I reckon you need all the friends you can get in life. You just never know what's around the corner and when you might need to call in a favour from one of your friends.

That was the reasoning behind me not letting any of my colleagues know about the lottery win. Not that I didn't trust some of my colleagues to let the cat out of the bag, but I knew that even if you told just one colleague, the likelihood of them accidentally telling someone else was quite possible. Then that person would tell someone else and so on. You would have the bush telegraph working overtime! Then could you imagine the pupils finding out? Life would be impossible for me in the classroom.

No, I was quite determined that no one from school should know. I might tell one or two of them once I'd left, but only when I was well away from the school. I knew I had to make up a story of why I was leaving. Should I say the story of getting some money from my Uncle Philip? Or that I was leaving teaching to go into a different career? Or maybe that I'd had enough of teaching and just wanted out before I made my mind up?

ADAM MERTON

* * *

One day something happened at school which I wasn't expecting, which caused me to play my hand earlier than I expected. It happened in March, just days before the end of term The Headmaster called me into his office at the end of the day. Being summoned to the Headmaster's office was still quite scary, even for the staff, let alone the pupils, but Bob Evans was a lovely man, who cared for all his staff, and would back them up to the hilt against any accusations from pupils.

'Gary,' he said to me. 'Come and sit down.'

I did as I was told and wondered what he was going to tell me.

'I suppose you don't need me to tell you, but as you no doubt will have heard, our deputy head, John Mitchell is coming up for retirement at the end of the autumn term. As someone who is highly regarded by his colleagues……' (I thought he was referring to John), 'I feel that you would be the ideal person to fill his shoes.'

I hadn't been expecting this. Plus, with all that had been happening to me in the last few weeks, I had completely forgotten about his imminent retirement.

'I don't know what to say!' I blurted out.

'Of course, you would have to put in a formal application to make sure everything is above board. But as long as you want it, the job is yours.'

I was shocked and more. I truly didn't know what to say. I really wasn't ready to tell him that I too would be leaving at the end of next term. Nor was it the right time. This really did put me in a quandary.

'That is very kind of you, Bob. I really don't know what to say,' I replied half-heartedly, repeating myself in the process.

'You sound a little hesitant, Gary,' he replied with more than a hint of suspicion in his voice. 'I thought you'd be jumping at a chance like this!'

'It's just that I never thought that I would be considered, Bob. I thought it would be advertised for someone outside the school,' I lied.

'Nonsense!' he interjected. 'You're putting yourself down. I think you'd fill John's shoes admirably!'

'That's very thoughtful of you, Bob. But I'm not sure if I'd be up to the job,' I lied once more, knowing full well that if I hadn't won the lottery, I would be clutching at his feet begging him for the job!

'You surprise me, Gary.' By now he was showing signs of being exasperated. 'Of course, you'd be the ideal person. You've got lots of energy that you put into the school. The staff and the pupils all respect you and you're a great leader. Need I go on?'

I was beginning to crack and then all of a sudden, he threw me a lifeline.

'Perhaps you'd like a little time to think about it?'

"Phew!" I thought. "He's throwing me a lifeline here. Grab it!"

'Yes. That would be a good idea. It's just a little sudden Bob. If you don't mind, I would like some time to have a think about it and discuss it with Tracy.'

'Fine. That's not a problem, though I would appreciate a swift response Gary as we need to get the advert in as soon as possible.'

With that he stood up, indicating that my time with him was up and he had other business to get on with.

"Wouldn't it be funny if I told him that he could stuff his job because I was leaving anyway," I mischievously thought. But I knew I would never do that. However, I did know that I would have to hand in my resignation sooner than later. Maybe I should have told him then and there about my plans for the good life, but I was always one for putting off the moment. It could've all been sorted if only I'd been a little pushier. But that wasn't me of course.

That evening I told Tracy what had happened, and she blasted me.

'Why on earth didn't you tell him you were going to be leaving?' she moaned.

'If it was me, I would have told him there and then. That would have got it over with.'

'There's a time and place for everything and today was not the right time,' I replied firmly. But she wasn't having it.

'You've really got to let him know tomorrow. No buts!'

She was right and after a poor night's sleep, I determined to tell Bob Evans that morning. There was just one problem. He wasn't in that day, so I had to wait until he was back in school.

In the end, being me, I waited until the Easter holidays came and then I wrote him a letter, explaining that I had been left some money by my late Uncle Philip and that Tracy and I had always wanted to live in the country and that it was an opportunity not to be missed, and so on.

I know it was cowardly thing to do, but I just couldn't face him in the flesh. I'm sure with all his experience of sussing out pupils who were lying; he would also be able to tell that one of his staff was lying too. I just couldn't take that chance, so once the dust had settled and he'd had time to take it all in, things might get easier for me.

* * *

For the first time in quite a few years Tracy and I went away at Easter for a holiday. This was partly to escape the reaction of Mr. Evans – if I was miles away, he couldn't contact me to discuss my letter of resignation; and partly for Tracy and me to thrash things out regarding who was to get what from the lottery money.

A couple of days after the end of the Spring Term, we took off from Manchester Airport for a week in Turkey. I suppose we could have gone for two weeks, but there was so much to sort out and organise with the money and who we were going to give it to. Plus, Lesley and Jon were now home for the Easter vacation and there was still a possibility that I might give in and tell them about winning the lottery. Being away for a week would give me more time to decide.

Whilst I was about to give in my notice at school, Tracy still had to do the deadly deed at her place of work. She had decided to wait until she got back from the holiday before doing it. We both reckoned that having a break would give us renewed energy for the next phase.

The holiday was a last minute thing and as such I managed to get a bargain with a five star hotel in the resort of Sentido. It seems funny now looking back at it, going for a bargain when I didn't need to, but my mind set was still in 'being careful with money' mode.

I think we both just wanted to get away from it all and hopefully look at things from a distance. As we had enjoyed our mini-break in York so much, we wanted to repeat it as soon as we were able.

Although the holiday was great and we weren't plagued by the thought of overspending and then being in debt when we got back, the lottery win was still in my mind every day we were away. We did discuss things a couple of times, such as whether the financial advisor was the right one for us and how we should invest all that money.

The question of who should get some of the money still reared its ugly head and it led to a heated argument about who on Tracy's side of the family should get it. In the end I said to her, 'What if I gave you a million of the winnings and then you can decide how much you'd like to keep and how much you'd like to give away?'

That threw her a bit, but in the end, she agreed that was the best course of action. I really wasn't too bothered about how much she gave away, just as long as she didn't mention the 'L' word. So, she agreed not to say where it actually came from, but that I had received the money in a legacy from a distant uncle.

Perhaps the biggest problem of all was how and when we would tell Lesley and Jon about the Lottery win. Naturally our two children would be the first to benefit from the lottery win, but the problem was 'When?' Tracy was all for telling them straight away, especially as they were now home for Easter, but I wanted to wait until Lesley had finished her finals and was back home from Bath University. I really thought that if she found out before she sat her final exams she might go to pieces and fluff her exams. Or she could also go silly and tell all her friends and put herself under pressure from everyone around her all expecting her to give them some of the money.

Jon was even more of a liability, being that much younger and definitely more immature than his sister. I was worried more about telling Jon than Lesley, as he could possibly go wild and start telling his friends, especially as he was so into all the different forms of social media.

In the end I won, as Tracy saw all the potential pitfalls of telling Lesley before she finished at university. Heaven knows what would have happened if she had two or more years to go, as was the case with Jon.

Another reason for holding fire with her was that I was as keen as possible for both Lesley and Jon to lead normal lives as possible. Would it be good for her to graduate and then never have to work for a living again? She could of course do that, but the only people who do that are members of the royal family and the landed gentry. Besides, Lesley was all geared up for a career as a pharmacist. Giving her shit loads of money at her age was downright irresponsible.

I was very keen for none of the family to lose a sense of the value of money, as that is when it can easily slip through your fingers and before you know it, it's all gone. That is what has happened to some previous lottery and football pools winners. They spent it all like there's no tomorrow and then it's all gone, and they come down to Earth with a very big bump!

We both agreed that it would be best to drip feed them with money, rather than give them a large lump sum which they might go and blow within a few months. They could have a car each and I would also buy them a house each when the time came for them to settle down and start having a family. Until then they would get a monthly payment into their bank accounts, so they didn't go silly.

The other question that we sorted, or at least compromised on during our holiday was telling the relatives and giving them some of the winnings. I knew on the second question that whatever we gave them, it would not be enough in some people's eyes. The financial advisor had advised us that rather than giving money to all and sundry of the relatives, it would be best to draw the line at the principal ones. So that meant my brother and Tracy's brother only. The onus was then on them as to who of their partners/children would receive a cut of that and how much.

Perhaps it was a little brutal, as it seemed to be passing the buck, but it helped with the question of telling as few people as possible about the lottery win. If only those two relatives knew about the win, it might be possible to keep it a secret from the rest, by them telling a little white lie and saying that they had been left the money in a legacy from a distant relative and leave it at that.

The question of "when" was where I would not compromise. My initial plan had been to tell Lesley and Jon first of all, before anyone else, but Tracy kept on at me during the holiday that we should tell our brothers first, on the promise that they would not tell a soul. Then if they said they would not get any of the money. Half of me thought that it was a silly idea; and half of me thought that it would be OK.

I just didn't want Lesley and Jon hearing from someone else in the family before we had told them, as that would screw things up big time. Tracy's argument was that they would be home near the beginning of July, so if we told Alan and Barry in June, there wouldn't be that much of a gap between the two sets knowing. Plus, as Tracy would have left her job by then, they might get suspicious. After all we didn't really want to lie to our own brothers, did we?

On this problem, I stuck to my guns and firmly, saying that Lesley and Jon would hear first, then our two brothers would be next. Tracy wasn't at all happy with this, but eventually she was pacified when I bought her a brand new MX5, which I shall tell you about later.

* * *

Before all that happened, I had my final term at school to get through. Like York, we came back down to earth with an even bigger bump as we both returned to work. Tracy gave her resignation in at the beginning of May and was soon fending off myriads of questions about why she was leaving. Our story about the legacy pacified most people, but some remained suspicious.

With me I was dreading coming face to face with Bob Evans, but when he called me into his office to discuss my letter of resignation, he was the perfect gentleman and said he now knew why I was so reluctant to take on the role of deputy head. He also offered to write me a glowing reference, should I ever need it. I felt terribly guilty about this, but it couldn't be helped if I was to keep the lottery win a secret.

Once I'd had my meeting with Bob, word soon spread round the staff room that I was leaving. It only takes one person to let the cat out of the bag and hey presto, the whole world knows. So as soon as I entered the staff room, I was cornered by several of my colleagues.

'How come you are leaving?' 'Why are you going to live in the countryside?'

'When are you moving?' 'How can you afford it? 'How much money were you left by your uncle?' These questions and others were all asked by them.

So, I told them my story of how I had always wanted to live in the countryside and grow my own vegetables, have a few chickens, and live the good life. As an uncle of mine had left me some money in his will, we could now afford to do so and that is why I had resigned.

The second rounds of comments though were not so much questions but more statements like, 'You're mad!' 'You're causing a large vacuum in the English Department' and 'Good luck to you!' In the end most of my colleagues accepted the fact that I was going, though I did feel a hint of jealousy from one or two of them. Not so much about my leaving, but more of being given some money, as if it was a crime. Heaven knows what they would have been like if they had known the truth. I'm sure some would have asked for handouts, but as I was advised by my financial advisor, I had to draw the line somewhere.

The worst thing about it all was that in many ways I felt like I was abandoning a sinking ship. We all struggled to get the best out of the children. With one of the most experienced and respected (if I may say so myself) teachers going, things would only get harder for most of them. On the other hand, my replacement might bring some fresh ideas into the school and shake the lot of them up.

I know I was being selfish leaving, but there was no point in staying in something that I was fast losing interest in. Now I had all that money I didn't need to work anymore. In fact, I didn't need to work ever again. Nor did my children, for that matter.

We finally told Lesley and Jon about winning the lottery a few weeks before the end of term, fairly soon after they had come home from university. We sat them down together and told them straight out.

As expected, Lesley was all cool about it, whilst Jon went a bit silly at first in his reaction to the news. We both emphasised to them the need to not say anything to anyone and told them to tell the legacy story if anyone asked. Lesley wasn't too happy about telling Mike, her boyfriend this story, but when I told her about what happened to lottery winners who went public about her win, she agreed to keep quiet – for the time being at least.

Once our children had been told, it was the turn of our brothers. One thing I did compromise on this was to let their wives in on the secret. I wasn't sure if this was a good idea or not, but how on earth could you keep a large windfall of money from your nearest and dearest?

For my brother Alan I gave £500,000 as he deserved it and from that he could decide how much he wanted to give to his two children Samantha and Adam. I didn't give anything to my sister of course, mainly because she didn't need the money, as she was pretty well off through her husband's work and the legacies he had received from his parent's dying. Also, besides which, I was hardly talking to her in this moment in time, with past upsets still raw in my mind.

I didn't ask Tracy how much she gave to Barry, her brother. That was her business. But I was concerned that she might not have emphasised how important it was to keep it all a secret from anyone else.

Tracy didn't mind too much about what I gave Alan, as she knew how hard he worked in his printing business, and like me hoped that he could possibly take early retirement from it and start relaxing a little more.

When it came to giving money to my best friends, she was less than enthusiastic. In some ways she was starting to see that the money was partly hers, which it was in a way - if I had decided to share it equally with her. But in reality, I hadn't. I had given her a cut of one million for her to distribute amongst her family and friends as she saw fit, but that was as far as it went. I decided to hold fire about what to do with giving money my friends. I would make that decision once the summer holidays came.

The rest - now less than ten million pounds - was mine and mine to do with as I saw fit. Tracy didn't see it like that, though. I really didn't want to have a big argument about it, but it seemed inevitable when she started questioning me about just who I was going to give money to and how much? Maybe looking back, I should have said that I wasn't going to give money any to them or tell her that it was a lot less than I did give them in reality, but I just couldn't lie like that to my own wife. It just didn't seem right. Though of course, I did lie to lots of other people - all in the name of protecting my privacy.

* * *

As I said earlier, I bought Tracy a new car once she had left her work. She had driven a small Nissan Micra for several years now and over time she had grown to hate it. Every so often something would go wrong with it and that would need replacing. Once we got back from our holiday in Turkey, I said she was free to choose whatever car she wanted. Being a woman of a certain age, a Mazda MX5 was something that she had wanted for a few years now. She chose a navy blue version with a 1600 cc capacity engine.

She loved it and in the early days drove it at the slightest opportunity. I must admit that when I eventually had a go at driving it, I didn't quite share her enthusiasm. I thought it seemed that you were driving along the surface of the road, such was its low chassis. Although I felt that it had a kick when you pressed the accelerator, it just did not win me over. I must admit though, when the roof was down on a sunny day it was quite pleasant.

I also followed Tracy in getting a new car, though I waited until after half term to do this. I had been very good about not splashing out on anything major, but I finally succumbed a few weeks before I left my school.

One of the things that I promised myself if I ever won the lottery was to buy the car of my dreams. That happened to be a Ford Land Rover 4 x 4. That was a car that I'd always wanted and which I'd set my heart on for years. I had driven a much smaller and less powerful car for years, namely a Vauxhall Vectra, which had been OK for me, though it was starting to get rusty and needed work on it from time to time. Certainly, it was time for me to get a new car and rather than wait until I'd left my job, I let my ego take over here, which led me to make a big mistake.

When I first got it from the dealers I felt as proud as punch, being above almost every other car driver on the road. It took some getting used to as it was so much higher, wider, and longer than my previous car. It was also much more powerful at 2,000cc and had a strong "pull" on it every time you accelerated. As I said, it took a lot of getting used to with me gingerly driving it at first, scared that I might touch some other car as it was so much wider than my previous car.

One thing that I found really hard was parking it. Although it had power steering, it was a nightmare trying to fit it into most parking spaces, as they weren't designed for large cars. In the end I found myself driving round and round car parks trying to find a double space, so I could fit it in easily. I must admit that once I got so frustrated in trying to find a large enough space for it, that I just gave up and parked in a mother and baby space at the local supermarket. I didn't half get a dirty look from a young mother with a baby in a pushchair coming back to her car in the same row.

Then, with just a few days left of term I stupidly drove to school in it, showing off to both the staff and the pupils. Of course, everyone was staring at me and to make matters worse, there just weren't any spaces in the school car park large enough to fit it in. In the end I had to embarrassingly drive out of school and find a space on the road near to school. Even then I couldn't stop thinking about whether it would be alright and not be scratched by a passing pupil or a careless motorist.

For those of you who have ever owned a brand new car, you tend to get rather paranoid about something happening to it for the first few weeks of owning it. I was no exception and after a few days I started to realise what a huge mistake I had made. For the rest of the term, I either got the bus into school or got Tracy to drop me off and pick me up.

* * *

One evening in early July, a few weeks before the end of term, and soon after the children had come back from uni, something happened which knocked me for six. I had just finished my tea and Tracy had gone out for the evening with one of her friends when the doorbell rang. It was a young woman in her late twenties I would say, who was holding a notepad in her hand. I thought she might be a plain clothes police officer, but then she explained who she was.

'Hello. Mr Whitemore?' she asked without pausing for breath. 'My name is Sarah Watkins and I'm from the *Evening Leader*'.

Immediately the alarm bells started ring in my head. Someone from the local newspaper was on to me!

'Am I correct in saying that you recently won the lottery?'

All sorts of thoughts shot through my brain of which the main one was, "How on Earth had she found this out?" swiftly followed by, "Who's spilt the beans?"
I had to think quickly.

I started to laugh, trying to sound as natural as possible.

'What on Earth gives you that idea?' I replied with more fake laughter.

'Oh, we had a phone call yesterday telling us that fact,' she answered, hoping I'd come clean and admit it.

'I think someone's been telling you porky pies, love,' I countered. 'I'm a secondary school teacher and I can think of at least ten different pupils who would try a stunt like that.'

Then I thought of a question which threw her.

'Did you actually meet this person?'

'Er no,' she replied sheepishly.

'Well how do you know if it's true or not then?' I fired back.

Then I came up with another shot.

'Anyway, if I had actually won the lottery, do you think I would still be living here in Chorlton in a three bedroom semi, still working every hour God sends in a tough comprehensive? No, I would be off like a shot, living in some mansion out in Cheshire. That's where you should be looking for your lottery millionaire!'

Luckily, my brand new 4 x 4 was parked further down the street as Tracy liked to put her car in the garage now that she had a decent car, and it was easier to keep the drive clear for her when she came home.

Finally, I fired one last broadside.

'Tell me,' I asked. 'Was it a male or a female who made the call?'

'I....I don't know.' she stuttered. 'I was just told to come and pay you a visit and find out more.'

'Well, you can tell your bosses that if they are stupid enough to believe an anonymous phone call and then send a gormless reporter round to an over worked teacher's house, interrupting him when he should be marking Class 8B's English books, then their newspaper deserves to go to the dogs!'

Her face went bright red, and her eyes dropped to the ground.

'I'm very sorry Mr. Whitemore. I won't take up any more of your valuable time.'

And with that she turned and went, whilst I broke out into a sweat, thinking will she still make up a story about me and just who made that phone call? I had a list of people in my head that might have done it, but there was no way I could find out which one of them it was.

That was the problem with trying to keep the lottery win a secret. Tracy and I had told just six people, apart from the solicitor; yet anyone of them could have told someone, who could have told someone else. Who knows? It shocked me to the bone and started me thinking about moving house sooner than later. Still, we had all the time in the world in a few weeks' time once I'd left school. I also got one of those doorbell intercom things fitted, so I didn't have to go to the door whenever the doorbell rang. I could check just who it was and tell them to go away if necessary. I'd become quite paranoid about who might come to the door. First, I had to go through the motions for a few more weeks and then say my goodbyes to everyone at school.

That final assembly at school was very sad for me, not just because I was leaving and saying goodbye to both my colleagues and all the pupils, but also because I was living a big lie; such was my need to protect myself from them all knowing about my lottery win.

Two other teachers were leaving that day with me, and the head had the grace to leave me until last. He gave me a great send off in what he said, and I said a few words to thank him and all the staff, but it was really hollow on my part, knowing the truth of why I was leaving. Looking back, I feel quite ashamed of the whole deception with the lies that I told, but back then I was so paranoid about people finding out about my lottery win, so that is why I did what I did.

The staff kindly gave me a present of an E Reader device with several classic novels already stored on it. I found it quite moving to be a recipient of their generosity. I could easily have bought one myself if I wanted to of course, but as they say, "It is the thought that counts".

5 GOING UP THE COUNTRY

Here I was then in the summer of 2012, starting to finally feel the benefits of winning the lottery. I had just quit my job and as it was the summer holidays, I was able to chill out sooner than normal.

Usually at this time I would finish off work at school during the first week of the holidays. Then I might chill out. Then I would go away for a week or two. Then it would be preparing for a new term. This involved going into school before the autumn term started to check timetables, sort out the textbooks for each year group and so on. Then the term would start, and it would be back to the grindstone. Only now I no longer had that pressure. Instead, I could look forward to the rest of my life so to speak. So, at the end of the school holidays my holiday would continue.

One of the first things I did in the summer holidays was to take the Land Rover back to the dealers. I knew within forty eight hours of buying it that I had been rather too hasty in buying this car. I now know that splashing out on something expensive was a natural thing for the average lottery winner to do. Spending lots of money on an expensive item such as a luxury holiday, jewellery or in my case a flashy car, was what most lottery winners did in the early days of their lottery win.

The look on the car salesman's face when I walked in was a picture! Although he wasn't happy, I was well within my rights to take it back. After some haggling, I was able to do a part exchange on a smaller and less powerful car.

So, that is how I came to be the driver of a nearly new blue Ford Focus RS. The registration plate was a 10, but at least it didn't stand out like a sore thumb on the drive, and it had only 12,000 miles on the clock. Tracy liked it better than the Land Rover as it was much smaller and didn't take up half as much space on our drive.

'At least I don't have to climb up ten steps to get in,' she joked on our first drive in the Sierra. It was a hard first lesson for me and from then on, I was a lot more cautious about spending big and flashy.

* * *

The next few weeks seemed to rush by. Every day I was glued to our new TV watching the Olympics taking place in London and the Home Counties. I did wish though that I could be down in London watching them in person. So, when one of my now ex-colleagues at school rang me up to say he had a couple of spare tickets for the athletics I jumped at the chance.

Although it was only for a morning session at the Olympic Stadium, it was still a fantastic experience to have been there watching history taking place so to speak. We had no problem finding a hotel as we could afford to stay where we liked. Through one of the receptionists at the hotel we were able to get some tickets to watch the table tennis taking place at the Excel Centre in London's Docklands, which was an added bonus.

I will never forget the feelgood feeling that I had being amongst everyone at these events. From the police through to the Games Maker Stewards, everyone was so friendly. We even fitted in seeing a couple of Tracy's old work colleagues whilst we were down there.

I WON THE LOTTERY...

No sooner than we got home we were getting ready to go on our third holiday of the year; this time up to Scotland. Neither of us had ever been there before, so we decided to go up there for about ten days as we thought about our next move. We drove in my "new" car which did itself proud and visited so many places including Edinburgh during the Festival, Glasgow, Inverness, Stirling, and Perth. The scenery was fantastic and the people friendly, even if at times you couldn't understand what they were saying!

* * *

It was only when September came that it finally sunk in that I had won the lottery. My life was now completely different in every aspect. I didn't have to wake up to the alarm anymore, which was a great feeling. I didn't have to put up with all those impatient drivers going to and from their workplaces each day, and I didn't have all that pressure that being a secondary school teacher brings.

In fact, I started to become more pleasant and laid back, seeing as I wasn't rushing here, there, and everywhere. The main things that took up our time during that autumn were meetings with our new financial advisor and looking for a new house to move to, which I will go into more detail about below.

It was nice being able to drive down to Bath to visit Lesley for the weekend on a Friday morning, rather than on a Friday evening straight after school had finished. In fact, Lesley was now living with her boyfriend Mike just outside Bath and enjoying her new job.

The same went for Jon. This time when he went back to uni in Lincoln, Tracy and I were able to stay over for a couple of days and visit this historical town, similar to York in many ways. Our life was now going at a slower pace and things seemed to be settling down.

Looking back, the biggest mistake I made after winning the lottery was moving to a new house to live in the countryside. It was not so much as the house, but more of where I decided I wanted to move to.

One of the biggest desires I had after winning the lottery was to buy a nice house somewhere in the countryside up on the edge of the Peak District, not too far from Manchester, but out in Derbyshire, near Buxton or Glossop perhaps? In my mind's eye I was imagining all that peace and quiet and all that lovely fresh air.

In retrospect, maybe I was too keen to move to a new house too soon, especially one in the countryside. If only I had taken my time a little more and thought things through in more detail.

Although moving out into the countryside was my dream, Tracy didn't quite share my enthusiasm and that was the beginning of the end of our marriage. She had her doubts from day one but got caught up with my enthusiasm and I guess went along with it because she too fancied moving up the social scale to a posh, detached house.

If only we had moved to somewhere nice in the suburbs, say in Cheshire, rather than in the Peak District, we might still be together, but with all that money in the bank, we charged into something that we hadn't quite thought through enough.

We both agreed that we would like to move to a detached house somewhere in the countryside, but that was about it. We hadn't thought about how many bedrooms it should have; how big the garden should be and what other rooms we wanted to have in the house. I suppose we both agreed that it could be old, as long as it had been modernised and didn't have any work needed to bring it up to scratch. But that was about it. Soon we would find out that there was a whole lot more involved in moving to a bigger house, further up the social ladder and in the countryside of course.

We started to look at potential properties on the internet and as soon as we started to contact a few estate agents to register our interest, things began to hot up. Once they knew we were cash buyers with no onward chain, they were falling backwards over themselves trying to sell us houses that were in no way suitable for us.

Also, we hadn't really thought about what our budget should be. It was more a case of finding a detached house out in the country somewhere east of Manchester, rather than saying we were looking in the £500,000 or even £1 million plus price band. There were all sorts of different detached properties that we needed to sift through. Some were houses with stables attached to them, which were clearly not what we were looking for. Others had acres of land, which again was a "no, no", as I really didn't want to be burdened with looking after all that land.

Many were in the wrong location, which was a pity as there were some that we both really liked. Then there were barn conversions, which we were both united in our dislike of such places. Whilst others had lots of work that needed doing on them before they were up to scratch. So, our choices began to become more limited when we discarded properties like these. In a way this sifting process helped us to see just exactly what we were looking for.

After a few weeks of looking, we knew when something suitable we liked the look of came up. The only problem was time. After that local reporter incident, I was keen to move as soon as possible, before anything else happened. Although we weren't in a chain as such and didn't have a deadline to meet, we both hoped we would be in our new house by Christmas.

That was the thing that spurred us on to try and find something we both liked, and preferably something that did not have a chain at the other end. The first two houses we looked at seemed fine on paper, but once we saw them "in the flesh", they weren't right. One had damp in the bathroom, which although you couldn't see it, you could certainly smell it! The other was overlooked by an even bigger house at the back of the garden, where you could hear young children playing noisily. Although I do not have anything against young children as such, I did want a house that was quiet and peaceful, which was the whole point of me wanting to move to the countryside.

'Third time lucky' is a well-known saying and in our case, it was the third house that we went and looked at that we decided was "the one". It was situated a few miles outside Glossop, within the Peak District National Park and was a former farmhouse.

The estate agent's description read like this:-

We are pleased to offer for sale this rare opportunity to purchase a unique and original stone built farmhouse, originally built in 1890. It was completely rebuilt and refurbished in 2004. It is located in a rural location within the Peak District National Park, near to the town of Glossop, Derbyshire and has stunning views over the local valley. The property sits on an approximately ½ acre plot and offers over 3000 square feet of living area. The accommodation briefly comprises of an entrance porch, hallway, downstairs WC, a large lounge, snug or second lounge, dining room and a luxury kitchen/breakfast room with attached utility room to the ground floor. There is also a large conservatory to the side. Upstairs there is a master bedroom with an ensuite and dressing room; three further bedrooms, one with ensuite, plus a study and two family bathrooms. Outside there is a double garage with driveway to front. To the side and rear are extensive lawned gardens, with two sheds and a summer house, all in approximately half an acre of land.

It finished with the words, "Viewings are advised to appreciate what this property has to offer".

There was so much going for it that we naturally both fell in love with it when we viewed it. I liked the fact that it had half an acre of land for the garden, which was just right as far as I was concerned, as I wanted to have a vegetable plot, with chickens to boot. Tracy liked the fact that not only did it have four large bedrooms, but two of them had ensuite bathrooms, so our two children would be catered for, should they come and stay or in Jonathon's case wish to continue living at home. Plus, there was a room where guests could stay.

Downstairs there was a large living room, a dining room, as well as a second reception room, which could be used as a games room or a snug. The kitchen was to Tracy's liking, although it didn't have a gas cooker, being out in the country. But this was only a minor compromise as far as I was concerned. I was sure that Tracy would soon become au fait with using an electric cooker instead.

We also liked the large conservatory at the side of the house, which faced east with views of Kinder Scout to die for. In fact, it was the views which sold it to both of us. I almost forgot to say there was a lovely grey slate patio on the back with integral barbecue, plus two sheds and a summer house at the end of the garden. Although the garden was mostly lawn, some of this could easily be ploughed up to make way for my allotment, with an area for chickens. I'd always fancied living the good life. So now here was my opportunity!

What about the price of this idyll? A mere £850,000 or near offer. As money was no object, I was tempted to offer the asking price, but when I mentioned this to my financial advisor, he advised offering £50,000 below the asking price and then raising our offer in £10,000 increments.

Wisely, Tracy and I both decided we needed to sleep on it and not rush into things. There was one thing I haven't mentioned which would put off most people. The house was half a mile down a country lane, with the next door farm a mile away across the valley. This was the one disadvantage and the thing that would lead to our downfall. The alarm bells did ring in my ears all through the buying negotiations, but I put them out of my mind, reckoning that we would soon get used to the isolation.

In the end the sellers - a middle aged couple who were getting divorced - a portent of the future perhaps? - came down £30,000 below the asking price. The fact that we were cash buyers helped swing it, according to the estate agent. Surprisingly, although they had asked for our address and other details in the early stages, they didn't question us as to how we could make a leap from a small semi-detached in Chorlton-Cum-Hardy to an £800,000 detached house within the Peak District National Park. I could only assume that our solicitor had a quiet word in their ears, saying we had recently come into a "legacy".

With our solicitor pulling out all the stops, we finally moved into *Hill View* (as we renamed it) in late November 2012. It was pouring down, and this was perhaps a portent of things to come. I couldn't wait to move, though Tracy didn't seem to share my enthusiasm. I thought we had "made it" moving into a detached house after my working class upbringing in a two-up, two down terraced house. Both Lesley and Jon had not seen the house in the flesh but had seen the details on the internet. Neither seemed that interested to be honest.

The first few weeks were spent settling in, getting to know Glossop, our nearest town and just exploring the countryside. As it was just about winter, the garden and the chickens would have to wait until next spring. Both our brothers and their wives came to visit us, as did some of our ex-colleagues from work. But as we had no neighbours as such, we soon began to feel the isolation, especially Tracy.

Before we knew it though Christmas had arrived and that kept us both busy. Jon said he did like the house when he first came home from uni, but for the Easter holidays the following year, decided to stay down in

Lincoln, which was perhaps his way of saying he didn't really like it. Lesley had decided to stay down in Bath over Christmas at Mike's parents and didn't see the house until well into the New Year when there was snow. I knew she was busy with her new job, but Tracy was cross with her for not making the effort.

We didn't have time to go away on holiday at Christmas, which we might have done, had we still been living in Chorlton, but we did get to go to one of Tracy's brother's Christmas parties which were always good fun.

It was one of those parties where everyone was talking at once and you couldn't hear yourself speak. We'd just helped ourselves to some food and went into another room which was much quieter than the kitchen diner. All of a sudden, this man in his sixties came up to me and said,

'So, you're the lottery winner then?'

'I beg your pardon?' I replied somewhat shocked.

'Don't deny it mate! Everyone here is talking about you behind your back.'

'I don't know what you're talking about!' I answered back, not very convincingly.

'What's it like with all that cash to burn? I bet you're a mean bastard. Surely you could spare me just a teeny bit of all that money?!'

I was lost for words but starting to get angry.

Tracy intervened, which put him in his place..... for about a second.

'How dare you use such disgusting language! You don't know us from Adam. Even if we had won the lottery, we certainly wouldn't give any of it to a slime ball like you!'

It didn't have any effect. Things were getting heated. He continued,

'Come on mate; just a thousand will do? That's all I'm asking. It would help me get out of a nasty situation. Ah come on!'

With that I stood up and was about to hit him, when Barry came in and said,

'You! Out now!'

The man reluctantly got up and moved away.

Barry escorted him to the front door.

He was still going on, 'I know they're millionaires. Jill told me!'

There was an awkward silence. Then Tracy burst into tears, and I put my arm around her.

'Come on darling!' I said. 'We're leaving'.

With that we got our coats and said goodbye to Barry who nodded sympathetically, whilst the irritating man sneered as we walked past him.

'I'm terribly sorry about all this. I really don't know what to say', was all that Barry could say.

Jill his wife, was nowhere to be seen, which was just as well, seeing as she seemed to be the source of the leak. I would've given her a piece of my mind if she'd been around.

Tracy was still crying when we got in the car.

I said 'Don't worry! It's over now'.

But was it? It left a bitter taste in the mouth, so to speak and caused a rift between Tracy and her sister-in-law for a long time.

The lottery had made its first wound of many wounds in our lives.

* * *

After that incident Tracy said that she no longer felt safe at *Hill View*, especially now that someone outside of our immediate family knew about the lottery win. I argued that it was a one off case and that we were miles away from where that toe-rag lived. Nevertheless, she said that we were vulnerable out here in the sticks, miles from civilisation. I tended to agree with her and decided that the solution was to have a dog. Tracy, much to my surprise went for the idea hook, line, and sinker. She said it would get us both out of the house more, taking it on long walks - clearly a dig at me, as over the Christmas period I had been stuck in front of the TV for a lot of the time and was gradually gaining a pot belly with all the food and drink I had recently consumed.

I went across the valley to ask our nearest neighbour on the farm if he knew of anyone who might have a spare dog going. A bit of a long shot I know, but I really didn't want to go through the rigmarole of going through a dog rescue place; what with all that checking up on you and the house. I liked to keep my privacy even more now.

A few days later the farmer rang me to say that he had heard of another farmer looking to rehome one of his sheep dogs that wasn't up to the job, so to speak. I jumped at the chance when I heard that and later that day Tracy and I drove over to his farm to check the dog out. She was a bitch who was five years old and had a heart defect which stopped her from running as much as she should, but apart from that she was still very healthy.

Tracy liked her and "Dolly" as she was called sniffed us carefully at first, before wagging her tail vigorously indicating that we had passed the test. We took her for a short walk to see how she handled on a lead and if she took to us. We both agreed that she seemed fine and that we would like to have her. After giving the farmer a generous donation, we put her into the back of the car and drove home.

As we drove home, we suddenly realised that as she had been a working dog she had no bed, plus she smelt like she needed a wash. So, we made a detour into Glossop to buy a bed, blanket, shampoo, and some dog toys to keep her occupied whenever we went out.

Once back at *Hill View,* we let her have a good wander around the house so she could get her bearings and start to feel at home. She sniffed around the house gingerly to begin with, whilst both Tracy and I talked to her, telling her that was her new home now. Then it was time for a bath, which she wasn't at all happy with, but once that was done and she'd had a good shake, she settled down.

We both agreed that "Dolly" wasn't the best name for her, so we threw different suggestions for a new name around until we settled on "Tess" after *Tess of the D'Urbervilles,* one of my favourite novels. As life continued at *Hill View,* Tess gradually became part of the family and Tracy started to feel more secure once more.

* * *

Those first couple of months at *Hill View* were what I would call our "honeymoon period", mainly because things seemed so idyllic. It was great to wake up naturally and not to the sound of an alarm going off in the middle of a dream. Then as soon as you opened the curtains in the bedroom, you had a view to die for – that is if it wasn't misty or foggy.

Perhaps that was the first crack to appear in the honeymoon period - the weather. Being in the Pennines the weather was rainy quite a lot of the time, but so was the whole of Manchester in fact! It was just the fact that as you were out in the country if it rained, a sort of gloom came over the place, which affected both of us. On the other hand, when it was sunny both our spirits were lifted, but being brutally honest, there were more rainy, gloomy days than sunny ones.

Then there was the isolation of the place. For instance, we didn't have our friends and neighbours popping round every five minutes as before. So, it seemed much quieter than at Chorlton. Also, with Lesley now living in Bath and Jon away at uni in Lincoln, the house was noticeably too big for our needs, and it started to seem empty.

The early days of living at *Hill Top* kept Tracy busy with changing the decor of the place. She chose to repaint the dining room and the living room and two of the bedrooms. We tried getting some painters in, but when we gave our address, they made excuses or never turned up to give us a quote. When we tried ringing them back, we found our number had been blocked. I guess it was down to the remoteness of the place. In the end we went and bought the paint and did the repainting ourselves, which kept us busy.

One big mistake that I made in buying *Hill View* was not having a surveyor's report done on the house. Stupidly, I thought that as the house had been modernised a few years earlier everything would be hunky dory; but that was not the case. The first problem we discovered was that there was damp in the utility room which faced north. The rendering that had been done on the outside wall had started to crumble with all that penetrating rain and so water had got in. Luckily through an estate agent in Glossop I was able to find a damp specialist who came in before Christmas and got the problem sorted.

Then, when some of the lights flickered in some of the bedrooms and then cut off the electricity in the house when I flicked a switch, I realised that the wiring was a little dodgy. That too needed sorting, and again we had to pay for that to be put right. The electrician started soon after Christmas, but it took him two weeks to get it sorted and he then charged a small fortune for his services. But again, I felt it was money well spent.

* * *

Gradually, the longer we lived in *Hill View*, the more our moods began to change. Tracy became irritable at the slightest thing going wrong and I found myself avoiding her when she was like this.

For instance, if we wanted a basic thing like milk, we just couldn't pop out and buy it from some corner shop down the road. We had to drive a couple of miles at least, to the mini-mart in Glossop and then drive back again. This took half an hour of our time rather than five minutes.

I think the isolation of the place got to Tracy much earlier than it did to me. We both accepted that we were now living a new lifestyle where we had everything we wanted, but in reality, we didn't have everything. The one thing we didn't have was other people's company. We needed different people in our lives, apart from each other.

Once the New Year of 2013 came in, things started to get worse for us month by month. I don't know if it was the fact that the year had a "13" in it, but they do say 13 is an unlucky number.

In January after it get very cold with the snow, we found that we had to have the central heating on all day just to keep the house warm. This wasn't a problem as far as I was concerned, but Tracy had always felt the cold more than me, coming from the South and so was not happy with this situation.

One evening Tracy was moaning that it was still cold, so I lit the wood burner and put a couple of large logs onto it.

"Now that should heat up the room," I thought to myself.

I was lying on the sofa, looking at the different flames that could be seen coming from the logs, thinking how pleasant it looked, when it all kicked off between me and Tracy.

'This is all so cosy,' I said to Tracy. 'Isn't it great living here?' I ventured.

'No, it's bloody not! she retorted. 'I really don't like it here anymore'.

I couldn't believe my ears! 'Had she really said that?' I thought.

'You're joking?' I quipped back.

'No. Sorry to disappoint you, but I'm being brutally honest with you,' she replied. 'I never really wanted to move here in the first place. What, with the problems with the damp; then the electrics going wrong. Plus, we never have anyone coming to see us anymore. I think this is the worse move we've ever made!'

I just could not believe what I was hearing. After all the time we spent looking at house details on the Internet and going to visit some of the places we liked. Then moving into a house which had every mod con and not ever having to work anymore. Surely the house had some saving graces.

'So, you want to move back to Chorlton then?' I snapped.

'Not necessarily,' came the reply. 'Just somewhere near civilisation. Somewhere where I can talk to the neighbours and not have to drive ten miles to buy some bloody milk!'

I could have continued the argument, but I thought better of it. I was not one for arguing in the first place, unless I really had too, and I wanted to have Tracy on my side. If she was getting fed up living here, did that mean that we would have to move again? I really didn't want to do that, so soon after spending all that money on this place. Plus, I did like it and wanted to give it a go.

'It's early days yet,' was all I could muster up.

With that she stomped off to bed whilst I sat there, mooching things over.

One of the major problems of living at *Hill View* was the lack of visitors. Although some of the family and our friends had come out to visit us in the first month of us living at *Hill View*, we started to notice the isolation. No one came to visit us at all during the cold snap we had in February, so it meant the only people we saw were each other for weeks on end. Naturally, we started to get fed up with our own company.

At our old house there were plenty of people around us, as well as lots of houses. Here there were neither of these and unless we drove into Glossop or occasionally

Hadfield, we never saw a soul. The postman was the only person who regularly came to our house, but even then, it was not every day. I had a feeling that he deliberately waited until he had a pile of post for us before he made a delivery.

It was obvious that there was now a new line dividing us from our friends. Although people were friendly enough when you rang them up, this didn't translate into them bothering to make the journey over to us. So gradually we saw less and less of them. We did however have Lesley and Mike come and stay for a few days in January. That lightened the mood somewhat, but once they went, there was emptiness in the house again.

Tracy did have the idea of opening the house up as a bed and breakfast, but after discussing the pros and cons of a b and b business between us, we decided against it. Whilst we had a couple of rooms spare for such a venture, the possibility that you might get some seedy person or troublemakers put us off. What if we had to call the police out in the middle of the night? It was a nonstarter without a doubt.

It was getting clearer that Tracy wasn't happy in the house anymore. She had started going into Glossop and further afield for beauty treatments and the like. She now had her hair and nails done once a week and she started attending a gym, partly to get fit, but mainly for the company, I guess. With her not around as much, the house seemed quieter than ever.

Meanwhile in all of this I was busy sorting out the garden. I set out an area to the side of the house in the garden where the vegetable plot was to go. I hired a small digger to dig up the ground as it was just too hard a job to do by myself. I built a couple of concrete sections at one end for a compost heap. Then we had a greenhouse built at the other end. This was delivered and erected by a local garden centre and looked quite impressive when finished.

Now all we needed were some plants to put in the ground and grow. Tracy and I visited the garden centre to stock up on a selection of seeds as well as some small plants that would hopefully grow into lovely flowers. I really quite enjoyed this as it gave me something to do and kept my mind off the isolation of the place.

Having the dog did provide us with plenty of amusement, as we could go out together with Tess for long walks, admiring the views and getting much fitter than we had been for many years. Having the vegetable patch or "allotment" as I called it also took up some of our time. It was fun digging up the weeds and removing stones to make the soil healthy again. Choosing what veg to grow and then nurturing it from a tiny seed into a juicy vegetable or fruit was also very rewarding.

One of the worst things that happened to us in the first six months was being trapped in our own house! Well not literally as you shall see. We had decided to go down to the local supermarket to get some food shopping. Tracy put the bags into the back of the car, and we started going down the lane from the house to the main road. As we were coming round the bend, which was not far from the main road, I had to brake pretty sharpish. The reason being was that some idiot had decided to fly tip a load of rubbish across the road. It wasn't just a few bin bags of rubbish; it was a whole lorry load and there was no way we could drive through that.

The only thing I could do was to reverse the car and drive back to the house and phone the local council. Driving in reverse along a narrow lane for almost a mile is not recommended. Several times I had to stop and go forward as I was about to go into the hedge. All the time Tracy was going on about how bad the fly tippers were and how they had no morals and perhaps it was not such a good idea to live in a house a mile down a country lane.

In the end it took the council over twenty four hours to come and remove the rubbish. The problem was they hadn't said they would let me know that the road was clear. So rather than driving down there in the hope of finding the rubbish gone, I had to take two journeys on my bicycle to check. The first time, later on in the afternoon it was still there. The next morning, I did the same thing again, and thankfully they had done their job, only this time the rain started to come down as I was coming home.

The experience of being trapped in your own home was quite worrying. Apart from Tracy continuing to complain about the whole thing, my imagination went into overdrive. What if there was a fire? How would the fire engines be able to get to the house? What if one of us was taken ill and we needed an ambulance? Again, the same scenario crept into my mind. Though I suppose they could have carried the trolley over the rubbish and then pushed it down the lane. Though by then Tracy or I could have died! It didn't bear thinking about.

On another occasion, we had a power cut. It was just after eight o'clock and Tracy was watching *Eastenders*. Everything went black and I stumbled to find my mobile phone and put the light on. Eventually I found some candles and lit them. So, there we were in this old farmhouse in the middle of nowhere, living just like it might have been a hundred years ago.

'This is fucking impossible!' she shouted and stormed off upstairs; presumably to bed. I didn't bother going after her as I knew that it would only make things worse, so I left her to cool down.

I sat on the sofa with Tess curled up next to me and tried to read a book in the dim light. Just before 10 o'clock the lights came back on and power was restored. I extinguished the candles and let Tess out for a wee, before going up to see if Tracy was awake and more importantly had calmed down.

When I went into our bedroom, she wasn't there which shocked me. I walked along the landing and saw the door to the spare bedroom was shut. Then I heard the sound of snoring coming from inside. "So that's where she is", I thought.

For the first time ever in our marriage we slept in separate beds in the same house. I was quite upset by it and wasn't sure whether to go in and wake her up to see why she had done such a foolish thing. I chose to let her be as it might have made matters worse. I didn't sleep well that night, I can tell you.

The next morning, she was all apologetic and said that she was so angry with missing her favourite soap that she decided to go to sleep and that she chose the spare bedroom to teach me a lesson. What lesson I was supposed to learn was beyond me, but it was obviously a sign of things going from bad to worse between us.

* * *

One bright light on the horizon for me was that City had got to the Cup Final for the second time in two years. This was something that I could not miss and through being a season ticket holder I was able to get one of the prized tickets. It meant that I would be out all day, though I suppose Tracy didn't mind that.

I went to Wembley on the train from Piccadilly on a football special full of city fans which meant there was a great atmosphere all the way to London. I had a great day apart from the fact that City lost 1-0 to Wigan Athletic. The homeward journey dragged somewhat. I did text Tracey to say I had arrived at Piccadilly station, but she didn't reply.

When I finally got back just after 11.00pm, there were no lights on in the house. Obviously, Tracy had gone to bed. "Pity she couldn't stay up to see me in," I thought.

As I came in through the door, I heard Tess growling and as soon as I put the light on, she came bounding over to me, her tail wagging a friendly welcome.

I quickly went into the downstairs loo for a pee, and then I went into the kitchen for a glass of water. I noticed a white envelope on the kitchen table. It said, 'Gary' on it, in Tracy's handwriting. A lump came into my throat. Was it what I thought it was? Surely not? Perhaps it was some bill that she wanted me to pay? Or some tickets for a raffle? All sorts of ridiculous thoughts went through my head, but instinctively I picked it up and opened it.

It said:

Gary

I really don't know how to write this letter, but the plain fact is I hate living here. I know you think it's fantastic, but I really can't spend another day or night here. I was hoping to just say that was the sole reason for moving out, but the truth is that I have found someone else to share my life with and I'm leaving you and moving in with him. He cares for me and I for him. There's no point in me continuing to live a lie. The plain fact is I don't love you anymore. I know I'm hurting you big time, but you can't change people's feelings. I'm sorry to be brutally honest with you Gary, but that is the way that I feel about you now. In fact, I have felt that way for some weeks now and I really can't go on like this. So, in our best interests I feel it is time for me to go and start a new life. Sorry, but that's the way it is. I'm sure you'll get over it and find someone else who suits you.

Goodbye.

Tracy

6 DON'T YOU WANT ME

That first day after Tracy left me, I was in a complete state of shock. I should have seen it coming I suppose, but I was too caught up in the house, the dog and myself. I had a terrible night not sleeping as you would expect and eventually got up at 6.00am, just as the sun was breaking through on the horizon.

I made myself a coffee to get my senses working, although I felt like shit. I'd sent three texts to Tracy and tried to call her numerous times last night, but naturally there was no reply. I went over and over in my mind what had gone wrong with the marriage? Was it the house? Was it the dog? Was it me? Was it the money? Or was it a combination of all these things? Yes. It probably was all these, and more. "What should I do next?" was the question going through my mind.

I decided to put Tess in the car and drive up into the hills and go for a long walk. That way the fresh air would clear my mind and wake me up, giving me a chance to work things out logically. Fifteen minutes later I was up on the moors with Tess at my side, walking purposely along a ridge with views of Derbyshire in front of me.

Part of me wanted Tracy to come back, hence the texts, and part of me said, "It's over. Time to move on!" My mind was like a pendulum swinging from side to side. Another question going through my mind was, "What about the children?" "Should I tell Lesley and Jon? Or should I keep quiet for the time being?" Seeing as Lesley was busy with her job and Jon was away at uni, I decided to hold fire for the moment. Mind you Tracy may well have told one or both of our children by now. What then? I of course had no control over this. Maybe if I just sent a text to Lesley, asking her to ring me....

I reached into my pocket for my phone to send a text to Lesley, but it wasn't there. Then I remembered that it was back at the house. The battery on it was nearly dead, so I had left it at home to charge. So, I couldn't send any texts or ring anyone. Although it might be seen as a negative event, not having a mobile phone with you all alone on the moors, miles from anywhere; in a way I felt like a sort of freedom up there without the safety of a phone.

Perhaps the isolation up on the moor would do me good? Or maybe it could have the opposite effect? Mind you, I was isolated enough anyway at the old farmhouse. My mind would not settle down. This was obviously a result of all the trauma of the past twenty four hours. My mind was like a pendulum, swinging in one direction and then the other. I just could not settle on making any decisions easily. But at least I was up on the moor away from all that negative energy that the house had caused. I loved the freedom of being up here, away from everyone. Clearly Tracy didn't, and that was one of the reasons why she had left. What if I said to her, "We'll move back to Manchester, and you can choose a house that you like?" Would she come round? Maybe that's what I should do?

Then there was the question of this other man. Who was he? Where did she meet him? What did he have that I didn't? Would it last? Maybe she would see what a stupid move it was and decide to come home to me? I went over and over in my mind the conversations we'd had and tried to see if there were any clues in what she said. I just couldn't think of her mentioning any other males. Perhaps he was someone at the gum she went to? Yes, that would fit. But how on earth was I going to win her back? After another twenty minutes of walking and turning things over in my mind, I made my way back to *Hill View* and to my mobile phone.

Once I was back home, I looked on my mobile to see if there had been any messages or missed calls, but there was nothing. I tried ringing Tracy once more, but this time I got a blocked message. "So, she has blocked my number now! How on earth am I going to contact her now?" I thought.
My knee jerk reaction was to text Lesley. I thought she'd still be asleep at this time of the day, so I just left a message, "Ring me when you get this call. Dad."
Should I do the same to Jon? "No," I thought. "He'd be fast asleep too."

I just sat there thinking and dozing with lack of sleep. I thought how much I loved Tracy. Surely, she still loved me, but the letter had said otherwise. I just could not believe it.

Soon after eleven o'clock Lesley rang me back.

'What's the matter Dad?' were her first words. I could tell she seemed worried.

'Have you heard from mum?' I asked sounding agitated.

'Why? What on earth's the matter? Has she gone missing?'

'She's left me Les,' I blurted out.

'What am I going to do?' I said trying desperately not to cry.

'Oh my God!' she shrieked. 'Are you sure?'

'Yes. Absolutely sure. She left me a note saying she's fallen in love with another man and has gone to live with him.'

There was a long silence whilst she took all this information in. Then she spoke again.

'Which man?' she queried.

'I honestly don't know,' I replied truthfully. 'I can only guess it's someone at the leisure centre in Glossop. She seemed to be going there a lot recently and I never suspected a thing.'

'Oh Dad! I don't know what to say. You don't deserve this,' she said sympathetically. Then after another pause, she asked, 'What are you going to do?'

'I really don't know Les', I replied, the tears starting to roll down my face. 'Try and win her back I suppose. I've tried ringing her several times, but she wouldn't answer her phone. Then I've just found out that my number's been blocked. Can you believe it?'

'Don't worry, Dad. I'll ring her right now and find out what's happening. I'll ring you straight back; just as soon as I've spoken to her,' she promised.

I felt a little better and a little more hopeful after ringing Lesley. She always did have a mature head on her shoulders. But after ten minutes she hadn't rung me back and I started to get worried. Had she got through to Tracy? Had Tracy turned her against me?

As these thoughts were going through my head, a text came through on my phone.

'Sorry Dad. I rang her twice, but no reply. I've left a message for her to call me, so will let you know if I get any news.'

I felt let down. Plus, it only made me more worried if she wouldn't speak to her own daughter. What if she turned Lesley against me? And Jon? Is this really the end of my marriage, or is there still hope? Was I over dramatising the whole thing? I was in such a state that I was thinking the worst about everything.

The first person I did call, apart from Tracy and Lesley, was my brother, Alan. Although he was busy with some friends round for lunch, he did listen and suggest that we should meet up for a drink. I saw him later that day at a pub in Oldham, roughly halfway between where we both lived.

'So big bro, what's been going on then?' were his first words.

'I really can't understand it,' I replied, 'I know we've had our ups and downs over the years, just like any other couple, but just lately she had got very tetchy, and you just couldn't reason with her. She didn't like this, and she didn't like that. First it was the smell of the plaster after the damp had been treated. Then it was the electrician who came in to sort out the electrics. 'I don't trust him' she said. "He might con us.' I thought she seemed to be happy living at *Hill View*. Well one minute she was and then the next she wasn't.'

'Well, isn't that a woman's prerogative to change her mind?' he suggested.

'Not when we agreed that it was the right place for us,' I countered.

'You know, Gary,' Alan replied, 'Things might have just been building up in her mind. You've mentioned about the damp and the electrics going wrong. Then there's the whole upheaval of moving house. It's bound to take its toll. Also, let's not forget the major change in your lifestyles that winning the lottery has caused.'

I nodded in half agreement, but I suppose in retrospect I was only seeing things my way and was not prepared to put myself in her shoes.

'Look. Isn't there some way that you can reach out to her? Surely after a few days apart she might start to regret what she did? Maybe you could meet up with her at a neutral place, say her brother's or a pub somewhere like this?'

'Easier said than done,' I argued. 'I've tried ringing her; tried sending her texts, but her phone is now blocked to me. I'm up against a brick wall, Alan and I can't do anything.'

I was starting to sound resigned to it being all over, but Alan had an idea.

'Maybe if I try to contact her myself? Surely she wouldn't block my calls or texts?'

'OK. But I wonder if she'll see you as part of the enemy. You can try, but I don't hold out much hope.'

With that, Alan changed the subject and started talking about his work and how things had got harder with his company starting to lose customers to a rival firm that had started up in another part of his town. I wasn't really listening, as Tracy was completely on my mind. So, he started asking me about the house and how the plaster was now, or if the electrics seemed OK?

In the end, I made my excuses and thanked him for agreeing to meet up with me, but I suppose nothing got resolved.

I made my way back to an empty house and loneliness.

After another sleepless night, the next morning there was a slight ray of hope. In between being awake and asleep a thought had come into my head. Seeing as Tracy had blocked me on her mobile phone and that line of communication was no longer an option for me, why not try sending her an e mail.

I was up in a flash and picked up my tablet. I started writing....

Tracy, Darling.

I really don't know what's happened to you these past few months. But please come home. I'm missing you terribly and can't stand being without you. If you want to move back to Chorlton or to a smaller house somewhere, we'll do that. Don't forget that you could live anywhere you want to with me.

Also, what about our two lovely children? Do you not realise the damage you're doing to them by leaving me? Think about how they must be feeling.

I don't know anything about this man that you've gone off with, but I forgive you for what you've done to me. Just please come back and we can start afresh.

All my love

Gary

I pressed the "send" button on my computer and hoped that the email might have some magic effect on Tracy. But within a few seconds of sending it, the email bounced back as undelivered, and I was devastated. It left me even more depressed than before I had sent it. I was at my wit's end and was fast running out of ideas to contact her. I tried going back to sleep, but it was no use.

Then I had this crazy idea that maybe if I drove into Glossop, I might just bump into Tracy. Then I could speak to her and maybe make her see sense and get her to come back home with me. I shut Tess in the house and drove like a madman all the way down into Glossop.

The most likely place I thought she might be at would be the Leisure Centre, so that is where I went. As I entered the car park, I looked around to see if I could see her distinctive navy blue MX5, but it wasn't there. I then got out of the car and walked into the centre and up to the reception desk.

'You haven't seen this lady today?' I asked the receptionist flashing a picture of her on my mobile phone.

She looked blank and nodded her head from side to side,

'No. I can't say that I have. Is there a problem?'

'No. It doesn't matter,' I replied, walking away in despair.

"This is hopeless," I thought as I struggled to think what to do next. Then the thought of Tracy having her hair and nails done at the hairdressers entered my mind. So, I drove to the main street and parked up, looking all the time for her MX5. I went into the hairdressers that she used. I didn't know anyone in there, so it was all a bit awkward.

'Has Tracy Whitemore been in today?' I asked hopefully.

'No. She hasn't been in for a few days,' replied a tall woman in her forties who I guessed must be the owner.

'I take it you're Gary?' she enquired. 'She's told us a lot about you!' she joked, and the other hairdressers giggled.

'Why are looking for her?' she went on.

I was flummoxed. I couldn't say, 'Cos she's left me,' so I had to think of something fast.

'She was meant to meet me about half an hour ago and she hasn't turned up,' I lied.

'Hope you find her,' was all that the owner could say, no doubt thinking "What's going on here? Has she left him?"

I walked out thinking they'd put two and two together and pretty soon the whole town would know my business.

I continued to drive around, but it was just a waste of time.

I started to get angry, thinking of her in the arms of another man. "I'll soon sort him out" I thought, but in reality, I hadn't a clue as to who "him" was, and probably wouldn't ever find out unless Tracy or someone close to her told me.

I reluctantly gave up the search and returned to *Hill View* to feed Tess and mope.

* * *

The next day I got a call from Lesley. It lifted my spirits immediately to see her name on my screen. I swiped the screen straight away.

'Hi Dad!' She said all bubbly.

'Hi darling,' I replied enthusiastically.

'Any news from Mum?' I asked expectantly.

'Yes,' replied Lesley.

'Well?' I couldn't wait.

'It's not good news dad.'

My mood immediately changed back down.

'She sent me a text last night. Seems she's been abroad somewhere with this other man, which was why she hadn't replied to my texts. No mobile coverage wherever she was. All she said was "It's over" and that she would call me in a few days' time when she's got her mind together'.

I was both hurt and angry at the same time. More angry than hurt really.

"Get her mind together! Christ she's had weeks to get her mind together" I thought.

I had gone quiet, and Lesley immediately became concerned.

'Dad. Are you alright?' She asked.

'No, not really,' I replied honestly.

'I really thought that you might have had some good news for me,' I admitted.

'Dad. I really think that she's not coming back, and you need to accept that!' She almost sounded brutal.

The problem was that I wasn't prepared to accept that it was over. All that was needed for Tracy to talk to me again and I'm sure I could persuade her to return to me.

In reality I was living in cloud cuckoo land and being the eternal optimist, thought everything would soon come back to normal.

'Does Jon know?' I asked, changing the subject slightly.

'Yes. I spoke to him the other day. Mum hasn't contacted him, so I let the cat out of the bag, I'm afraid'.

'That's ok, Les. He had to know sooner or later.' I didn't want to alienate Lesley.

'How did he take it?' I queried.

'Noncommittal, I'm afraid. He went all quiet on me. He really didn't give much away'.

'Ok,'

'I'll let you go, but please keep in contact Les. I love you.'
'And I love you too, Dad.'

Later on, after taking Tess for a walk, I went back into Glossop and spent most of the rest of the day sitting in my car at the leisure centre car park. I figured that as she had been abroad with this guy, she must be back in Glossop again, or wherever he lived. I just hoped that I might see her distinctive navy blue MX5 drive into the car park. Then I could speak to her and make her see sense.

I was like a private eye on a surveillance mission. But it was all a waste of time. I then spent another pointless hour in the main street of Glossop watching the traffic pass by and then I gave up.

Despondent I returned to *Hill View* and put the TV on, trying to take my mind off the situation. I needed someone to pull me out of my despondency; but who? Only Tracy could do that, and this was clearly not going to happen. I drank a bottle of wine and fell asleep on the sofa, going into a fitful sleep, finally going up to bed at 2.00am.

I knew that I couldn't go on like this. If I was brutally honest with myself, I knew that Tracy was never going to come back. I needed to put my mind onto other things. Yet no matter how hard I tried to put my energy into *Hill View* I found that it made me more depressed.

I noticed it first when I went outside to work on the garden. I knew I was struggling with the garden as I was by myself, whereas before I would have had Tracy to help me. Then I started struggling with the house. Doing the cleaning really snapped my energy, although it did keep me occupied. If the house had been in a built up area, I could easily have paid for a cleaner to come in and do the household chores, but being so isolated meant this was a "No, No."

Another thing that I thought about was my old school. I thought that if I was still teaching my mind would be busy on school things and I wouldn't feel half so bad. I would have the support of my colleagues, and would no doubt be able to get some counselling if I wanted it. Plus, I would still be living in Chorlton with my neighbours and friends nearby, all there to help lift me out of my depression. "If only I hadn't won the lottery", I thought, "then this would never have happened."

Here I was with shitloads of money. I could buy anything I wanted. Yet the one thing I wanted; no amount of money could buy. Quite ironic really! As I didn't have the support of anyone nearby to lift me out of my depression, I began to get worse day by day. I soon found myself becoming addicted to watching daytime television – all those current affairs programmes or house buying and selling programmes. I would find myself transfixed in front of the tele, usually eating biscuit after biscuit with Tess lying down asleep in front of me. It was me feeling sorry for myself and fighting against the notion that Tracy was gone for good.

One ray of light in all this depression was Jon coming home from uni for the summer. I had to go and drive down to Lincoln to pick him and his gear up in early July. Usually, I would have stayed overnight and made a short break of this, but now I was so afraid that I might miss Tracy should she decide to come home, that I did the journey there and back in a day.

Once Jon was back home my mood did lighten somewhat, seeing as I had company once again in the house. But my constant pestering him as to whether he had heard anything from his mother eventually got to him and he announced one day that he was going to do a tour of Europe by train with his best mate, Andy. I could not deny him this experience and so reluctantly drove him to Piccadilly station one morning in August.

* * *

Back at the house my mood plummeted again. I tried to keep busy in the garden with the vegetable patch and the chickens, but it no longer held any delight for me. I did take Tess on long walks most days where I felt happiest, but eventually they all seemed to feel the same.

Normally, I would go away at this time of the year with Tracy somewhere, but as there was no Tracy I couldn't go. I should have gone by myself somewhere, but I just couldn't bring myself to do it.

I tried reading; buying some e books for my e reader, but I really couldn't get into reading. I tried doing some cycling, but again my heart was just not in it. So, I slipped back into watching daytime TV and nibbling away on sugary foods to get my energy levels up.

When the new football season started, I just couldn't be bothered going to see my beloved Man City play at home. Although I was still a season ticket holder, I now associated going to see City play with the day that Tracy left me, which was silly. But such was my mood of despondency that this is how I behaved.

Once Jon had come back from his trip round Europe and I'd taken him back to Lincoln for his final year, things became even more desperate. One day as usual I was moping about wondering where my life was going, when I head a car pull up outside. I looked out in the vain hope that it might be Tracy. It was actually Alan, and he had a pleasant surprise for me.

'Hi Big Brother!' he called out as he got out of his car. He seemed so happy, so full of life.

'I've got a surprise for you!' he said.

'What?' I replied half-heartedly.

'We're going away for the weekend! A change will do you good!'

My heart sank. I didn't want to go away. There might be a chance that Tracy could come back I thought in my misguided brain.

'What about the dog? It's too late to book her into the kennels,' I argued.

'Don't worry about that. We're taking her with us. Sue has said she can stay at our house whilst we're away. We'll drop her off on the way.'

'Are you sure?' I half protested.

'Don't worry brother! It's all under control. Just go and pack some clothes for two nights away'.

I still wasn't sure about leaving *Hill View* for two nights, but deep down I knew a change would do me good. So, I reluctantly packed a small suitcase of clothes, as well as some dog food and blankets for Tess. It was very hard for me to think what I should take, as I normally have plenty of time to think about things before going away.

Half an hour later we jumped in the car with Tess on the back seat and Alan zoomed away down the narrow country lane, with Oasis blasting through the speakers.

After dropping off Tess with Sue, who promised to take her for plenty of walks, we drove back down the M66 and onto the M62 going west. I still had no idea where we were going but the further west we went, I guessed that it must be Liverpool and I was right.

We stayed at a nice hotel on the waterfront with views out across the river Mersey to Birkenhead. During the weekend we went on the ferry across the Mersey, visited several Beatles sites and even managed to get tickets for the Saturday match at Goodison Park to see Everton play Aston Villa. Then in the evening we went for a few drinks before ending at a gig where an Oasis tribute band were playing.

I actually enjoyed the change, though I still thought of Tracy at times, admittedly not as much as if I had been at *Hill View*. I found listening to the music at the show the hardest part of the weekend as normally whenever I have been to a gig it was usually with Tracy by my side.

Soon after eleven on the Sunday morning we departed from the hotel and drove east again back to Bury. Sue had kindly prepared us Sunday lunch, which was the first proper meal I'd had since Tracy had left and that too did me good, actually having a nice square meal for a change.

Being in the company of Alan and Sue and all the various people we came across in Liverpool made me feel happier - the happiest I'd been for several months. I finally began to realise just how isolated I really was in that old farmhouse.

Maybe that was the reason for me being so depressed, and not just because of Tracy going. I foolishly put that thought out of my head though and started to think about what to do next as Alan drove Tess and me back to the house.

To be sure, I wasn't glad to be going back to an empty house without the presence of Tracy in my life anymore. As we got closer to *Hill View,* I began to get a knot of dread in my stomach. Then as Alan's car turned up the narrow country lane, I swore I could see lights on in the house. Surely Tracy hadn't returned, had she? Or could it be burglars?

As the car came to a stop outside the front door, I got out and looked for Tracy's car, but it wasn't there. I did hear a thud thud of loud rock music, and then it dawned on me that it must be Jon home. But why come home now in the middle of term? Maybe he'd got some news from Tracy that he wanted to tell me?

Alan came with me into the house to the deafening music coming from the lounge.

Yes, it was Jon, and he got a shock as Alan and I entered the lounge.

'Well, this is a surprise!' I shouted above the din.

Jon looked up shocked and turned the music down.

'Hello Dad,' he replied sheepishly.

'Hello Uncle Alan.'

Alan knew something was up but sensed that Jon and I needed to be alone, so he made his excuses and left. Before he went, I gave him a big hug and thanked him for the weekend.

The fact that Jon had come home in the middle of term told me something wasn't right.

'What's going on?' I snapped.

'Dad, you'd better sit down while I tell you,' he replied.

I'd hardly stepped in through the front door and already things were amiss.

'Go on then,' I said.

'Dad…..I've dropped out of university,' he half mumbled, obviously fearful of my reaction.

'What!' I half shouted, just like Mr Bumble in *Oliver Twist*. 'Why?'

'Well because I've had enough,' he confessed. 'I'm not enjoying the course anymore and I'm finding the work hard. Since you and mum split up, I've found it hard to concentrate on my work, as well.'

'But you're throwing away your future,' I reasoned.

'You've got your whole life ahead of you. Please don't waste this opportunity!'

'I know, but I just don't think I'm cut out for student life anymore. I'd rather make my own way in life without a degree.'

What he said horrified me, especially after all the sacrifices that Tracy and I had made to pay his student fees. I knew that wasn't a problem anymore, but when I thought of all the sacrifices my parents had made for me, I became angry.

I then had the thought that what he said didn't quite ring true. Jon had always been like me; hard working and focussed. We'd talked in the past about what he'd like to do after a degree, and he seemed quite settled when I'd dropped him off at the start of the autumn term.

'Are you sure there's not another reason for dropping out Jon?' I asked suspiciously.

Jon was never any good at hiding things and he then admitted what the real reason was.

'Yes Dad, there is.' He paused and then came out with it.

'Some of the other students found out about the lottery win and they've been hassling me, pestering me for money. I keep telling them that I didn't win the lottery and that it was you and that you haven't given me any of the money yet, but they don't believe me,'

A lump came into my throat. "So, this is what winning the lottery does to your children," I thought. I became calmer as the reality of it all sank in.

'Thank you, Jon, for coming clean with me. I appreciate that. But have you not gone to your tutor or someone else in authority to tell them about this?'

'No. I think it would only make things worse. I just couldn't stand it anymore, so I came home.'

'OK. You're safe here', I said. 'But how did the other students find out about the lottery win? I presume you didn't tell them?' I asked.

'No Dad. But I did mention it to my flatmate Jake as I thought I could trust him. I guess he told someone else and then they told someone else and pretty soon the whole campus knew about it.'

'That's what happens with any secret, I'm afraid. Once you tell someone, unless they're 100% trustworthy, the secret gets out.' I tried not to sound judgmental, but it seemed like it.

'We've got to have a think about what to do next. I take it you don't want to go back to uni?'

'No way!' he replied. 'It's just hell there right now'.

'OK. Let's have a good old think about it and whatever you decide to do, I'll back you up.'

'Thanks Dad. You're great!'

That was nice to hear that, but I had one more question for Jon.

'Does your mother know about this?'

'No. I haven't told her yet.'

'Well maybe we need to wait a bit before we do that.'

Jon stayed at *Hill View* for another couple of weeks and then decided that after his jaunt round Europe he wanted to see even more of the world. During the time he'd been at home, he'd concocted an itinerary where he would travel round the world with an old school friend backpacking. He would fly east to India, then Singapore, then Australia and New Zealand, before coming back across the United States. Part of me was quite jealous, as I would have loved to have done that in my younger days, but not now. The other part of me was quite worried, as it was such a long undertaking and in any particular place he could be in danger. Mind you the same could be said about some places in this country.

In the end I reluctantly let him go, knowing that he would be staying with a friend whilst he was in Australia, and a promise of ringing once a week to keep me updated of his progress.

* * *

As soon as Jon had departed, I immediately went back into depression mode with a vengeance. It wasn't long before I was back on the sofa watching those daytime programmes, tucking into chocolate biscuits and other snacks. Once in a while if the sun was shining, I would get in the car and drive up onto the moors and take Tess for a long walk, which she loved. Although it lifted my spirits a little, I soon came back down to Earth with a bump as soon as we got back to the house. It was as though the house had a negative energy which I didn't notice. Whenever I was in the house my mood would change to a depressed state and no matter how hard I tried I just could not shake it off. I did try reading a little bit, using the Tablet that I'd received as a leaving present from my colleagues at school, but even that didn't lift my spirits.

"This is crazy!" I thought. "I have lots of money and I'm desperately unhappy. Where did it all go wrong?" I knew the answer. It was moving here to this place. Completely the wrong move. Too far away from my friends. Too isolated from any neighbours. Too far from the shops. Then the fact that I didn't have any human company was the final nail in the coffin.

Yet, there were two more things that occurred that would push me to the brink of extinction

Just when I thought things couldn't get any bleaker for me, I got a phone call from my sister to say that my mother was on her last legs. Although I had driven over to Bolton to see her in her nursing home about once a week before the move, the gaps started to get longer and longer. It became once a fortnight, then once every three weeks, then once a month. Stupidly, I had let the move take over everything else in my life and so I had neglected seeing her. Something I now regret greatly now that she has gone.

The next morning after the phone call I took Tess to the kennels and drove over to the nursing home to see her. She hardly recognised me; such was the effect of the morphine upon her. My sister was her usual cool self and her husband didn't even talk to me. Alan was going to pop round later that day as soon as he could get away from work.

I held her hand and she smiled weakly.

'I thought you said that you would get me out of this place', she mumbled.

I went bright red and hoped that Dawn and Nick couldn't hear what she had just said.

I felt she was slipping away and yet I had neglected her badly. I felt so guilty.

Neither Dawn nor Mum knew about Tracy leaving me, so when Mum asked where Tracy was, I had to lie. I just couldn't face talking about it, not even to Mum.

It was doubly hard for me to make conversation with Mum or Dawn. I did try and talk about when we were small and how we went on trips to the seaside or into the country. That lifted both Mum's and my spirits a little.

After an hour I was mentally exhausted and needed to get away.

I promised mum that I would come back tomorrow to see her, but that never happened as she passed away in the night. In many ways I regret not being with her at the last, but I really didn't want to see her in this state. Of course, Dawn and Alan were there at the end, so I got another black mark against me from my sister. But we're all made of different stuff and react to death in our own way. Mine just happened to be different to my siblings.

Dawn made all the funeral arrangements which I was happy for her to do on this occasion. As a gesture of good will she invited me to read the lesson at the service, whilst Alan did the eulogy. I just couldn't do something like that with the state I was in. By now everyone in the family knew about the marriage break up and seemed quite sympathetic to me, though one or two relatives did bring up the subject at the wake. I tried to shrug it off and change the subject, feeling quite prickly about it all.

Once it was all over, I was actually quite glad to get back to *Hill View* with Tess waiting patiently for me at the kennels. Apart from my children and brother, she was the only thing that kept me going at the time.

The final nail in the coffin was me receiving an official looking letter one day. On the envelope I could see the words; "Little & Webb – Solicitors" and immediately my heart sank. I knew what was in the envelope before I even opened it. I put it on the kitchen table to open once I'd had my breakfast, but my curiosity got the better of me and I opened it straight away.

The contents read as follows:-

Dear Mr Whitemore,

In accordance with instructions from your estranged wife, Tracy Alison Whitemore, I am instructed to inform you that she will be seeking a divorce from yourself at the earliest opportunity.
According to the law you are within your rights to contest this application, though from what she tells me, she is set on her chosen course and will not be interested in reconciliation.
My advice to you is to find yourself a solicitor who specialises in divorces to represent you.

Yours sincerely,

James Little,

Solicitor

The inevitable had happened. In just over two years my life had gone from one big high to the lowest of the low, or so I thought. As the solicitor suggested in the letter, I knew I had to find a solicitor of my own. Should I fight or should I accept that it was inevitable? I was confused to say the least and went straight to the internet to see what I could find. The only problem was that there was no internet signal, so I was forced to drive into Glossop and sit in a freezing cold café looking things up.

With my depression getting worse, I began to feel trapped, not just in *Hill View* as a place, but in my life as well. I felt that I had messed up big time and that there was no way out, which was a stupid thought really. I had all this money, most of which I really didn't need, to live as comfortably as I did, yet it wasn't solving my problems.

Only people could solve them. What I wanted most of all was for Tracy to come walking in through the front door and say, 'I've made a terrible mistake, Gary. Please will you forgive me? I love you!'

But that wasn't going to happen in a million years. I just couldn't accept that Tracy was gone forever and out of my life for good. I was still hanging on, hoping that it would all get better.

The solution was me of course, but I couldn't see that in the mental state I was in. As each day went on, my despair increased. 'If only the phone would ring,' I thought. 'Or someone could text me. Couldn't they?' I seemed incapable of making the first move and being proactive in the situation I was in.

Inevitably, the only thought that I had, was that of ending it all. Even sillier, yet I thought this would be the best way out of this mess for me. Then perhaps Tracy would see how much she had hurt me. I didn't for one second think about the effect killing myself would have on those who did love me - Lesley, Jon, Alan, and some of my friends. I just thought none of them cared anymore. I wouldn't accept that they all had their own lives to live and would be terribly shocked and hurt if I did such a thing.

Next, I began to think of ways of actually committing suicide. Maybe I could take lots of paracetamol and just fade away in my sleep. Or I could go and lie down on the nearest railway line and wait for a train to come along. I didn't think of the trauma it would cause the train driver, not to mention those who had to clear up the mess. Perhaps I could drive out onto the moors and find a high cliff to jump off. I would be dead in seconds. Again, what about those who found me? Or I could drive my car at speed along the motorway and then turn off at speed down an embankment.

It doesn't bear thinking about now, but in those dark, desperate days that is how my mind was working. I resolved to do it sooner than later, especially with Christmas coming up. I just couldn't bear the thought of my first Christmas without Tracy. So, I set the ball rolling and rang up the kennels to leave Tess there 'for a few days.' I'm sure they would find a good home for her once I was gone.

The next morning, I didn't feel any better. It was as though I was being pushed along this road to destruction and there was no way that I could turn around and escape. Overnight, I had decided to take large amounts of paracetamol as my way out of this nightmare. That way there wouldn't be any mess to clear up and whoever found me might think that I had died naturally in my sleep. I didn't realise that the paracetamol would damage my liver first and not necessarily finish me off immediately.

I put the lead on Tess who thought that she was going to go for a walk. I then drove the three miles to the kennels and dropped Tess off, saying I had to go away on business and would be back in two days' time. I tried to be as casual as possible, but the thought that I would never see Tess again played on my heart strings. As I drove away, I could see her being walked to the cubicles in my rear view mirror. I was back at the house in less than half an hour.

It all seemed so quiet. No wife, no dog, no future. I was ready to end it all. The time had come.

I wasn't sure if I wanted to write a suicide note or not. I debated in my mind that I should write something, so in the end, I simply wrote,

Tracy. You finished me off.
I'm sorry Lesley, Jon, and Alan.

I just didn't want to write a detailed explanation of how and why I had got to this point. I figured that most people would know the reasons. Next, I decided that the best place to do the deed would be on the sofa in the main living room. That way I would be found much easier.

Then I went upstairs and into the bathroom. I took two new bottles of paracetamol out of the cabinet which I had bought over the previous days and went into the kitchen to get some water. Before I took the tablets, I decided to take one last look around the house and went in each room as if I was saying 'goodbye'. I also went into the garden and looked out over the moors. The sun was just emerging from behind a cloud and illuminated the valley below. 'Why are you going to let all this go?' was the thought I had. But the other part of me was determined to continue with the suicide.

I sat down on the sofa and opened one of the bottles of paracetamol and poured some of the tablets out into my other hand. It was time for me to take them. The end wouldn't be long now…….

7 END OF THE BEGINNING

I held several tablets in my hand and was about to put them into my mouth. Then more thoughts came into my head. "Stop! This is stupid!" they said. "You are throwing your life away over a stupid relationship. There's much more to life than this. What would Lesley and Jon be like if you weren't around?" I paused and thought, "Yes. This is stupid. It's not going to solve anything. It'll just make matters worse."
But then a much stronger thought said, "Go on do it! It won't take long. Everyone will be glad when you're gone. No more pain. No more heartache. Swallow the pills!"

I slowly lifted my hand towards my mouth ready to end it all and then my mobile phone rang. It was like an alarm clock waking me up from a deep sleep, such was the way I was thinking. I didn't recognize the number but picked it up anyway.

As soon as the voice spoke, I realised who it was. It was Stuart the lottery winner, who I had first talked to over a year ago on the advice of the man from the lottery.

Stuart ringing me up out of the blue like that was a godsend.

When he heard my voice, his first words were,

'Christ Gary. You sound like death warmed up!'

He could obviously tell things weren't right. As he spoke, he coaxed out of me what the matter was and helped me to forget what I was about to do. He listened as I poured my heart out to him about all that had happened and then proceeded to give me some good advice.

'If I were you mate, I would get the hell out of that place. It sounds like it's dragging you down. It's not as if you're stuck there, mate. You could go and live any place you like.'

I sort of agreed with him. I knew that this place was bad for me. It had turned into a black hole for me, and I had been swallowed up by it. What should have been Heaven for me had now turned into Hell. All that I had left was Tess, who was ever faithful and loving to me. All the possessions I owned and the house I was now living in didn't mean a thing to me anymore.

'I know you've spent a lot of money buying this place. But what use is it for one man and his dog?!!'

He was right. I couldn't really live here anymore in this now massive place all by myself. Sure, it was lovely here in the summer, but in the winter, it was quite frankly depressing. I'd learnt a very hard lesson buying this place.

'What do you think I should I do?' I asked him.

'You need company mate,' was his blunt reply.

'It looks like Tracy has gone out of your life for good now, so best accept that and start looking for someone else to share all your money with.' he joked.

I was slightly offended by what he said, but deep down I knew that he was right. Tracy was never going to come back, no matter how much I still loved her. Loving her was just a waste of my time and effort. I wasn't the first person to split up and get divorced and I wouldn't be the last. It was time to move on.

'Not only do you need to find a new soul mate, but you also need to find a place to live that's actually in civilisation!' he continued.

'Us humans are not meant to live by ourselves. I know some do, but that's the exception rather than the rule. It's time to make a new start. Preferably where there's signs of life!'

He was always sarcastic and blunt, but funny with it.

'Now if you ever need to talk to me, just call me. Anytime you like, mate! Just remember you *are* someone. Just remember. The world is your oyster. So, start enjoying life. I'd get out of there fast if I were you!'

I was taking in all that he was saying and as he spoke some of the depression started lifting from me, as though he was working his magic on me. I was starting to see light at the end of the tunnel. Yes. I did need to get out of this house. Yes. I did need company. Yes. I was going to do something about it.

I thanked him for remembering me and for all his advice and then I ended the call and put the phone down. I looked around the room and at the two bottles of tablets on the table next to the sofa. I shuddered when I thought about what I was doing just ten minutes ago. Yet now I was a different person - almost. I had reached rock bottom and now the only way was up for me. It was time for a change in my life.

In all the time that I was talking to him, I was still holding the tablets in my hand. By now they had become powdery and flaky, so the first thing I did was to put the tablets back into the container and then throw it in the bin. That was an important step for me. In fact, I guess it was the first step onto the ladder which would take me away from all this depression and the suicidal thoughts.

I washed my hands as if I were ritually cleansing myself of the suicidal thoughts. I was just thinking about what to do next when I heard the noise of a car engine getting closer to the house. "I bet that's the postman," I thought. "I wonder if there will be something from Tracy?" Obviously, my attitude to Tracy hadn't yet changed.

The engine stopped and a door slammed. I got up in anticipation for the bell which was about to ring. It did and I walked to the porch to open the door. When I opened the door, it wasn't the postman, but Alan. My jaw dropped.

As soon as he saw me, he said, 'What's been happening? You look in a right state!'

'Nothing,' I lied, but he was having none of it.

'Come on big bruv. You're not looking right. Is it to do with Tracy still?'

I couldn't lie to him, never in a million years. Plus, despite my phone conversation with Stuart, I was still pretty low.

'Yes,' I mumbled and then a tear started to flow down my cheeks. Plus, I had a lump in my throat.

He guided me back into the house, shut the door and sat me down on the sofa, where a matter of minutes earlier I was about to end my life.

I started crying properly now and he put his arms round me, comforting me.

'Let it all out, bro,' he said gently.

As I cried, he noticed the other bottle of paracetamol on the table next to the sofa.

Then he saw the suicide note next to it and started to read it.

'Oh my God!' he cried out in horror.

I looked up from my tears and saw the note in his hand and the second bottle still there and felt so guilty.

He now knew what I had been thinking of doing and obviously still thought I was about to do it.

'Please Gary. You're worth much more than a broken relationship. Your life is precious and I, Sue, Lesley, and Jon still love you and want you in our lives. Can you see that?'

'Yes Alan. I know that, but I'd had enough and would have done it if it had not been for Stuart ringing me up a few minutes ago.'

Then I explained about Stuart's call and him making me see sense about this place and my life.

'You're packing your bags and you're coming with me!' was all he could say.

It was like a re-run of the Liverpool weekend a few months earlier, only this time I didn't have the strength to argue with Alan. He was giving me a lifeline and I was glad to take it. As I went upstairs to pack some things, I could hear his voice – clearly, he was speaking to Sue and letting her know the situation.

I was immediately concerned about Tess. What should happen to her? But then I remembered that I had put her in the kennels only that morning. Perhaps she could stay for a few more days whilst I sorted myself out?

It was a strange feeling getting into Alan's car. In my mind I knew that I was leaving *Hill View* for good, but what was going to happen to me now? I knew I would have to come back sometime for my car and other belongings, but I had made up my mind: I couldn't stay living here a day longer.

The journey to Alan's house in Bury passed quickly, though I was deep in thought for most of the time. I did ask Alan why he happened to come along when he did. His reply was that he had come over to Glossop on business and was going to pop round later in the day, but his contact cancelled at the last minute, so he came straight away. I also asked him never to say anything about this to Lesley or Jon about it.

You never know what I might have done next being all alone in that large house. For all I know I might have slipped back down into that suicidal mind frame being there on my own. I definitely needed someone to grab me by the scruff of the neck and take me to a better place and thank God that Alan was that person.

I mustn't forget Stuart too for his phone call, which I suppose in a way actually saved my life. I could have been lying on that settee a lifeless corpse for several days with no one there to find me for all I knew. It didn't bear thinking about.

Once we arrived at Alan and Sue's, the first thing that Alan did was to get me in at his doctors with an emergency appointment. Although I wasn't resident there, when Alan explained the situation, they suddenly became very accommodating, and I saw a doctor later that afternoon. He prescribed anti-depressants as you would expect and suggested that I go for counselling. I turned him down on the latter suggestion, arguing that I was over the worst of it and would talk things through with my brother and his wife, who I could be more open with as opposed to a stranger.

* * *

For the next few weeks, I was a "guest" at my brother's home. Luckily, he had a spare bedroom that I could stay in and as it was Christmas I wasn't left alone that much. In fact, both of them watched me like a hawk all the time.

Whilst I had all the company and food and television I could want, I missed Tess terribly. I agreed with them that it would be best for her to stay in the kennels over the Christmas period; then I would make a decision about what to do with her. I felt that Sue was not that keen for her to stay at their house, which I could understand. At the same time, I wasn't ready to go and live somewhere by myself. So that was one issue that played on my mind over the Christmas period.

The other issue was what I should be doing with my life now that I had given up *Hill* View. The house and the garden had taken up so much of my time over the past year that it had almost become a full-time job for me. Yet the earthquake that went off with Tracy leaving me had stopped me from putting much effort into the place anymore.

Stuart's phone call had galvanised me to start thinking about what I should do next. Although I wasn't immediately convinced that leaving *Hill View* was the best thing for me to do, I had reached a point in my life where I knew I couldn't go on living like this. Whether I was going to be reconciled with Tracy or not, I knew that ultimately leaving *Hill View* behind was the best thing for me to do.

The idea of finding a new place to live had started the ball rolling in my mind soon after speaking to Stuart, and whilst I was at Alan and Sue's I started thinking more and more about where I would like to live. Would I stay in the Bury area to be near Alan, or would I be a burden to him if I were living on his doorstep? Perhaps I should move down to the Bath area to be near to Lesley?

I suppose that as my roots were in Manchester I should stay in the area. That was where I had lived for the majority of my life and there was so much going on in and around the city. Plus, there was the added attraction going to see Manchester City play. In fact, Alan had taken me to see them play Liverpool on Boxing Day, which was just the tonic I needed on the road to normality. Now I just needed to be happy in myself about taking the plunge and moving out of Alan's.

Although Tracy was still in my mind - though not as much; both Alan and Sue had started to convince me that I needed to move on from all that. It was hard for me to accept that of course, but I could see that they were right. Tracy wasn't going to come waltzing back into my life – I had finally started to change my thinking on this. But there were lots of regrets and questions running through my mind. What if we had stayed in Chorlton? Would things be just the same as before the lottery? What if we had bought a smaller house than *Hill View*? Would that have made things better? Had I alienated her by moving out to the country? Was I not man enough for her? Had she cheated on me before? And so on.

The other thing that both Alan and Sue kept trying to impress on me was that I needed to do something to fill the void of living by myself. Not just a hobby, but something more akin to a job, as that is what I had been doing for the past twenty odd years. I knew I would go mad again if I just stayed in an empty house or flat all day long, so I started to look for ideas on the internet; something to do that would keep me busy and perhaps make some money on the side.

I considered selling something online from a website, but I was put off by having stock that needed storing somewhere and then having to get it delivered to the customer. Then I thought of buying a restaurant or some other retail business, but I really didn't think I had the nous or energy to do such a thing.

When I told Alan about my dilemma, he suggested property developing.

'I've got a friend who's a property developer. Well, several actually. They buy old houses around Lancashire for peanuts and then do them up, before selling them on for a profit. Perhaps you might like to try that as a business venture?' he suggested.

I had often watched the TV programme, *Homes Under the Hammer*, so had a good idea of what it involved. I could easily afford to buy some of these dilapidated houses; it was just finding the tradesmen I could trust.

'Maybe if I put you in touch with my mate Darren, he could show you what he does and let you put your toe in the water to see if you like it or not?' suggested Alan,

'I'll say that you took early retirement from teaching because of high blood pressure and you want to try out something new.'

'What about me living here with you? I argued.

'He doesn't have to know anything of your circumstances. I'll tell him that you are now living in a flat near me in Bury after the breakup of your marriage and that you are interested in starting up in property developing. That's all he needs to know. What else you tell him is up to you.'

'But won't he see me as a potential rival?' I said seeing all the pitfalls.

'Don't talk nonsense big bro. There's so many cheap properties available all over the Northwest, that even he couldn't buy them all!'

I suppose I had nothing to lose. So, after chatting to Darren on the phone to see if he was OK for me to shadow him one day, we met a few days later at an auction house in Rochdale. He was a nice guy; well built, with a shaved head.

He let me watch him bid on a couple of properties that interested him. He was successful on one of them and after completing the paperwork, took me in his car to view another property that he had been renovating. It wasn't too far – just on the edge of Rochdale and was a mid-terraced house.

Inside was the smell of drying plaster on pink walls with wires hanging out of them. He explained that he got the property for £140,000 and after his costs of around £20,000, he expected to make a profit of upwards of £80,000 after tax.

'Not bad', I thought, but I wasn't convinced. Although the financial rewards were good, it all seemed so much to do, especially with getting the workmen in to do the job and perhaps fighting all that red tape from the council.

After asking him a few questions and discussing the ins and outs of his work, I thanked him for his time and made my excuses. "It's just not me," I thought in the taxi on the way back to Bury. I was no nearer to finding a "job" to get me back into life once more.

* * *

However, I had other things to take my mind off my situation. Just after Christmas I had my end of year "report" meeting with my financial advisor in Manchester. It did me good to get away from Alan and Sue's; not because I was fed up with being there – they had been so supportive to me, but because I needed to have some space from their home and see a bit of the world again.

I caught the tram into town. It was the first time I had been on public transport for ages and a big step forward for me. I quite enjoyed it. I suppose it was being with real people again, of all different backgrounds and accents. In fact, it was probably the first time since I had been teaching that I was mixing with "real folk" - not that my brother and his wife weren't that - but just the mixture of different ages, nationalities and backgrounds showed me a side to life that had been missing in mine. I found it quite exhilarating, and it made me realise how much I had been apart from the "real world" so to speak. I needed to get back in there I guessed.

It was also well over six months that I'd had a meeting with Adam and although the last time we met was after Tracy had departed, I hadn't actually told him about it. This time I was more upfront with him and when he asked me if there had been any changes in my circumstances since we had last met, I told him straight away.

'Well in that case I would suggest that you change your will as soon as possible, Gary,' he suggested.

'Although separation and divorce is not a pretty thing, it is important to hold on to what is yours and make sure the people you care about get your money, should anything ever happen to you.'

I completely agreed with him, though talking about Tracy immediately opened up old wounds. I knew it would take a long time to heal, but I didn't realise how raw I was inside about her after all this time. In my mind I was still torn between loving her and hating her for what she had done to me. But I did take on board what he said and made a mental note to get in touch with my solicitor, especially as I'd ignored the letter from Tracy's solicitor about the divorce.

He also warned me that I should be prepared for a fight with her over my fortune. I really didn't see it that way, but from his experience he knew that divorce settlements could go on for ages, particularly if the other partner felt that they should get half of what you had, as the law stated. He also asked me what my plans were as regards my situation. Again, I was totally honest with him.

'I'm really not sure to be honest,' I confessed. 'This separation business has taken a big toll on me. I do know now that living in a big house in the countryside is not the right thing for me anymore.'

'True,' he agreed. 'I presume you are going to sell it then?'

'Yes. It's just become like an albatross around my neck.'

'Where are you going to live then Gary?' he queried.

'Well at the moment I am staying at my brother's in Bury until I find something that I like. I was thinking of moving back into Manchester somewhere.'

'May I suggest that you rent somewhere first before you decide to splash out on buying a property?'

He was quite forthright in his advice, but then that is what I paid him to do.

'Yes. You're right Adam. I don't want to go charging into something I haven't really thought about,' I agreed, thinking of my mistake in buying *Hill View*.

Talking to someone who was an expert in his field helped me to become more focused about finding somewhere to live, though his advice didn't stretch to finding me something to occupy my time with.

He talked more about how my shares and investments were doing and how much profit they had made, which really didn't interest me. Then it was time to go back out into the wide world.

It was now rush hour as I left his plush office building in the Spinningfields area of central Manchester. City workers were coming out of the office blocks in their droves, and it was quite hard to dodge them all as I made my back to the tram stop.
Suddenly I heard someone shouting my name,
'Gary! Gary!'
I turned round to see who it was that was calling out my name and recognized a face that I hadn't seen in a long time, Tom Webster from my university days. I knew he lived in Manchester, but he had been out of my life for several years and obviously he didn't know anything about me winning the lottery.
'Hi Gary. How are you?' he boomed as we shook hands. 'It's been a long time.'
'Fine,' I lied.
'What are you doing with yourself these days?' I asked, quickly changing the subject away from me back onto him.
'Doing pretty well,' he enthused. 'I work as a corporate accountant for one of the big firms based here in Manchester. Life is pretty good right now,'
Before he had a chance to ask me what I was doing in my life, I jumped in with a suggestion.
'Do you fancy a drink? Then we could have a good catch up. That's if you've got time?'
'Yes. That'd be brilliant. I've just finished work and I normally have a swift half before going home. So yeah. Let's find somewhere!'
His energy shocked me, yet I suppose if he was happy with his life, this is what it must be like. I was quite jealous.

We found a quiet pub in the next street and continued where we left off. I explained about my coming into some money from a legacy and moving out into the country to live the good life, how it hadn't worked out and how Tracy had left me and that I was thinking what my next move would be. He too had been married but was now divorced and clearly had got over it. He seemed so full of life and zest.

'Hey Gary. It's great here!' he boomed. 'There's so much happening, you wouldn't believe it! Since I've been living here, I've made so many friends and everything is on the doorstep. Not like where you lived. You'll love it if you move here!' he boasted enthusiastically.

'You certainly sound like you're enjoying life!' I concurred. 'I just need to find somewhere suitable. Maybe put my toe in the water first?'

'Why don't you come and stay with me then?' he offered. 'I've got a spare bedroom where you can sleep. You can stay as long as it takes. It'll just be like being students again!'

'That's really kind of you Tom. I don't know what to say.'

'Just say, "Yes". Then you can get back to being with the living!'

We talked for about another half hour catching up on each other's news until we were interrupted by my mobile buzzing. I looked at it and saw that it was a text from Alan asking me where I was and if I was alright. He was so protective! I texted Alan back to explain the situation and then told Tom that I would have to go but promised to think about his offer. We swapped numbers and then went our separate ways…..but not for long.

* * *

When I got back to Alan's, I told him about meeting Tom and his offer, but also about how I enjoyed being on the tram amongst all those people again. He said that it was a step in the right direction, but about moving in with Tom he said that I should sleep on it first, which I agreed to do.

I also mentioned about what the financial advisor had said about changing my will and seeing a solicitor to help me through the divorce action. He suggested using his one in Bury and although I still had thoughts of my long-standing solicitor in Chorlton, I agreed that using him might be easier.

The next morning, I felt so much better. No doubt meeting Tom had given me more hope and direction. I was starting to feel that living with him in central Manchester could well be my next step on the road to recovery, though persuading Alan and Sue might prove difficult.

In the meantime, I had to start the ball rolling with selling the house and what to do with all the furniture inside it. I soon decided that putting it into storage for the time being would be the best option and told Alan of my intentions. He did support me on this but was still wary about me moving out of his house.

'Maybe stay a few more weeks?' was his suggestion.

I agreed, but my hunger to move and be independent once again grew with each new day.

With the question of selling the house, I decided to stick with my solicitor, Tim Watson despite what Alan had suggested, as I was starting to become more independent again. So, I arranged a meeting with him the next day – I was keen to keep the momentum up you see. Getting over to Chorlton was a lot harder by public transport from Bury, so Sue kindly offered to drive me there and wait for me whilst I had my meeting.

It was quite painful speaking with Tim, as Tracy was the main topic of conversation; especially as he had known her in a professional capacity, as well as me for many years. He agreed that selling the house was the best option, though he agreed with Adam that selling it by auction would probably be quicker and easier than through an estate agent, especially in view of its remoteness.

I also showed him the letter from Tracy's solicitor about the divorce. I could tell from his reaction that he should have been told about this earlier, but it had got forgotten about with all that had been going on. By now I had accepted that divorce was going to happen, so I agreed to let him handle the case.

Like Adam, he did warn me that Tracy may well seek to get as much of my fortune as possible and that legally she was entitled not only to half of the proceeds from the sale of the house, but also half of what I had in the bank. This horrified me, particularly as she was the one who instigated this whole thing in the first place. Also, I had generously given her a million pounds in the early days to do what she liked with. Surely, she hadn't spent it all.

'The Law is the Law, Gary,' was what he said.

'It might be prudent to "get rid" of a large part of your money, otherwise she may be able to win half of it if the divorce judge decided on the 50/50 scenario," he warned me.

I didn't quite get what he meant by "get rid of" at first, but then I realised that he didn't literally mean that, but that I should find someone who I could trust who could keep the money in their own bank account until the divorce case had been settled.

There was only one person I could think of who fitted all these criteria and that was Alan. I knew I could trust him, but I when I told him later that evening, (out of Sue's ear shot), he said, 'No way, bro.'

So, that was something else for me to worry about. I thought I had made progress in the past few days but seeing the solicitor had knocked me back a little.

Then there was the question of Tess. She had been in the kennels for too long I thought. So, I had to decide whether to keep her or let her go. The offer of Tom to go and live with him in central Manchester still appealed to me and seemed the only option open to me, apart from staying at Alan and Sue's indefinitely. Whichever one I chose, meant no Tess and that was very hard to take.

Letting go of Tess was the biggest wrench of all in this wretched business. She had been a great companion to me in those long months of despair, showing unconditional love and faithfulness to me, yet I knew I just could not hold onto to her. She was a country dog and needed plenty of exercise. I could no longer give her that commitment anymore, as I knew back in civilisation I would be going out socially and it just wouldn't be fair on her leaving her locked away in a house for hours on end.

After much deliberation, I contacted the RSPCA and agreed to sign her over to them. I knew that she would be looked after well and would eventually go to a good home, where she would have an owner who would be able to give her the quality time that I could no longer give her. They were fine about it and assured me that I was doing the best thing handing her over to them. They said that sadly this happened a lot nowadays when couples split up. So that was one more thing that I had to let go of in all of this and a hard one to take.

* * *

Alan drove me back to *Hill View* in mid-January to do the dirty deed. I was also going to pick up my car and drive back to Bury by myself, with him following, seeing as I hadn't driven my car for over a month.

We picked Tess up at the kennels and she was overjoyed to see me, licking my face profusely. I could see that she had lost some weight, but apart from that she was the same Tess that I'd known for almost a year. Even though it wasn't that long by most dog owner's standards, I still felt a special bond that I couldn't describe in human terms.

When we got to the house, nothing seemed to have changed and as we went inside it seemed so cold and so silent. It definitely seemed as though I didn't have a connection with it anymore and it made me a little sad to think of how different it had all been a year ago. There was also a small plie of post to pick up. I decided to leave opening it up until later.

On Alan's advice I had arranged for an estate agent to come round later that morning to take photos and measurements for putting it up for auction – once Tess had gone. Then in the afternoon the removal men were going to come round and pack the rest of the furniture and my belongings and take them to the storage place. I would be able to access it any time should there be something that I needed.

Within half an hour of arriving at *Hill View*, a small white RSPCA van came up the drive and parked by the front door. After I'd signed the forms, I said my goodbyes to Tess and handed her over to the RSPCA officer. She obediently jumped into the cage in the back of the van, unaware of what was in store for her. "I'm sure she will be much happier with her new owners whoever they may be," I thought. Then as the van drove away down the lane I broke down and cried like a little schoolboy. To me it was as though she had died. In a way she had, as she was now no longer a part of my life

Alan gave me a few minutes to pull myself together, then made me get on with collecting more clothes and personal belongings that I hadn't taken previously. As I went into each bedroom, the mood of the place seemed to engulf me and I found I had to go outside into the fresh air to compose myself.

Perhaps the place was cursed? Or even haunted? After all it was old farmhouse, over a hundred years old. It was funny how the previous owners had got divorced and that was why they sold it. There seemed to be a pattern here. "God help the next people to live here," I thought.

Alan came back inside with me and helped me to finish off the packing. As we were doing so the doorbell rang. It was the estate agent, who was earlier than I expected. He apologised for being early, explaining that as the place was out in the sticks, he'd left the office early, just in case he got lost!

He reckoned the house would fetch at least £700,000, if not more. A hundred-thousand-pound loss then! It was not a surprise to me, as who would want to buy a house in such an isolated godforsaken place? Only a fool like me!

Then it was just a case of twiddling our fingers until the removal men arrived. Whilst we were waiting, we ate some sandwiches which Sue had kindly made, and drank from bottles of water. Alan tried to take my mind off the place by reminiscing about our childhood days and how we would go and play in an old, deserted house near to where we lived. How we never came to serious harm I will never know.

This cheered me up a little and as soon as the removal men came, things seemed to go quicker. The house echoed so much once the furniture had gone from the rooms, and it seemed even colder than when we arrived that morning. You could see our breath even inside the house.

I just couldn't be bothered to go round the rooms one last time. Not only did it remind me of that horrible day when I nearly ended it all, but I was now beginning to believe that there was some malevolent presence in the house. Probably my imagination, but right now I just wanted to get shot of the place.

It was starting to get dark when the removal men finally left. The next time I would use the furniture again would not be for another two years, though I didn't know it at the time.

As I walked out of the front door and onto the drive, I didn't seem sad in the slightest bit. It was more a case of "bring on the future", as I'd had my fill of living in the country. I got into my car and the engine started straight away. Alan had brought along some jump leads just in case it wouldn't start, but he didn't need them.

'Let's get the hell out of this place!' was all I could say.

He nodded his head and said, 'Take it easy bro,'

And with that we left *Hill View* behind for good.

8 CRAZY CITY

The very next day I contacted Tom about coming to stay with him for a while, as I reckoned that I was ready to leave Alan's and start living in the big wide world again. Although both Alan and Sue were reluctant to let me move out, I really felt ready to do so. By now I had come off the anti-depressants and after several long chats with Alan and Sue, had managed to climb out of the mire of depression that I'd been in a month ago.

Within a week I had moved into Tom's flat which was bang slap right in the city centre. He had bought a penthouse in a tall block of flats which gave him great views not only of the city, but also the surrounding areas. He was certainly living the highlife and I was soon to be following him on that score.

For those of you who don't know Manchester, the city centre is boarded by two main railway lines that run from west to east. To the north of the city centre is the railway that goes through Manchester Victoria, and to the south of the city centre is the line which goes through Oxford Road station and onto Piccadilly station. Tom's flat was right bang slap in the centre of these two lines, where all the night life and the action was. Talk about going from one extreme to another! I had moved from the peace and tranquility of the countryside to the noise and vibrancy of the city.

Tom in all his enthusiasm showed me a side to life that I wouldn't have gone near with a barge pole in my previous life as a teacher, but due to circumstances beyond my control I had been flung like a missile into a completely new and in some ways uncontrollable lifestyle as you shall see.

For a few weeks I lived with Tom before I found a place where I could happily live on my own. After all the months of living by myself I had become quite independent in many ways. Then when this was followed by the weeks at Alan's and Tom's, I began to long for some privacy and time on my own.

Whilst Tom went off to work during the day, I spent my time staying in the flat surfing the internet, reading, and watching movies, plus I was talking to Alan every day as he was still concerned about me. I also spent a lot of time trying to find a flat of my own. This involved looking for suitable ones on the internet, followed by meetings at estate agents and then viewings of potential flats.

Following the advice of my financial advisor, I had decided it would be better to rent one, rather than buy one as I wanted to test the water and see if I was happy with where I was situated. Plus, I really didn't want to lose a lot of money again by buying something unsuitable.

So, after several false starts I finally settled on a place also in the city centre, not far from Deansgate, with all the nightlife it had to offer. The flat came with its own furniture, which helped me considerably, seeing as all of the furniture from *Hill View* was in storage, waiting there until I knew what I was going to do with my life.

The rent was quite high – over £500 a week - as you would expect for a penthouse flat in the centre of Manchester, but it was what I wanted. If I wanted to buy a similar flat, it would have cost me around half the price I paid for *Hill View*. No way would I risk all that money again. As it was already furnished, I really didn't need to bring much stuff with me; just some books and DVDs and the odd small piece of furniture, which Alan helped me retrieve from the storage place.

My penthouse flat was everything you would expect a newfound bachelor to have. It was open plan with views to the south on one side of all the various shiny office blacks and the old red brick university beyond that. When I looked to the east, I could still see my beloved Pennine Hills in the distance, which brought back memories (mostly good) of the beautiful scenery there and the walks and the views.

The thing I liked best of all was the fact that if I needed anything it was all less than five minutes away. Say for instance if I wanted some milk, all I had to do was get into the lift and go downstairs, leave the building, and turn right and walk a few yards down the road to the supermarket. So, all my eating and drinking needs were met. When you compare this to living in the country, if I needed some milk there, I had to get in the car, drive several miles into Glossop, find a shop, buy the milk, and drive all those miles back again.

Plus, out in the country there was hardly anyone living within a mile of me. My new life in the city meant that I had tens of thousands of people all living and working right next to me. If I wanted to go anywhere, all I had to do was get on a tram or take a train from either Piccadilly or Victoria and I could visit anyone I liked. Or if it was a local trip, I might just take a taxi.

I had got rid of my car soon after arriving, partly because there was limited parking space in my building and partly because the public transport was so good. If I ever needed a car, all I had to do was hire one from several companies based in central Manchester. They would even deliver it to the front entrance of my block, and they dealt with all the paperwork.

* * *

Living in the city, meant that I soon started to move into Tom's circle of friends and have a lifestyle to match. All of them worked in offices based in and around the area of Spinningfields in such areas as investment, insurance, and banking. They all worked hard and also played hard.

One of them, Sam, was a City fan and it was he who introduced me to going to see them play away several times. That season we went to see City play at Norwich, Hull, and Arsenal in the Premiership, which did me good, mixing with ordinary folk once more and taking me out of myself. I couldn't make myself go and see City play at Wembley in the League Final in March though as it would be forever etched in my mind with the day that Tracy left me.

Stupidly, I still had a faint hope of a reconciliation with Tracy, but as I was blocked on her phone and email, the only means of communication was either through the children or via her brother Barry. In a way I felt sorry for him as he was torn between the two of us. Although he had been a close friend for many years, he would naturally be on the side of his sister. As they say, "Blood is thicker than water". Mind you, I really wanted to forget the fiasco of *Hill View* and Tracy leaving me and start living a life again. "Life is for the Living" so they say.

I was still keen on finding an activity to keep me occupied during the day and some of my time at Tom's was spent on more research into possible "day jobs" for me. After my brush with property investing, I decided that I was more inclined to find something that didn't take so much physical work and was free of all the council red tape.

So, after reading a newspaper article about people who invest in stocks and shares from home, I decided that I wanted to find out more. Rather than go and discuss it first with my financial advisor, I jumped straight in and joined an online broker club, where I put up £10,000 to invest and see what happened.

I suppose it was another form of gambling, but then again isn't that what it's all about - putting some money into something and hope that it will eventually make a profit? I tried to take it slowly, but once you're in, you get sucked in even more. I liked it partly because I didn't physically have to go anywhere, so I just stayed in the flat "playing" the markets; and partly because I wasn't tied down by people telling me what to do.

To me, it was more of a game rather than a serious effort on my part to make money. I had so much, so it didn't matter if I lost some of it. I was pretty naïve doing this and after a few weeks, although I had made some small gains, in reality I had probably lost getting on for £30,000. I know it sounds a lot, but for me with all those millions in the bank it was peanuts.

I really needed someone to come into my flat and say, 'Don't be so stupid, Gary!', but there was no one, and in the end the only reason I stopped doing it was through boredom. I found that it needed a certain type of brain to be able to play the markets successfully and clearly my brain wasn't the right type!

* * *

It was at night-time that the biggest change to me happened. Little by little I was becoming a night owl, who was awake more at night than during the day. At first Tom and I just went out for a drink at the many pubs in the city centre, but as I got to know some of his work colleagues, I gradually got drawn into the seedier side of the city centre.

Although Tom worked during the week, at the weekends he would certainly let his hair down. So, on the second Friday night of me staying with him; he suggested that we went out to a club for a change. Only this club wasn't a normal club with a disco and lots of people dancing, it turned out to be a pole dancing club! We ended up there placing ten and twenty pound notes into the dancer's garter. Also, as I was starting to drink more - not just pints now, but also shorts and cocktails - my inhibitions were starting to go out of the window.

Then there was the drugs....

I was fascinated to find out how Tom seemed so full of energy all the time, so one day I asked him.
'How come you have so much energy all the time, Tom?' I asked him one night, when we were out drinking.
'I was wondering when you were going to ask me?' he replied with a grin on his face.
'Speed mainly. And sometimes Coke. They both have the same effect of making me more awake, more energised. Simple as that,' he confessed.
I wasn't in the slightest bit shocked, as I half suspected that was the case.
I just nodded my head in agreement, indicating that I thought that was the reason.
'Want to try some then?' he asked.
That threw me. I was certainly tempted, as in some ways I was jealous of Tom and how he seemed to be on top of the world all the time. Plus, nothing seemed to faze him – his marriage breaking up and getting divorced, his work and all the stress that it brought him; he actually seemed pretty happy with life. All this made me want to be like him, but at the same time I knew it was a dangerous and stupid thing to do.
'Not at the moment,' I replied, indicating to him that I *was* interested, but also a little afraid of taking illegal drugs. After all I had been quite depressed for most of last year. I didn't want to mess up my mind even more.
'You know Gary,' he said. 'I was just like you a couple of years ago; down and depressed after my marriage failed. Then when I started taking speed, I instantly became so much happier. It'll do you good.'
It was if he was throwing down the gauntlet to me.

'I'll think about it,' was all I could say.

I could definitely see that he seemed so much more alive than me, but what was all that drug taking doing to him inside? He didn't look like a junky, sure. But he could be one for all I knew.

Being with him and his mates on a regular basis, I suppose that it was inevitable that I would start taking recreational drugs just like him. It was a couple of weeks later that I threw caution to the wind and actually snorted some speed when he offered it to me a second time. Admittedly I'd drunk quite a lot that evening, so my inhibitions had gone. But within ten minutes of taking it, I began to feel so good and actually couldn't stop talking all evening. The only problem was when I eventually got home about 3.00am, I just couldn't go to sleep.

I knew that I'd crossed that fine line into the world of drug taking and within a few more weeks I was trying coke which seemed even more powerful. Tom supplied me with whatever I needed and although I didn't take half as much as him, I found that I started to need it more and more. Plus, the cost of the drugs was eating into my lottery money little by little.

The other temptation, apart from drugs that my new lifestyle threw at me was sex. By now, with me gradually accepting that there was not going to be any reconciliation with Tracy, I had started to become attracted to the opposite sex once more. Going to one or two lap dancing clubs had started to influence my thoughts. It was well over six months since I'd last had sex and all the turmoil had affected my libido, but now it was starting to grow again, so to speak! Although I wasn't after a serious relationship right now, I was interested in one night stands. In the clubs I was visiting there was no shortage of beautiful women around, and they weren't all taken.

My first few visits to the clubs were spent on getting to know the club, such as what was the clientele like? Where there people of my age frequenting them? Or was I too old for them? Luckily, with the support and experience of Tom and his mates I soon decided that *Stacy's* and *El Grande* were my favourite clubs.

Both were gaming clubs with plenty of action going on around the roulette and backgammon tables, but that sort of gambling had never been of interest to me. Instead, I preferred the plentiful supply of slot machines available.

I did have one rule however and that was that I would limit myself to £100 an evening. If I won something - great. If I didn't - no problem. Once my supply had gone, that was enough for me. I definitely didn't want to become hooked on gambling. I just wanted to make sure that I didn't stand out like a sore thumb and make myself conspicuous.

On one of the evenings that I visited these sorts of clubs I got chatting to one of the pretty ladies standing by the roulette table. She was called Marcella and was in her late thirties I would guess. She had long blonde hair and just the right amount of make-up. She was slim and had adequate breasts and seemed quite gregarious. She was wearing a long green evening dress with a slit up to her thigh, backed up with sparkly gold coloured high heels. I realised that I was quite attracted to her.

I found myself saying 'Hello,' without really checking to see if she was with anyone. She replied straight away with a 'Hello handsome!' which made my heartbeat go much faster. Clearly, she was a bit of a flirt. She told me her "companion" for the night had gone off to the men's room and deserted her, so she was at a loose end. Being naïve to all this I didn't quite get the gist of what she was saying, but I did realise that she was an escort girl, who had been paid to accompany someone for the evening and possibly for the rest of the night.

We chatted some more, and she explained that she was paid by the hour for however long the client wanted her to be with him. I could tell by the way she spoke that she was not some cheap call girl, but quite intelligent and from a middle class background. I was intrigued by her but didn't want to push her too much about why she was in this business, what with all the people around and her companion possibly due back at any moment. However, before I said 'Goodbye', she gave me her card which had the phone number of the escort agency that employed her, as well as their website. Very business-like if you ask me.

* * *

The next day I logged onto the escort agency website and couldn't believe my eyes. There were lots of girls on its pages; all in varying stages of undress, making it pretty clear what they were there for. You could choose according to age, nationality, figure, and colour of their hair. If you pressed a particular girl's profile you could find out a lot more about her, including her age, the colour of her eyes and hair, her breast size and nationality. Most important of all you could find out how much she charged for her time. I looked at several profiles and noticed that most charged between £75 and £100 upwards per hour.

Some girls had the letters "GFE" next to their picture. I hadn't a clue what this meant and looked it up on the internet. I soon learned that it stood for "Girlfriend Experience", meaning that the girl wouldn't be available just for sex, but would behave like your girlfriend, talking to you, kissing you and showing you affection. I decided straight away that was the type of girl I would hire.

After looking through pages and pages of several escort websites I finally settled on a girl called Miranda. She was thirty three according to the blurb and had size 38 DD boobs. Not that it mattered. I liked the look of her from the photos and rang the number on the site. A male voice answered. I explained that I was interested in booking Miranda and that this was my first time.

'Sure mate. No problem. When did you want to see her?' was all that he asked.

He then went into detail about how it all worked, explaining that I was paying for her time and could take her to any place I liked such as a club, a show, or the cinema. What we got up to after that was entirely up to us, though if sex took place, wearing a condom was compulsory. Plus, you had to pay in advance by card or cash before anything happened.

Although he didn't ask for my address, he did want my first name and my mobile phone number. I told him my name was "Tony", not wanting to give him my true identity. He told me that I would get a phone call from Miranda later that day and if she felt happy after talking to me, then we could proceed.

I was actually quite excited with the thrill of it all. It was unknown; possibly dangerous and not the sort of thing you would tell your children. The other thing that I had made up my mind about, was that to begin with I would prefer to go to a neutral place, rather than the escort girl's flat, or perhaps she could come round to my flat. I just wanted to be sure that it was actually a girl I was meeting and not some thug ready to rob me.

All afternoon I was on tenterhooks waiting for my phone to ring. Finally, just after five o'clock it finally rang with the words, "private number" on the display screen. I knew it was "Miranda" and as soon as she said 'Hello.' my heart rate shot up. She sounded so sexy on the phone.

Miranda asked me a little about myself and where I worked. I told her Tom's workplace and said I'd only just got home. I was a single male aged 38, who had recently got divorced and was looking for someone to accompany me for the evening.

After talking some more, she agreed to be my escort for the night, and we agreed three hours of her time. There was just one thing – as it was my first time we would have to meet at the agency's office where I would make my payment and then we could go out together. I agreed straight away without thinking and arranged to meet her at 9 o'clock at the escort agency offices, which were just round the corner from where I lived.

I spent the rest of the evening on tenterhooks. Before anything else I went down to the cash machine near my flat and took out £500 in cash, which I thought would cover me for the evening. I really didn't want to use my card – just in case it turned out to be a scam. When I got back, I had a shower and a shave, put on some aftershave, and made sure I looked good. I hadn't taken so much care of what I looked like for years! Then I took the plunge and went round to the offices of the escort agency. It turned out that it wasn't an office as such, but rather someone's apartment in a plush block of flats.

When I rang the intercom, a male asked for my name and then let me in. I went in a lift up to the fifth floor and rang the bell of the flat number I'd been given. He shook my hand and introduced himself as Phil. He then asked me, how I wanted to pay, and I handed over the money. Phil then went over a few things in a business-like manner before letting me know that Miranda was on her way and wouldn't be long.

After about ten minutes his intercom rang, and he spoke into it. A couple of minutes later Miranda came into the apartment looking gorgeous. She had black high heels on and wore a pale pink long coat which was open, revealing a black mini dress beneath it. She had dark brown hair which touched her shoulders and she looked even better in the flesh than in her photograph. Phil introduced us and we kissed each other on the cheeks. I smelt her perfume straight away which was quite strong, but still pleasant.

Then she asked, 'Where are we going Tony?' in the same sexy voice as she had on the phone earlier.

'I thought we might go to *Stacy's*', I said, trying to sound confident.

'Wonderful,' she replied. 'I like it there.'

'OK. Let's go then,' I replied.

Again, I tried to sound confident, but inside I was all butterflies. This was the first woman I had been out with since all those years ago when I first went out with Tracy and I was obviously rusty.

When we were in the lift, she spoke first to break the silence.

'I can tell that you are nervous, Tony,' she said in the sexy voice of hers. 'Don't be!' and with that she kissed me briefly on the lips. She was obviously flirting, but I loved all the attention. Tracy was never like this!

She put her arm through mine as we walked down the street. I felt ten feet tall with a beautiful, sexy woman next to me. Some male heads turned which boosted my ego even more.

When we got to *Stacey's* we spent the first half hour watching people on the roulette table and playing some of the slot machines. All the time she was very touchy feely with me. We did talk some of the time; mainly small chit chat, but I could tell she had class and wasn't some cheap call girl.

After about an hour she said,

'Would you like to go somewhere quieter Tony?'

I could tell what this was leading to and replied,

'Sure. Your place or mine?'

'I think seeing as this is your first time, your place might be the best place. I'm sure you'll be more relaxed there.'

So, within an hour of arriving at *Stacy's* we were leaving. I ordered a cab. Although it was only a few streets away, I felt it gave a better impression going to my flat by taxi, rather than walking.

In no time at all we were in my flat and kissing passionately. She was clearly up for it! I lead her into the bedroom, and she undressed ever so teasingly down to her suspenders and stockings.

You can guess the rest!

Miranda left soon after midnight, getting a cab downstairs at the front of my block. It had been fantastic; almost like the first time I'd had sex. Only this time we both knew what we were doing and so enjoyed it all the more. The only thing I didn't like was wearing a condom; something I had never really done before, apart from experimenting with one in my teenage days. Not that it put me off sexually. The high I got from the sex was so much better than the coke or speed, and after Miranda had left, I knew that I would be doing this again very soon!

* * *

My life was not all partying, though. I did go to see some big artists at the Manchester Arena like Kylie. For the Kylie show I took along an escort, Rachel for the evening. Plenty of heads turned as we went to our seats and it made it worth all the money that I had spent on her. Naturally, after the show she came back to my flat and stayed all night.

I also went down to London every so often, mainly to see an artist who wasn't playing in Manchester. The good thing about it was that I was able to get a train 1st class and be booked into one of the nicer hotels in London in just two and a half hours.

Over the course of the next year, I went to concerts at Wembley Stadium, the 02 and the Royal Albert Hall. Some of the time I went with my brother or Tom or one of his friends; though once or twice I arranged for an escort to go with me. Not so much for the sex, but more for the company. It was still very expensive though.

There was one thing that helped me keep in reality and down to earth and that was going to see Man City play both at home and away. I had started using my season ticket again after neglecting it last year. I knew I could have bought a hospitality box if I wanted to, but that wasn't really me, and besides, I would be apart from the true fans, with all the singing and the atmosphere.

In years gone by, I had occasionally been to see City play away, usually in the North West like at Liverpool, Everton and Stoke. I even went to a few games in London when I was a student down there. Now with all that money I was able to go and see them play at any of their away games if I wanted to, seeing as season ticket holders got away match tickets before anyone else.

Soon, I started going on the away coaches from the City of Manchester Stadium as it was then called. I ended up going to places like Southampton, Newcastle, and Norwich. Quite long journeys, which could be a little boring, though I usually took my e reader with me. The one positive from all this was to make a whole lot of new friends who had the same shared interest as me.

Into my life came Brendan - another forty something fan, and Jack - a much older guy who had been watching City play since before I was born. We had a good laugh and although we didn't socialise outside of the away scene, it did me some good in that it helped me to forget my other life.

* * *

With my renewed interest with the opposite sex came a desire to make myself look as attractive as possible to the opposite sex. I stated going to a men's hairdressers near to where I lived. Not only did they do haircuts, but they also did shaves, eyebrow shaping and Indian Head Massage. I was gradually moving away from a traditional working class male into a sophisticated, style obsessed male who wanted to look good and attractive to the opposite sex.

Another thing about my appearance that I wanted to change was my teeth. I noticed that Tom had had his teeth fixed and they looked pretty good. I asked him the name of his dentist as I had a snuggle tooth which I thought was not flattering and as I wanted my teeth to look perfect, I asked Tom for his name.

He was called Mr Askew and was based in Bramhall, where he serviced all the rich and famous in the north Cheshire area. I looked his practice up on the internet and rang them up, making an appointment for an exploratory session. Although it was quite expensive by my old standards, now money was no problem, so I was quite happy to go and see what could be done.

He was quite a charismatic character, who was very good at name dropping, telling me some of his famous clients including City and United players and their Wags, as well as some of the top lawyers and businessmen in the North West, most of whom I'd never heard of.

'And what do you do Mr. Whitemore?' he probed as soon as he had finished taking X-rays of all my teeth.

'I work in banking,' I half lied. 'I specialise in investments,' which was half true, as this was making use of the money I had.

'Oh. What's the firm called? I might have heard of them?'

I was starting to get uncomfortable, not in the teeth department, but in his probing questions. Clearly, he thought I hadn't got the money for his place, but when I answered, 'I don't actually work for a firm anymore, as I made a killing through some major investments. I now work from home now.'

'And where is that?' he asked.

When I told him the name of the block of flats I lived in, it seemed to pacify him, and his attitude immediately changed.

He then got on with his job, much to my relief.

The long and short of it was that he could remove the snuggle tooth and put an implant in its place, or he could file down the whole top row, where it was and put veneers along which would also make my teeth much whiter. I had been thinking of getting my teeth whitened but had been put off when I found out that I would have to wear a special mould for several nights to get rid of forty plus years of stains. This second option seemed a lot more attractive, so I told him without really thinking things through that I would go ahead with that option.

'It'll be something in the region of eight to ten thousand pounds, Mr Whitemore. The receptionist will give you a detailed breakdown.'

'That's fine,' I half boasted. 'How long will the treatment take?'

'I will need three sessions; one to make a detailed mould of what's to be done, one to put in a set of temporary veneers over the stubs and one to put the finished veneers from the factory. Once it's done you will look fabulous!'

Over a period of several weeks, I would take a train down to Bramhall and back from Piccadilly. I quite enjoyed the journey; not that it wasn't far, but it was nice to get out of the city for a change. Plus, the actual town looked attractive to me and sowed the seeds of maybe one day moving out to here or to somewhere similar.

When he had finished the job, I thought it was worth all the injections, filing and drilling. My smile was different and much brighter with the new veneers. It did my self-confidence a lot of good and definitely made me look more attractive to the opposite sex, which was all part of the plan.

During the treatment, Mr Askew had begun to call me by my first name, which I didn't mind. He said I could call him Luke if I liked and so the dentist/patient line became blurred. I think he did a great job and told him so at the end of the treatment.

Strangely, our paths would cross again sooner than I thought.

* * *

Although I had let Lesley and Jon know about moving to the flat, I actually hadn't seen Lesley for well over six months, such was the fact of living two hundred miles apart. So, when I get a text from her to say that they were going to the Lakes for a holiday and could they pop in and see me on the way up, I was overjoyed.

At the same time, I was dreading it, aware that she hadn't seen me in my new guise of drug taker and sex addict. I could easily clean up the flat and make myself look presentable, but would she see through the facade? Also, I had to be careful not to mention my "secret life" of escorts and drugs that none of my family knew about. I would have to tread carefully so as not to let it slip.

It was one Saturday in April, when Lesley and her boyfriend Mike popped in to see me. Naturally, I had been out the night before, getting in around 3.00am, but when the intercom rang at half eleven, I was still asleep. It was only when Lesley called me on my mobile, did I finally rouse myself. I was going to set the alarm but had completely forgot!

My flat was a little like a scene from a farce with me rushing round the flat trying to get dressed and tidying things up, whilst they were coming up in the lift. It was a good job that I had abstained from the escorts last night or they could have come face to face with one of my "lady friends".

As soon as I opened the door to the two of them, Lesley's first words were,

'Had a late night Dad?'

I kissed and hugged her with genuine affection, but I noticed a slight pulling back as she caught a whiff of my breath.

'Sorry Les. I completely forgot to set the alarm last night and as I had a bit of a late night…..you know…..' I was lost for words.

'So, you seem to enjoying life again?' she queried.

'Yes. I'm quite settled into my new life in the city,' I replied, trying not to sound too conceited.

'That's good. You seemed so down at the other place. I could never have lived there.'

'Yes, I know. I suppose it was a big mistake moving there. Still, you live and learn.'

I tried to change the subject, as I was sure that Tracy would come into it.

'Fancy a cuppa? How was the journey?

'Yes. That would be great,' she said. 'The journey was fine. No hold ups.'

'So where is it you're staying then?' I asked.

'Oh, it's quite near Coniston,' she replied. 'Mike loves walking and the fresh air.'

I had almost forgotten that Mike was there, so I tried to draw him into the conversation.

'A man after my own heart!' I half joked.

Mike laughed and then looked at Lesley.

I made them both a cup of tea, whilst I made myself a strong black coffee, hoping it would wake me up properly and get rid of the alcohol in my body. When I brought it to them and sat down, I noticed Lesley looking nervously at Mike.

'Dad there's something Mike and I need to tell you,' said Lesley seriously. She looked again at Mike and then they both looked at me.

I thought it was going to be something about Tracy, but it was nothing of the sort.

She held out her left hand and pronounced, 'Mike and I have just got engaged!'

Such was my state of panic that I hadn't noticed the engagement ring, sparkling on her first finger of her left hand.

'Congratulations!' I said, trying to sound pleased, though inwardly I was confused, thinking how she could want to do this seeing as her parents were getting divorced. This made me think of Tracy and I blurted out,

'Does your mother know yet?'

'No. You're the first to know. In fact, I haven't had much to do with her since she left you Dad.'

That was sort of comforting for me to hear that, but then the alarm bells started ringing inside.

'Have you set a date for the wedding yet?'

'Yes. It'll be in April next year.'

'Well, I'll help you with all the reception just as much as you want me to Les, I offered.

'That's so kind of you Dad.'

Inwardly, I was making plans about what might happen if I came face to face with Tracy, but it was a long time away.

* * *

Before all that though, I had a court hearing to attend in Manchester regarding the divorce settlement. Tracy was still popping up in my life despite the fact that I no longer had anything to do with her.

Through the efforts of my accountant and my solicitor the eight million pounds that Tracy was after had mysteriously disappeared into a new account I had set up in Alan's name. Reluctantly, he had changed his mind about it when I said that Tom was happy to "look after" the money. I was glad of that because with Tom not being family, you never could tell. Now all I had left of the eleven million plus pounds of lottery winnings was a little over two million.

On the morning of the court case, I was super nervous, especially with the distinct possibility of seeing Tracy face to face after all this time. There was only one thing that I could do in a situation like this and that was to snort two lines of coke before the proceedings began.

Alan had promised to be there as moral support, but at the last minute he sent me a message to say that he couldn't make it due to a crisis at work. Poor Alan. He was finding it increasingly hard to make his business work, but he refused any more money from me. If only he'd give it all up and retire. He would be so much happier.

The hearing couldn't have gone any better, with the judge awarding Tracy half of what I had in my bank account, including the proceeds from the sale of the house, (which finally went for £750,000 to a Buddhist group wanting it as a place for retreats). At least I could keep the eight million, even if she did get another million out of me. As you would expect I had to explain why there was so little left of the initial fortune. The judge believed me, partly because I seemed so confident thanks to the coke, and partly through my solicitor, who used all his legal speak to convince the judge of my integrity.

One thing which surprised me though was the non-appearance of Tracy. Her solicitor had said that she was flying in from Australia, "where she now lived", but that her flight had been delayed and she wasn't going to be able to make it in time. So that was where she had gone. Probably trying to get as far away from me as possible I shouldn't think!

With that major hurdle out of the way, it was now business as usual with me going down to *Stacy's* to celebrate. My life was now a continual round of drinks, drugs and sex all eating into my fortune and doing who knows what to my brain. I had now become one of the rich boys on the Manchester scene and I revelled in it, mixing with the rich and famous who frequented the same clubs as me. I even got to know some of the City players, though they really didn't want to talk shop; just enjoy themselves.

One blip on my current lifestyle was that Tom was being transferred down to London with his job and so he couldn't supply me with my drugs anymore. Instead, he put me onto a new dealer one night before he went; someone I knew already, namely Luke Askew, my dentist.

Although on the one hand I was shocked to see him doing this, on the other I wasn't as drug dealers can still be respectable citizens on the surface yet have a dark side underneath. Over the next few weeks, we become closer as he supplied me with whatever I wanted, with ever increasing amounts of drugs to feed my habit, until it all went wrong one day.

A few weeks after Tom had departed for London, I woke one morning about half eleven and as usual I felt like death warmed up. My head was throbbing, and I felt sick, but that soon passed. I drank a glass of water and felt better. I needed some fresh air, but where would I find that in the middle of one of Britain's biggest cities I thought?

I felt a sudden urge to get out of Manchester. It was almost like a panic attack. Maybe deep down inside I was starting to rebel against my current lifestyle. I didn't know why I was thinking this, but it was so strong that I skipped breakfast and walked to Manchester Piccadilly station, still feeling pretty grotty. Once there, I looked up at the information board on the concourse which showed 'the next train to...' and how soon it would be going. I scanned the board, looking at the various destinations - Liverpool, Sheffield, Chester, Plymouth, and London. None of these tickled my fancy and most of them were too far for what I was thinking.

I looked again and the name 'Hadfield' shot out at me. I knew it as a small town, east of Manchester and not too far from Glossop. I also knew it was on the edge of the Pennines and would take me out into the countryside. I suddenly realised that I hadn't been out of Manchester by myself since moving into my flat; apart from going to see City play away of course, and to the dentists.

It struck me there and then that going into the countryside once again might do me some good. Clear my head perhaps and help me put my feet on the ground once more. There was a train in ten minutes time going to Hadfield, so I went and bought a ticket and got on the train.

Just over half an hour later I was walking along the Longendale Trail footpath which follows the old Woodhead railway route to Sheffield. I wouldn't be walking that far of course, but the taste of fresh air was certainly therapeutic for me.

As I walked along, I tried to analyse my situation and blow away the cobwebs which had formed over my life with all the partying and excess living I was now doing. The drugs, and now the sex were starting to get a hold over me and I really didn't like that. I was also starting to become more aggressive and starting to swear quite frequently, something I hardly ever did in my previous life as a school teacher. At football matches I would be the one effing and blinding at the referee when he made a decision I didn't agree with. I knew it wasn't really me, but I just couldn't help myself anymore. I was still hurting inside after the divorce from Tracy, who I had always loved and been faithful to. Yet it had all come to an end and in reality I suppose that I just couldn't face that fact.

I looked to my right and saw the Pennines stretching out ahead. Then I looked to the left and saw a massive reservoir with several birds flying up over it. It struck me that birds were so free. They could go anywhere they wanted and weren't hemmed in by all the rules and traditions and expectations that human beings have. It made me think of the Beatles Song, *Free as a Bird*. It played itself in my head and the line, "Whatever happened to the life that we once knew?" seemed to fit perfectly into my situation. How I longed to be free like the birds that I was observing.

The idea of freedom was something which began to eat away at me. I had all this money and yet I wasn't free. I certainly could go anywhere I wanted to go with all that money in the bank, yet I wasn't free emotionally. In fact, I was becoming more trapped in my emotions. I couldn't escape. I needed help! Yet who could I turn to?

My mother was now gone. I didn't have a wife to turn to anymore. My brother was so busy with his business all the time. He had been so supportive to me, but I didn't want to burden him just now. My children were both far away. I could call them, but they were still so young and not worldly wise. I had lost the support and camaraderie of my colleagues at school. It seemed as if there was no one who could help me.

I kept walking and breathing in the fresh air which seemed so different to the polluted city air of Manchester. It felt good to be out in the countryside once more. My mind went back to those times as a child when the family would come out onto the Pennine Moors and walk for miles, singing and joking and playing amongst the bracken and the heather. That was life was all about. Not all this partying and spending money like there's no tomorrow.

This is what I needed, yet it had all gone so wrong just over a year ago with that hell house not that far from here. I knew deep down that I needed balance in my life. I was playing with the self-destruct button that controlled my body. Having all that excess was not good for my body, yet if I came out to live in the countryside again, would I end up just the same as I was - all depressed and lonely? At least in Manchester I had plenty of friends. Or were they friends?

As usual I my thoughts were swinging to and fro from one extreme to the other, At least when I was married to Tracy there was balance. Now I was living at one extreme. If only I could get balance again. Maybe having a steady girlfriend might make me more balanced, but to be honest I really didn't fancy settling down again. Part of me liked the high life and that was the part that was winning in my mind. I had reached a turning point. I knew what I had to do. Either I stop all this high life living and escape to some normality, or I keep going the way that I was doing and end up destroying myself. It was so hard for me in the state I was in. I needed someone or something to make me stop this lifestyle, but there was no one. I turned round and made my way back to Hadfield station and waited for the next train back to Manchester.

As I walked out of Piccadilly station, I picked up a free newspaper that was being handed out by the street vendors. I glanced at the headlines at stopped dead in my tracks. It said,

"TOP DENTIST ON DRUGS CHARGES"

I read the first few lines of the page and realised who this dentist was. It was Luke Askew who had been arrested and I suddenly started to panic. 'What if he squeals? What if they've been watching him and know who his customers are?' I began to run against the thronging crowd making their way into the station. I had to get back to my flat as soon as possible as I had a stash of coke hidden in one of the tea caddies in my kitchen.

Ten minutes later and breathless I arrived at the entrance to my block of flats. I walked past the front door and round the side to the back entrance, checking that there were no police cars parked in the street. Then I went in through the back entrance and into the lift.

I opened my door and checked that everything looked the same as when I left the flat earlier in the day. Then I made straight for the kitchen. I found the tea caddie and lifted off the lid. There was getting on for a grand's worth of coke in it, but I took it straight to my toilet and flushed it all down the pan. 'What a waste!' I thought. But it was better than being arrested for possession of a Class A drug. I then washed the container in liquid soap and boiling hot water to destroy any traces of the drug. Then I popped it into a dark plastic bag and went down to the street where I found a waste bin and got rid of it. The whole episode hadn't just shocked me; it had frightened me as well. I didn't want to end up in prison as Luke would surely do.

That evening, I decided that I would actually stay in and not go to the pubs and clubs, partly after the shock of Luke getting busted and partly after my "revelation" out on the moors. I sat down to watch the news, which I hadn't seen for days. There were items about the state of the economy, an earthquake in China, some celebrity's new film and various sports items. It was all so depressing. I was finding it hard to concentrate; such was the effect of the cocaine. My mind was restless I and couldn't think straight. I started browsing the internet; just looking here and there, not really bothering about anything.

I needed company, but not my usual sort of company. I also needed to get back to being a "normal" person and not being the party animal, I had become. I tried to go to bed "normally" at eleven o'clock, but it was so hard getting to sleep. Eventually I did, but I knew I needed help to achieve "normality" in my life.

The next night though, I was back at *El Grande* with an escort on my arm and some fresh coke supplied by someone I met in the gents. I was back to my old ways, which I found comforting, but I suppose in reality I was comforting myself over the breakup of my marriage and the failure of *Hill View*. I needed another earthquake in my life to make me come to my senses and very soon that is what did happen.

9 THE ONLY WAY IS UP

A few days later, at about 11 o'clock one morning I was woken from a deep sleep by my mobile phone ringing. I was in a dream where I was being chased by burglars through the streets of Manchester. Then I realised that I was one of them and we had just robbed a bank and there was money in our hands dropping out onto the pavement as we ran from the police. All the time I could hear the bank's alarm going off. Then I woke up.

It was my mobile phone ringing. I was still quite intoxicated from last night and dozed off until the phone rang again. This time I woke up properly. As I made my way across the bedroom to try to pick up the phone from my jacket pocket, I felt my head throb with yet another hangover. 'I need to sort myself out' I thought.

By the time I reached my jacket and felt into the pocket, it had stopped ringing. I looked to see who it was and was surprised to see that there were four missed calls from Sue, Alan's wife. 'That's strange', I thought. She never ever rings me, although she's got my number, just in case I can't get hold of Alan, or vice-versa. The fact that she had tried ringing me four times started a panic in me. It must be something to do with Alan.

I pressed the redial button and got through straight away. 'What's up Sue?' I enquired. 'It's Alan, Gary. He's had a stroke'.

The words hit me like a rocket piercing through my brain. To say I was shocked was an understatement.

I had to sit down as Sue's words sank in.

'Is he OK?' I enquired. 'What happened?'

'Luckily, they caught him quite soon after it started', she replied. 'He was at work in his office and his secretary went in to find him slumped in his chair with his face not quite right. Luckily, she remembered the advert and rang for an ambulance straight away. He was in the hospital within half an hour of him being found, so he was lucky.'

'Which hospital is he in?' I asked, sounding more and more concerned.

'Fairfield General,' Sue replied.

'Right. I'm on my way!'

I felt so guilty that I hadn't picked up my phone earlier, but as I didn't get in 'til four and then crashed out, it was hardly surprising. Although I had the mother of all hangovers, I knew I had to see my brother straight away. I quickly got myself a black coffee and rang for a cab. I was at the hospital half an hour later.

On the way I mulled things over in my mind. Talk about wake-up call. Adam having a stroke was the big wake-up call that I needed to wake me up out of the stupid mess my life had got into. Yet, why should it be something as serious as this to bring me to my senses? Once I was at the hospital, I soon found the stroke ward. I think some of the staff might have thought I was the one who should be admitted, such was the state I looked! Anyway, as his brother they allowed me into the stroke ward, even though it was midday and not yet time for visiting.

I'm not one who is easily shocked, but even I was shocked at the sight of him lying flat on his bed. He had a drip coming out of his left arm up to a saline bag hanging from a frame. On his right hand was a cannula ready for all the bloods they had to take out of him to check his cholesterol and other things.

It was his colour that got to me though. He looked so pale and when he saw me, he raised a smile - if you could call it that. More of a slight lip movement. He couldn't talk yet and it was only in his eyes that I could see my brother of old.

"Hiya bro" I said. A grunting sound came out of his mouth and it was then that I realised he couldn't talk. That really threw me as I hadn't expected him to be that bad.

I pulled up a chair so I could sit beside the bed. A male nurse came to the other side of the bed and started taking his temperature, looking at his watch as he did it.

'How is he?' I blurted out, forgetting that whatever the nurse would say to me, Adam would hear every word of it.

'It's early days yet. We have to see the effect of clot buster drug that we've given to your brother. We should know what sort of recovery he will make within the next twenty-four hours. Most stroke patients are like this for up to forty-eight hours after the medicine enters their body. What you are seeing is mainly the effect of the drug on your brother.

From the scan he had, we could see that a blood clot entered his brain on his right side, but the effects of the damage will be seen mainly on the left side of the body. It's just a case of waiting. Most stroke patients make a full recovery depending on how soon they are admitted into hospital.'

I certainly got a full answer from the nurse, but I knew it would take a long time for Alan to recover. I was so glad that he had been caught in time and wasn't in a coma or even worse.

The effect of seeing Alan like that released a feeling of brotherly love for him from me that I hadn't realised existed within me. I had always been close to him and respected him tremendously, but as for loving him, I didn't realise that I had it in me. It was as though a part of me had been broken off. Although it hadn't happened to me, I felt the shock as well as the emotion that a major health scare brings. "There but for the grace of God go I", is the saying that comes to mind here and I was sure glad that I was not in his shoes.

Looking back, this episode in my life really shook me up and made me think about what my life was like and just how precious life is. I started to realise how selfish and stupid I was; living the lifestyle I was leading. What if something like that happened to me? He was only three years younger than me and look at him now. What if he died? I would be distraught to say the least.

He had been a rock for me in all my depression. Then I had abandoned him in a way, by hardly seeing him in the past few months. All the booze and drugs and women had become more important to me than my own family. What a selfish bastard I had been.

The guilt flowed right through me and started a chain reaction in me that would lead me to making a complete lifestyle change. The only problem was I couldn't do this change by myself. I needed help.

In that hospital I began to realise that life is precious, and it can all go in the blink of an eye. What if Alan did die? Then I would lose my rock, the person who understood me most of all in the world; the person who had known me the longest and who helped pick me up when I fell down. Plus, what about getting that eight million quid back?

In a way I realised that I needed to stand on my own two feet more, but most important of all I realised that the life I was living wasn't good or right for me. It was all very fine living the champagne lifestyle with the women and the drugs, but I knew deep down that it was destroying me. I didn't need to live like that, not if I wanted to survive and flourish.

Surely there was someone out there who could help me? Someone who wouldn't judge me but could point me in the right direction and help me to overcome the need for the three demons in my life - drink, drugs, and women.

I WON THE LOTTERY...

After that first initial visit, I was more prepared for the sights and sounds of that stroke ward. In all my concern for Alan I really hadn't noticed the other patients around him the first time, but now on this second visit a few days later I did see them and was shocked and saddened by what I saw.

There were some who didn't look too bad; some who were sitting in chairs by the side of the bed staring into space, but others were lying very still on their beds with drips and other lines attached to their bodies. There was a smell of urine in the air, as obviously someone had wet themselves on the way to the toilet. There was also an eerie silence, broken only by the constant beep of blood pressure monitors or patients buzzing for a nurse to help them.

At least Alan looked a lot better than previously. This time he was sitting up in bed, though he was still attached to a drip. He also seemed a lot more coherent and I could have a near normal conversation with him. He told me that the stroke had happened soon after he'd taken a stressful call with a client who wasn't particularly happy with some work that his company had done for him. He reckoned this might have been the trigger for his stroke. That and all the worry that I caused him, no doubt.

They still couldn't say how long he'd be in hospital for, but the consultant was very happy with the progress he was making. The stroke hadn't done any serious damage as far as he was concerned, but he still could not stand up yet, let alone walk. That would take longer.

It was when the nurses came to Alan's bed to wash and change him that a ray of light opened up for me. I was asked to wait outside whilst they cleaned him. One of the other nurses saw me standing around and told me that there was a relative's room just down the corridor where I could wait. So, I decided to go in there for a few minutes until they had finished.

There was no one else in there, but it had a settee and two chairs with a pile a magazines on a table. On a wall were various posters of different organisations and events taking place. As I was scanning through them, I came across one that made me stop. It was for counselling and said:-

Professional Counsellor available for consultations in the South Manchester area.

I deal with all sorts of problems including depression, anxiety, addictions, and low self-esteem. For an informal chat please ring Richard on……..

This was just what I was looking for. Someone above was looking down on me perhaps. Here at last was someone who might be able to help me. I took down the details and made a mental note to call him when I got home.

I was as good as my word and did call him when I got back to the flat later that day. The counsellor answered the phone more or less straight away and took down my details and said that he would definitely be able to help me, just as long as I was willing to be helped. I said a definite 'Yes' to this and made an appointment to visit him at his practice in Cheadle the next week.

* * *

A week later I was there at his house, a large Victorian, red brick semi with room for several cars on the drive. For the first session with Richard, I was naturally quite reticent and nervous, but he soon put me at my ease. I was asked to sit in a large brown leather chair which I found quite comfortable.

What he said first of all threw me completely.

'I would like you to close your eyes if you are able'.

I was beginning to think that he was about to hypnotize me, but it was nothing of the sort. He continued.

'Just imagine that you are looking down at yourself from up in the sky, Gary,'

I was about to say, 'Really. Are you sure?' but thought better of doing that.

'By doing this, you will be detached from all the problems that are going on in your life. It's as though you have two parts to the person that is you, and one part is describing to me, what this person called Gary Whitemore is doing with his life.'

I shut my eyes and tried to look down on myself from above. It was surprisingly much easier than I could have believed. Also, I thought we would be talking mainly about my drugs and my drink habits, but I couldn't have been more wrong. Instead, we went right back to my birth. Well not literally, but we concentrated on my family, such as what my parents were like, what backgrounds they were from, what jobs they had, where we lived and probably most important of all my relationship with my brother and sister.

Richard soon learnt about how I got on really well with my brother and not at all with my sister. To be honest, it wasn't so much of him asking me questions as more me telling the story of my early life.

As he had promised in our initial chat, he didn't pass judgment on any of the things I had done but listened quite a lot of the time and occasionally threw a question to me, which caused me to go into myself and think more deeply about how and why I had done such a thing.

I did actually find it quite therapeutic, as in a way he was releasing all the things from my early childhood that I had bottled up inside me. Once or twice, I bought up my drink/drugs taking, but he always replied, 'I don't think we're quite ready to go there just yet'.

It was only when the session was coming to an end, did he finally talk about my drink and drugs problems - I wasn't prepared to talk about my sex life just yet. That could wait.

When I asked him about how I was going to stop my drinking and drug habits, he answered,

'Everything you do is all in your mind first of all. You have the thought that you would like to do something. Most thoughts are OK, but there are some thoughts which are negative and not OK for you. So, whatever you do with your body, comes from your mind first.'

I understood that completely.

He went on, 'Whenever you feel the need to have a drink or take some drugs, try and imagine that the desire you have is like a light switch in your body. You have the power to turn this light on or off as you choose.'

I could see that and nodded my head.

He continued, 'When you are not drinking or taking drugs, the light is on in your body, and you feel great. When you start taking the drugs or drinking to excess the light will go off and your body will be in darkness. This is not the state that your body will want. Your body will want the light to stay on and fill up your whole body with light. So, tell yourself that you want that light to stay on and you don't want a drink or to take drugs. Just remember this each time you are tempted and try seeing this actually happening in your mind.'

Richard added, 'You might also try and avoid situations where you may be tempted to have drink or drugs. I know it's easier said than done but think about the places that you frequent where you will be tempted to have a drink or take drugs. If you really do mean business, you owe it to yourself to avoid these places.'

That was tough talk, and I knew he was right, but could I do it myself? Could I withstand the temptation to have a drink, snort a line or hire an escort girl?

He seemed to be reading my mind.

'Gary. I have had scores of people in this room who have been in a similar situation to yours; several of them have been in a worse state than you. Yet they have managed to overcome their addictions, or fears, or habits. When push comes to shove, it all comes down to you and what you choose to do with your body. You can choose to take drugs, or you can choose not to take drugs.'

That was encouraging. He continued.

'Personally, I don't think you're half as bad as some of the people who've come through these doors. So, yes. I think you can do it. Certainly, it will take time and a lot of determination. But keep asking yourself, "Do I want this for myself? Is this the best thing for me?" Everything in life is about choice. Choose Life, not Death!'

What he said galvanised me, as I knew that ultimately drink and drugs could lead to a premature death, and I didn't want that. I understood the words he had said and knew more than ever that it was up to me.

He said that he would see me in two weeks' time, and I readily agreed to that.

On the train back to Manchester I went over in my mind all that he had told me, as well as thinking about my life so far. What had I done with it? A mixture of things, I suppose, both good and bad. Some of it was happy, and some of it had been sad. Some were sensible and some were stupid. I knew that it wasn't going to be easy to break all these habits, or even addictions, but from what Richard had said, I could do it. I knew that I could do it, but it would take a lot of effort on my part and more visits to Richard.

I continued to visit Alan at the hospital almost every day. The only days when I didn't visit him were when I went on the coach to see City play away and when Simon from my teacher training college came up to Manchester for the weekend and I was busy showing him around. I was careful to avoid the clubs I frequented, so it was just having a drink at pubs and much earlier nights.

I know I should have avoided the pubs, but I felt guilty about keeping him away from them, seeing as they were the places where I felt it was best to socialise. I did compromise myself a little and limited myself to just beer and stayed off the shorts and cocktails. It was difficult though when you looked around a pub and saw people doing shots and whisky chasers. Once I'd made that decision, it wasn't too hard to follow it through when they next round of drinks came up.

We did spend a lot of time chatting about things like the breakup of my marriage and what was going to happen next. I didn't mention going to the counsellor though, but did talk about my desire to move out of the centre

After three weeks in hospital, my brother was finally allowed home. He was obviously much better than when I first saw him lying there helpless in that hospital bed; but he was still in a bad way. He could walk – just about, with the aid of a stick and all his movements were slow and laboured. Also just walking from the ward to the car near the front of the hospital soon got him out of breath.

I came along with Sue, partly to help and partly to take my mind off the withdrawal from the drink and drugs. Whenever I began to think that I'd like a drink or some coke, I would think of my brother and the state he looked. It was like having smelling salts put near your nose when you are about to faint. It made you come round to reality straight away.

Once Alan was home and in through the door, I knew that he and Sue needed some peace and quiet, as well as time for Alan to settle into being home once more. It wouldn't be long before the physios would be round to start the next phase of his recovery. I did promise to him though that I would be there for him whenever he needed me and pretty soon, we would start going for walks again, just like we did when we were children.

I got a cab from Alan and Sue's back into the centre of Bury and then took a tram back into Manchester. There was the world and his wife on that tram. Old, young, posh, poor, seedy and everything in between. And me. I thought of how I fitted in or didn't fit in with all these people, all on their own unique journey through life.

On the journey back I started making plans for my next move as by now I knew that I would be leaving the city centre as soon as I could find somewhere that suited me. I didn't want to go right back out into the sticks, but far away from the temptations of the city centre to help with my recovery. I just couldn't continue with the way I was living life as a wild, out of control bachelor. It was time to stop all that. Stop the drugs, stop the alcohol, stop the women, stop the reckless spending, and settle down into a normal life. I just wanted life to be like it was before my lottery win if that were at all possible. Well not quite like it was, but with a lot more normality in the picture.

* * *

After that first session with Richard, I had wasted no time in looking for somewhere different to live. This was partly due to Richard's advice, and partly as a result of a conscious decision I had made after Alan had suffered his stroke. Both these pointers helped me focus both on who I wanted to be and where I wanted to be.

As a lottery winner I could go in all sorts of ways and I think this was my big problem. With Tracy no longer in my life I didn't have the boundaries and her influence to guide me. It was now up to me to say, "Enough is enough!" and "I'm not going down that road anymore". It was easy to make that decision after what had happened to my brother, but much harder to put it into practice.

Although there were still several months left of my contract on my flat, I decided that I needed to move out and live somewhere away from all the temptations that the city held. I chose the Oldham area as it was close to the M60, so I could easily get to wherever I wanted to go to in the Manchester area. Plus, it wasn't far from the moors, especially Saddleworth Moor, which although it is just fifteen miles from the centre of Manchester, it is still a wild and invigorating place.

I chose a two-bedroom end of terrace house in a pleasant street in the village of Greenfield to the east of Oldham. It was the place where I would go on the train as a boy with my father and brother to walk in the countryside. Going back to my roots, so to speak, when life was so much simpler.

This time around I would be near to the countryside, but still surrounded by people and houses. My house had a spare bedroom if anyone needed to stay. The street wasn't full of cars and I could look out onto the moors from the back of the house. Yet it was cosy enough for me to not have too much around the house to do, so I could keep on top of everything.

I could easily have bought the house myself or a whole host of other houses in the village, but I deliberately chose to rent somewhere as I needed some time to think about things and it wasn't too far from Richard's place. Plus, if I didn't like the neighbours, I could quite easily move out and find somewhere else. I felt most of all that I wanted to be in a working-class community again to keep me grounded and to see where it led me.

I also bought myself a car again. It was just a basic family saloon, second hand of course, so it blended well with the other cars in our street. As it had now been almost a year since I last drove a car, I was a little rusty at first, but it soon came back to me. I realised how much not having a car had impacted on my life.

Having a car again gave me a certain type of independence which I'd lost when I was living in Manchester. It meant I could go anywhere I wanted to when I wanted to and not have to rely on someone else to transport me like taxi drivers, but also the trams or the trains, which ran to a timetable that I had to fit into.

It also meant that I could start seeing both Lesley and Jon again, as I'd seriously neglected seeing them. Jon had finally come back to Britain just before Christmas, so he stayed with me in my flat, seriously cramping my style. During our time together he did confess that when he had been staying at a "friend's house" in Australia, it was actually with Tracy, as I half realised when the court hearing took place.

He didn't stay with me long though and announced that he was going to move down to Bath to live nearer Lesley. He had decided that he wanted to get into acting and had found a course that fitted his needs down there.

Meanwhile I was gradually getting back into becoming "normal" again thanks to Richard. In fact, one of the first journeys that I made in my new car was to see Richard again for our second session. In this second session we began by talking about my relationship with Tracy - how I met her, what attracted me to her, how I fell in love with her and how I wanted to marry her. It was a little like living the experience again, as Richard managed to get me to go deep within myself and examine all the motives that I had.

Richard asked how I felt about Tracy now and I replied that I really wasn't bothered about her anymore and was accepting of the fact that we would never get back together again.

'Would you say that you have forgiven her for all that she has done to you?' he challenged.

'No. In all honesty I suppose not,' I replied.

He went on, 'If she were standing right in front of you now, would be able to tell her that you forgive her?'

'I would find that pretty difficult,' I admitted.

'How about thinking of it like this? They say forgiveness is the best form of revenge.'

I was shocked as I'd never thought of forgiveness in that sense before.

'You see Gary, when you truly forgive someone, you actually let go of all the hurt that they have passed onto you through their actions. You break the chains that have been binding you to them in your anger and hurt. To do that you have to show love for them in a way. Not necessarily love in the form that you had for Tracy before she left you, but more a general type of love, accepting of that person no matter what. It's really unconditional love – love without any conditions. You give out love without expecting anything back. Really it comes down to love, acceptance and forgiveness in that order'.

'I'm not sure I'm ready for this just yet' I confessed.

In fact, all this talk of love and forgiveness was making me quite uneasy. Richard had always said that the sessions might be hard going and yes, this one certainly was. So, I tried to change the subject a little. I brought up the subject of me and the escorts. I knew I would have to tell him eventually if I was ever going to be free of this type of sex addiction, so I forced myself to tell him.

He didn't bat an eyelid, such was his cool, calm, nature. He just reiterated what he had said in the previous session about not putting out the light. I must admit that giving up seeing escorts was the hardest vice to give up of the three, though I was gradually getting more focused on what I wanted in life. Forever spending my money on high class call girls was not one of them. I suppose I was hankering after a settled relationship again, but the fear of being hurt was playing on my mind.

'What I find interesting is how you came to move from being a Secondary school teacher out into a big house in the countryside and then back into a penthouse in the city. You must have had some money to be able to afford all that?'

'Yes. That all came from a legacy I received from my Uncle Philip who was quite wealthy in life and who left me and my brother a tidy sum of money'.

I was expecting him to ask, 'How much?' as they usually did, but instead he said,

'I'm not really bothered about how much money you received, Gary. But I do know that it has obviously had a detrimental effect on your life, or you wouldn't be here'.

I felt relieved that he was probably the first person apart from my Mum who actually wasn't bothered about the amount. Clearly, he wasn't worried about money like the rest of us.

He went on,

'Do you sometimes think that you would like to go back to how it all was when you were a teacher before all these massive changes in your life?'

'Yes, I would' I said, but then I countered this with, 'Most of the time'.

'So, you are grateful that you received this legacy then?'

'I suppose I am in many ways, as it has given me a lot of freedom that I wouldn't have if I were still working as a teacher'.

He was on the attack.

'Ah…. But money isn't everything'.

'I totally agree with you there, Richard'.

'So, if I said to you that you can go back to being married to Tracy, working as a Secondary school teacher, and struggling with money, would you jump at the chance?'

He knew what he was doing as I fell for it hook, line and sinker.

'No. I don't think I would anymore, Richard. Too much water has passed under the bridge. I might have when I was all alone in the farmhouse in Derbyshire. But I have moved on from there'.

'Good!' he replied. 'You're showing me that you want to move forward with your life and not live in the past anymore. I think we can progress even more in our next session and help you to be healed from all this hurt that has gone on in your life'.

Richard had shown me that in spite of all that I had been through, I no longer wanted to turn back the clock and go back to how it had been before the lottery win. Instead, I was starting to look to the future again.

* * *

As Richard had suggested to me that I needed to start having new interests and new hobbies and new challenges, I found that I wanted to get fit again and lose some of the weight I had put on with all that personal lack of discipline.

So, one of the things that I changed in my lifestyle as I approached fifty was that I started exercising again. Although I could easily have bought lots of gym equipment and installed it in the spare room, I decided to join the local gym. This was also a way of me being able to make new friends, especially ones of the more down to earth variety, which I needed in my life.

I had never been one for jogging, partly because I didn't fancy the idea of all that running in all weathers, around uneven streets with holes in the road or pavements to trip you up on. Plus, as you know Manchester and the surrounding area is notorious for it always raining. Who wants to have a cold shower whilst running??!!

The idea of doing my exercising at a local fitness club in a warm and dry environment seemed quite attractive. Also, there was always someone on hand to check you didn't overdo it on the running machine and set you the right targets for your fitness ability. The other thing about being a member of a fitness club was that it got me out of the house and led me to making several new friends.

Several months of regular exercise helped me tremendously both physically and mentally. Physically, I managed to lose a stone and a half and actually weighed less than before I won the lottery. I had probably indulged too much in the staffroom with doughnuts and cakes whenever it was someone's birthday.

Mentally, it was even more rewarding, as the targets I was set by my trainer gave me something to focus on away from the withdrawal from the drink and drugs. Maybe not so much on the sex side, though using up all that energy did curb my sex drive somewhat.

Another of the advantages of going to the gym during the day on a weekday was that as a male I was in the minority with lots more than women. So, it was on the cards that I would start asking someone else out. After my experiences with the escort girls, I was much more confident around women and wasn't stuck for words when it came to communicating with the opposite sex.

I wasn't really interested in one night stands anymore and was putting my toe in the water so to speak regarding a new relationship. Although I enjoyed having sex, I now wanted it to be set against a romantic background and not some seedy one-night stand, of which I was now an experienced participant.

However, when a dark-haired woman of roughly the same age as me started giving me the eye, I became interested in where it might lead. The problem was that she was married, although I was not aware of this when we started chatting to each other in the café. She didn't have a wedding ring on, and I think she led me on, especially when she invited me back to her house the following week.

Although the alarm bells were ringing in my head, I allowed myself to be led by her, instead of me taking the lead and finding out more about her first. When I did relent and go to her house, it was obvious what she wanted. I was tempted for sure, but it was not what I needed or wanted.

We were only just getting started when a car pulled up outside.

'Quick!' she almost screamed. It's my husband back home early! Follow me now!'

I didn't need any coaxing. I was out of that back door at the drop of a hat and out on the pavement just as her husband was walking into the house. My heart was beating faster than a pneumatic drill I can tell you. I walked quickly to my car, locked the door, and tried to catch my breath. If I'd given in to my temptations it would have been a case of being caught "in flagrante delicto" and a receiving a beating up most likely.

It was a hard lesson for me to learn. I needed to take things more slowly and think things through more when it came to the opposite sex. After that, I changed the day I went to the gym and from then on, I made it a rule never to get caught out like that again. If I was going to have a relationship, it would be conducted in neutral places until I was sure it was OK to continue.

* * *

Little by little my life was changing, and I was starting to feel contented again; not happy as such, but calmer and more focused on what I wanted. It was at my third session with Richard that I finally came clean to him about winning the lottery. I still wasn't going to tell him when we started the session, but in a way, he unlocked the door inside me that was keeping it all hidden away.

'Gary. I have to say that I have gradually been peeling away the layers that surround the real you, but I still haven't quite got there'.

He was carefully probing my mind and then went in for the kill.

'Is there something inside you that you are hiding from me? I know that it's hard to really open up, but is there anything else that I should know?'

I couldn't keep it hidden any longer. It was now or never. So, I decided there and then to come clean with him.

'Yes, there is', I confessed. 'When I said last time about receiving a legacy from my uncle, I wasn't quite telling you the truth'.

'I thought as much. Go on'.

'Well, I did receive a lot of money a few years ago, but it wasn't left to me in a will. I actually won the lottery'.

He didn't flinch or say 'Wow', but simply nodded as if saying, 'Please continue'.

'The amount I won wasn't just enough for me and Tracy to give up our jobs and never have to work again. It was much, much more than that. It was enough to buy a large expensive house and give lots away to our family and friends and still have plenty left', I explained.

I was still expecting him to say, 'How much?' just like all the rest, but he didn't.

'So that's why all these feelings of guilt have been coming out', he replied. 'I'm not going to ask you precisely how much? That's your business. But I can see how it has scarred you emotionally and made you into the person that you are, sitting here before me'.

He had hit a nerve deep inside me and much to my surprise I burst into tears for only the third time in my adult life. I didn't care that he could see me as a quivering wreck in front of him. It was all coming out of me. All the guilt as he had suggested. But also, all the pain, all the anger, all the frustration and all the hurt.

It was quite a cathartic experience for me and was like a weight being lifted from me. I was emotionally naked there in front of him and I didn't care. All that mattered was to pour out of me all this toxic mixture and be rid of it. He patted me on my shoulder and waited.

I didn't cry for that long, but when I stopped, I immediately felt a strange sense of freedom. I had finally faced all my demons and let them go. I could move forwards now and not be worried about the past. I could start again and not look back, but from now on I would only look to the future.

Richard had finally got to the truth and as we talked more, I began to realise that I was finally free. I could now accept winning the lottery as being something that gave me freedom and was no longer a burden to me. I knew that if anyone asked me where I had got all my money from, I wouldn't be afraid to tell them the truth.

It was nearly time to stop seeing Richard, but he agreed to one more session at my asking as there was one final thing on my mind.

* * *

In June I got the letter through from my solicitors that said my divorce had finally been completed and I was now a single man once again.

I had spoken to the solicitor a couple of weeks earlier.

'Rest assured, Gary,' he said. It will all be finalised within the next two weeks. I really can't see any problems'.

What he didn't tell me was that there would be an invoice for his services in securing the divorce which came to nearly £15,000!

'What!' I said out loud, sounding shocked. I looked again at the invoice and then at the next page which had itemised every phone call, every email, and every meeting I'd had with him. He was charging me £150 an hour for his work. No wonder you never hear of a poor solicitor!

I wouldn't have a problem paying it of course, but what about the poor sods in the same position as me who would really struggle to find that kind of money? At least I could now draw a veil over what I saw as the worst experience of my life.

The fourth session with Richard was a type of finishing off session as we both felt that we had managed to "untangle" me and sort myself out now. We went over a few things about my past and how it was important to "let go" of the past and old emotions that stopped me from moving forward. We also talked about the importance of living in the "now" and enjoying the moment, and not letting concerns about the past or worries about the future affect me.

"Life is what you make it" was a phrase which Richard used several times over the course of our counselling sessions and I gradually began to accept that teaching. What happened to me in the past was the result of the choices that I made, and I was now a lot more of a positive person, who would savour each moment of my life as precious and not to be wasted or messed with. I certainly felt a whole lot better emotionally as a result of seeing Richard for these counselling sessions.

One thing about Richard that intrigued me was how he seemed to have this air of calmness about him, and nothing ever phased him. I wanted to know his secret.

'Can I ask you about how nothing seems to faze you and you seem so accepting about everything? You seem to be a very peaceful person? I enquired.

'Ah. That's because I practise a thing called "Mindfulness", which is a type of meditation', he replied.

I instantly had a vision of him sitting cross legged at home and chanting a mantra.

He picked up on my thoughts.

'It's not a load of chanting and sitting in the Lotus Position if that's what you think,' he said, 'But simply sitting still somewhere quiet and getting your mind to clear itself of all your worries and anxieties and the clutter that's in your head. Anyone can do it and with practise it becomes much easier.'

'So that's your secret – Mindfulness?'

I had heard the word but had never investigated what it meant.

'But "mindfulness" sounds like your mind is "full"?' I queried.

'Yes. Many people think that. But it's completely the opposite. It's not the best word to use for this practice, but many people who have tried it, swear by it. The 'mindful' part comes from being mindful of things and not getting drawn in but watching them from the side. A bit like our first session when I got you to look down on yourself'. It made perfect sense to me. He went on, 'Without sounding sexist, it's not just a feminine thing either. Both men and women can do it.'

I was intrigued and asked if I could try it there and then.

So, he guided me through his way of doing the practice and surprisingly I found it pretty easy to do. He said that he always did his mindfulness first thing in the morning, either before or after breakfast.

'In that way you set yourself up for the day,' he told me.

'The important thing is to try and make sure that you get rid of all the worries and concerns that you may have. These may "fill up" your mind first of all, but these should be exhaled as you breathe out. In fact, using the correct breathing is the key to it all. Then once you have got rid of these worries out of your mind, you can start filling it with positive thoughts such as thankfulness for all the good things in your life'.

'I can understand that now,' I replied. 'My father always used to say, "Count your blessings!"'

'Precisely,' agreed Richard. 'That just about sums it up. The more positive thoughts you have inside you, the better able you will be to face all that Life throws at you'.

I was glad that I'd asked for that extra session with Richard. From then on, I tried to practise Mindfulness each day. I even read some books on the subject from my local library. It helped made me a better, more confident person, able to look forward each day and be thankful for my life.

* * *

In July, the biggest event of my year took place, namely Lesley and Mike's wedding down near Bath. I was dreading what was going to happen in view of the fact that Lesley had invited Tracy, even though she hadn't replied, indicating that she might not come. But then she could show up and how would I react?

This was also the first time since mum's funeral that I saw some of my relatives. Most were fine to me, though some on Tracy's side avoided me and those who did speak to me seemed distant and aloof. Tracy did not show up in the end, which was a great relief in spite of my newfound positive side. I guess coming all the way from Australia was a factor, though it was quite easy to get in a plane and fly back. I guess she just couldn't face seeing me again after all that had gone on between us. I was sad for Lesley though, as she had sided with me through it all, it must have been tough for her not to have her mother there on her special day.

Making the speech as the bride's father was the hardest part of the day for me. I was nervous and remembered all that Richard had taught me which helped calm me. It all went past in a flash though and after that I relaxed, though

I did steer well clear of alcohol. I was determined never to touch the stuff again.

Over the course of the year that I was living in Greenfield I was gradually coming to terms with the end of my marriage and starting to think what I really wanted out of life. I had gone from one extreme to the other over the past few years, like a boat tossed on the waves in a storm at sea. Now the storm had passed, and I was back in calmer waters. I knew that I would like to settle down again and start living a normal as life as possible, preferably with a steady partner. I felt that I knew myself better than at any time in my life, thanks to the help of Richard and the various crises that had happened in my family.

My life was precious, and I was determined to make the best use of it. I didn't need to live to excess like I had been doing in the centre of Manchester. Balance was now my keyword. I had all this money, most of which I really didn't need, so I felt that maybe it was time for me to give something back and help those less fortunate than me. There were plenty of people and organisations who would be grateful to receive any money from me, but it wasn't just money that I was prepared to give. It was my time as well and with this in mind I started to think seriously what I might be doing in this respect.

Whilst I did like Greenfield immensely, I felt that ultimately it wasn't the right place for me to put my roots down in. I really needed to live in a town or in its outskirts at least, in a house of my own. Not some massive palace. I'd tried that and it hadn't worked. I now realised that by moving to *Hill View* I was trying to be someone I wasn't. They say you learn though the mistakes you make and that is so true in my case, though I must say I learnt a lot more than I would have imagined!

I started to look at properties again, mainly to the south and east of Manchester, though not as far out as Glossop. I needed to be near to the M60, so I could visit my family and friends wherever they lived. I knew that I needed to be proactive and seek out friends both old and new, rather than be waiting in vain for people to come to me.

I felt so much more positive as a result of the sessions with Richard, plus with the mindfulness I was much calmer and peaceful and didn't get angry easily. Of course, there were odd things that still got me angry at times, but I could deal with them in a calmer way and not bust a gut about them.

I was a "New Me" I had decided, and wanted to embrace every new thing that occurred in my life. Things were finally looking up.

10 MOVING ON

After a year of gradually re-adjusting my life to near normality in rented accommodation, I finally made a decision and settled on a place I would like to live. That place was Hazel Grove. It was still in the Greater Manchester area, but to the south east of Stockport town centre, which meant that I could easily get to the motorway if I wanted to go south to London for a concert or to Bath to see Lesley and Mike.

There was also a railway station less than a mile away, which was great for getting into Manchester or for going further afield. Most important of all was the house itself. It was a three bedroom detached house in a close with a few other similar looking houses. The street wasn't overrun with cars, as everyone parked them on their drive. There were a few trees and grass verges which helped to make it more environmentally attractive to me.

I had deliberately chosen a house that wasn't too big, or too small, yet big enough to accommodate my children and grandchildren whenever they might visit. Plus, I was keen to seem as "normal" as possible. No way did I want to be a 'show off' millionaire living in an opulent house with flashy cars outside. If my dad could see me now, he would say I had gone up in the world and was "well off", but hopefully not a snob like my sister and her husband. I would also hope that he could see that I was still firmly connected to my working class roots, although I was now living a middle class lifestyle.

I finally moved into the house about a month after the sale completed. This was because I wanted to make sure that before I moved in, everything would be sorted and decorated as to how I wanted it to be. This time round I made sure that I didn't get caught out with things like damp and the electrics not working, so I paid for a full structural survey on the house. As the house was still quite new, all the snagging problems had been sorted out and no major issues came to light.

Even so, I went through the house room by room looking for anything that I thought needed doing. Mostly it was decorating, though things like the light fittings, blinds and curtains were all changed before I moved in. Also, with this house, it was much easier to get tradesmen to come and do the jobs that needed doing. After all the problems I'd had at *Hill View*, things were done quite quickly.

I also managed to find a retired chap to do my gardening in the summer; mainly cutting the lawn, but also putting in some nice colourful flowers and bushes in the borders to brighten up the garden.

A week before the day that I actually moved in, I paid a visit to my storage place to go through all my belongings. Seeing all that furniture that Tracy and I had bought new when we moved into *Hill View* made me a little sad, but definitely not sentimental. There wasn't too much that I wanted to keep, so I got the removal men to take the remainder down to a large charity shop in Stockport that specialised in taking in good quality used furniture. The majority of it was the new stuff that Tracy had bought for *Hill View*, and I really didn't want that connection and the memories that went with it in my new place. I knew that someone somewhere would appreciate them in their home.

Compared to my time in Chorlton this new house was minimalist, not because I chose so, but because we had so much rubbish in that house that we really didn't need. I was more aware of only having what was useful to me and I filled up any big spaces with house plants. I suppose at first that the house did seem a little large for me but compared to *Hill View* it was tiny.

I was also more conscious of making sure that I kept myself busy *and* sociable, so I would invite some of the neighbours in for a cup of tea or even a meal on the odd occasion. I become good friends with a couple called Pete and Frankie who had moved up from the south with Pete's job. He was a Chelsea fan so we were able to talk football and he would often come round to watch games on my TV. It was things like this that helped me to begin living *normally* again. But I still needed to go out more, so I started going to a daytime adult education course. It was worth it as the next piece in the jigsaw puzzle of my life was found there.

It was whilst out shopping at the local supermarket that I came across a stand full of booklets advertising a local adult education college. I picked one up and put it into my trolley, intending to look at it once I got home. But it was actually a few days later before I finally got round to looking at the brochure. As I turned the pages my curiosity was ignited with the choice of courses available. There were all sorts of courses including photography, accountancy, IT Skills, Spanish, and dress making.

The one that tickled my fancy though was Art. I was looking for something that would bring out my creative side as Richard had suggested and one that was not too taxing on my brain. Art and in particular painting were something that appealed to me. Although I hadn't done any painting since my schooldays, I was keen to commit myself to something that would get me out of the house and mixing with other people.

It meant a commitment of ten weeks every Tuesday morning for a couple of hours which sounded fine to me. So off I went one April morning, armed with a set of paintbrushes and several tubes of oil paints.

The art group was a motley crew of mainly retired types in their sixties and seventies, but that didn't bother me. In fact, I was the youngest apart from a mixed race lady who seemed slightly younger than me. The first lesson was about colour and we had to try to create an abstract painting with just three colours based on a specific shape such as a square, triangle, or rectangle. We were allowed to mix these three colours into any colour we liked. I really enjoyed this first lesson and managed to produce a mainly green triangular shaped painting.

I soon began to look forward to going to my art class, not only for the stimulation it gave my creative side, but also for the company. Everyone seemed to get on well, apart from one grumpy old man who seemed out of place. Luckily, he dropped out after the third lesson.

From the various painting forms that we encountered I discovered that my forte was painting landscapes. I wonder why?!! I decided that I preferred the softer water colours as opposed to the tougher acrylics and that is what I tend use now when I paint at home. Two of my water colour landscapes are now hanging in my house as I was so pleased with them. They both show different views of places in the Peak District, which I so love.

Another attraction for me at the art class was the other "youngster" who I mentioned above. She and I got on well, partly due to our age and partly as we liked the same sort of art, mainly abstract works. Gradually over the length of the course we got to know each other more and more, until one day I plucked up the courage to ask her out. It wasn't to go to the cinema or out for a meal as you would expect, but instead we went to visit Manchester Art Gallery one afternoon. I figured that doing something together that we both liked would help us both get an idea of where we stood, and whether we could take the relationship further.

That afternoon we learnt more of each other and tested the water as to whether we could take the relationship to the next level. She was called Ann and was originally from Preston. Like me, she was divorced and had a grown up son in his twenties who lived down in London. She told me she hadn't come off too badly out of her divorce from her husband, who'd had an affair, which put an end to the marriage. Although she didn't say just how much she got in the divorce settlement, she told me that she lived in another town near Stockport a few miles to the west of me and that she was quite settled where she lived.

I told her about my life and how I came to be divorced, so straight away we had something in common. I explained about moving out to the countryside as a result of receiving an inheritance from my uncle in his will, but I didn't feel ready to say about the lottery win – just yet. She had been an accountant and had worked in Warrington, but when the divorce came through had packed it all in, and with the proceeds of the family house she decided to try and start afresh with a new career, hence her doing the art course. She thought she would like to try being an artist as a living, which I thought was quite feasible after having seen some of her paintings. She still did some accountancy work on a freelance basis to pay for her bills. We agreed to meet again, this time for a meal at a restaurant in Stockport. We would take it from there.

* * *

On the home front I was gradually settling down in my new house. The neighbours knew me as someone who had taken early retirement. They knew that I used to be a schoolteacher and that I was divorced, but was comfortably off, hence the house that I lived in. I didn't own a flashy car, which I believe would have drawn attention to me. Instead, I thought that I blended in nicely in this environment and was now living life as a normal person, with the added bonus of no money worries.

I suppose I could have been living in a little, terraced house in a small town somewhere in Lancashire, hiding away from everybody, living like a hermit. But again, that wouldn't be me. I do know one or two lottery winners do live like this, afraid that someone will discover who they really are. I do feel that it is usually best to live in a way that you feel comfortable and happy with, not trying to be someone you are not, which is what I did in the early days.

I just had to sort out a few things from my past.

One morning soon after I had moved into my new house, I had a sudden urge to get in my car and go for a drive. So that's what I just did. Within ten minutes I was on the M60 going in a clockwise direction. I had no idea where on earth I was going, but I just had that urge to drive and go somewhere. I checked my petrol gauge and there was about three quarters of a tank full, so I knew I would be OK for a while yet.

I passed the turn offs for the M56, the M62 and kept going. The next turn off was the M61. 'Should I leave the M60 here?' I thought. 'This road goes all the way to Preston and beyond. Surely I've had enough of motorway driving?'

Then it dawned on me I wasn't that far from Bolton and the home of my sister. 'Why don't I go and see her? I haven't seen her for a few years. Yet she doesn't live that far from me'.

So that's what I did and twenty minutes later I was ringing the doorbell of her house. If she wasn't in, I would just get back in the car and drive off somewhere else. Dawn opened the door and her jaw dropped in shock.

'Hello Dawn. I was just passing…..'

'Come in Gary,' she replied still shocked. 'It's lovely to see you.'

I stepped into the immaculate house, not a sign of dirt or dust anywhere.

We went into the lounge, and she started up the conversation.

'Well how are you? Where are you living now?' she asked.

'I'm OK. How about you?' I fired back.

'Fine. Just starting to get the first twinges of arthritis in my knees, but nothing to worry about'.

'Where's Nick?' I asked.

'Oh, he's out playing golf down the road at the golf club. He won't be back for ages.'

Then the conversation went cold. I knew this was the moment; the reason why I had *really* come to see her.

'Dawn. There's something I need to say to you', I said nervously.

'I'm sorry for the past and how I've treated you. I've been a complete bastard and I regret it now', I blurted out.

I couldn't believe I was actually saying this. Her reply was instant.

'That's OK Gary. I forgive you. I've been just as bad myself. Let's put it in the past and make a new start!'

With that we hugged each other, and Dawn started crying. Although I tried not to, I too shed a tear as we embraced.

Yet another weight hanging from me had been released and I instantly felt great. Much better than a cocaine high I thought. We spent the next hour catching up on each other's lives and news. I knew I had to tell her about the lottery win and as soon as I mentioned it, she said, 'I know Gary. Tracy told me!'

"The bitch," I thought. But then I remembered what Richard had told me and I released the thought and explained how it had changed my life to what it was now. I didn't go into too much detail about my time in Manchester, but I think she already knew from Alan.

When it was time to go, we hugged each other quite openly and I knew that another milestone had been reached in my dealing with the past. Listening to my intuition had well and truly paid off.

From then on, we became like a proper brother and sister once more, chatting on the phone once a week, visiting each other from time to time and just being OK with each other, rather than being estranged from each other, which happens in so many families nowadays.

* * *

When Alan had his stroke, it made me realise that however much money you may have in the bank, that is no protection for something going wrong with your health.

'Money can't buy your health' is a saying I am well aware of. But on the other hand, there is no harm in making sure that everything is working ok inside and if you can afford it, then make the effort to do it. To this end I decided to pay for one of those 'Health MOTs' at the local private hospital.

I went along soon after I had moved into my new house, ready to hear the worst, expecting that something had gone wrong with my body thanks to all that booze and coke. They checked my blood pressure, my heart for a heart disease risk assessment, my lungs, my arteries and took blood samples to check for all manner of things. One of these was my PSA level which checks for possible prostate cancer. Well, you hear so many stories of men getting this nasty disease.

To my surprise, virtually everything came back as OK, though the main thing was that I was overweight for my age and my muscle mass index was more than the recommended level. Also, my blood pressure was slightly higher than it should be, though of course the doctor said that it could be the stress of all the tests going on and it would be a good idea to have it done at my local GP's surgery in a couple of weeks' time, just to double check.

Considering that I had been treating my body so badly over the previous couple of years, I was lucky that I hadn't damaged it too much with all that excess. I hope that giving up alcohol had helped, as well as the mindfulness, and learning to calm myself down also played their part.

Incidentally, before I had this health check, I did go to an STD clinic when I was living in Greenfield. I just wanted to check that I was OK after all that sex I'd been having with the escort girls. Not that I was suspicious of anything nasty going on down below - it was more of a way of drawing a line under all that had gone on.

I felt that the 'New Me' didn't want to continue with that sort of lifestyle, no matter how much fun it had become. Yes, on the one hand it was quite enjoyable, but on the other hand it wasn't natural, and could have put me at risk. Here I was spending all that money on escorts; (or where they really prostitutes?) all for a quick sexual fix.

Also, I was taking all sorts of risks meeting them. I was laying myself open to blackmail if they knew how rich I was and that I lived alone. Those that did come to my flat knew where I lived and could easily pass on details about me to a third party.

By now the idea of paying someone for sex had started to repulse me. I now thought that this isn't really a natural relationship. It's just a sordid business where in many ways the man is exploited just as much as the female is.

Last of all I was now starting to think in terms of finding a regular girlfriend who would treat me as an equal and not just as a way of making some money. If I was going to settle down in the relationship department again, I wanted to make sure I was clean down below.

After an anxious wait of several days the results came back as negative, so I was greatly relieved. It was now up to me to forget the past and start living in the present.

* * *

Another of the new activities that I got involved in, was helping the homeless in Stockport. Like any large town, there were a number of homeless people sleeping out on the streets. (I hate the term 'rough sleepers' by the way, as it sounds like they are choosing to sleep out on the street).

After my move I soon got involved in a local charity which was actually doing something positive for these people, unlike the government. Although I could have just given some of my money to the charity, I decided that I would like to give them my time, which in a way is more valuable to them.

By doing this, it meant that I got to know some of these vulnerable people, who think that nobody cares about them. The charity has a shelter, and I gave my time to be at the shelter and spend time listening to these people.

Their stories are varied. For some it is an addiction to alcohol or drugs or both which has led to them being on the street. They have lost everything; jobs, family, friends, possessions – all because their addiction has taken over their life. Something I can relate to, though thank God I didn't end up going as far down the road as some of them did.

For others it has been the breakdown of a marriage or long term relationship. Something again I can relate to. They ended up sleeping at a friend's house and then they had to leave when their friend got fed up with them being there. So where else could they go, but out onto the streets?

This refuge was helping them to get the best advice as to what they should be doing with their lives. It was also giving them a step back up on the ladder to finding somewhere to live apart from on the streets.

The charity also did regular fund raising events like collecting for the charity at local supermarkets or doing sponsored events such as bike rides or walks, or something silly like having your hair shaved off. Little by little I felt proud to be part of something that was helping these people to turn their lives around and make a new start. If only more of us cared and then these people wouldn't be where they are.

After going a couple of times, I got the surprise of my life when in walked my old friend Jim McKeith from my school days. It was over twenty years since I last saw him. He recognised me first and we hugged each other straight away, rekindling that bond we had before he joined the army.

It turned out that he had once been homeless in central Manchester, but people from another branch of the charity had got him off the streets, helped him to quit the booze and get him back into "normal" life once again. We instantly became best friends once more and he now knows about my lottery win and I have helped him in some ways where he wouldn't have been able to do so.

* * *

By now Ann and I had both fallen in love with each other, though this time around it wasn't the all-consuming love that I'd had in my twenties, where I couldn't bear to be apart from Tracy. It was still a deep feeling inside, but being older and wiser, was more of a respectful love where we took things more slowly. We were both naturally a little hesitant as we both didn't want to get hurt again. But those heart strings had such a hold on us that falling in love was inevitable.

Also, I knew that sooner or later I would have to tell Ann about my lottery win. Whereas in the past I would have spent days or even weeks lolling it over in my mind, the New Me was going to tell her early on in the relationship. Deep down inside, I knew that she was right for me, but I also knew that there could be no more lies in my life. It was time to stop keeping things hidden from the people in my life, or they would come out later at the worst possible time.

So, one evening when she was round at my place for a romantic meal, I told her. I was prepared for her to walk out on me if she wished, but I hoped that she would see it as a sign of commitment from me.

I wasn't worried about her wanting me for my money as I believed that she wanted to be with me out of a genuine love for me. After all, she had told me that she loved me just weeks into the relationship. I naturally had responded with a 'I love you too darling.'

'Ann there's something important that I wanted to tell you,' I began. 'Something that I want to get off my chest'.

She looked puzzled.

'It's not serious,' I went on, hoping she wouldn't take it in the wrong way.

'So, you haven't got some awful illness then?' she questioned.

'No, it's nothing like that. Remember when I said that I had come into some money through a legacy?' I continued.

'Yes. What about it?'

'Well, it wasn't quite true,' I confessed.

'So, you're not rich after all?'

'Well actually I am. The money I received wasn't from a legacy.' I hesitated with nervousness. 'It was from a lottery win…'

I expected her to say, 'How much?' but she looked more shocked than anything else.

'It wasn't just a small win,' I went on. In fact, it was over ten million.'

Now I had finally got it out, I felt relieved.

'You're having me on!' she half laughed.

'No seriously. I'm telling you the truth. I held back telling you about it as it's been such a big thing in my life, and I needed to be sure I could trust you before I could tell you.'

Now she really did look shocked. In fact, she was speechless, so I continued.

'It's been both a blessing and a curse in my life and I have found it hard to open up to a lot of people about it. I have tried to keep it quiet as much as possible, so only my close family and friends know.'

She kept silent as various thoughts went through her head.

'I truly love you Ann and I really don't want this to spoil our relationship. But I knew it was important to come clean with you, seeing as we are now serious with each other, and I want you to understand that you are the most important thing in my life now.'

She continued to stay silent as if she was mulling it over in her mind. Then she said,

'Are you really telling me the truth, Gary?'

'Yes. I am, Ann. It's something that I couldn't hide from you, even if I wanted to.'

'It seems so unbelievable. This house and your car. They don't say "millionaire" to me,' she said doubtfully.

'That's because I don't want to be all flashy like some people. That's simply not me. I don't want the big house and the posh car anymore. I've been there. Done that. I've tried that and it didn't work. I want people to accept me for what I am. Not for any money I may have.'

'Well in that case, Gary. I'm happy to be stuck with you!'

With that she leant over and kissed me slowly and passionately. She continued,

'It's you I love and you, alone. Not your money or anything else about you. That's secondary to us.'

I inwardly breathed a sigh of relief and looked at the wonderful sight before me.

She said one more thing.
'Do you really have ten million pounds to your name?'
We both broke up in fits of laughter.......

After my confession to Ann, I felt so much happier and calmer. I had been on edge for several days before I told her. I even began to think that a fix of coke would help me, but as soon as that thought came to me, I dismissed it as part of my old self which was now dead and buried.

The openness and honesty that I showed to Ann paid off; our relationship deepened more and more. We became inseparable, almost like teenage lovers. It was a strange feeling. I'd had it before with Tracy and I really didn't believe that I would ever experience such a feeling again in my life. When Tracy left me, I was so distraught and thought life would never be the same again. Yet, with Ann things have become even better if I dare say so. Who needs millions of pounds when you have the love of a good woman?

I suppose it was inevitable that we would move in together. In fact, we had slept at each other's houses on and off for several months now. The question was, 'Whose house should we set up permanent home in?' Again, I was afraid of jumping the gun too soon and it all going 'pear shaped', so I held off for as long as possible. In a way it was as big a commitment as anyone would make, choosing to set up home with someone; almost like getting married, but without the certificate.

It was a risky idea, as it could make or break a relationship. A good friend once told me, 'If you're thinking of getting married, try living with someone for a year and then see if you still want to spend the rest of your lives together!' Well, at that stage of the relationship I wasn't thinking of marriage, but it was still relevant advice as it would help us to see if we wanted to stay together on a more permanent basis.

We had first made love only after we'd been 'going steady' for six months. Again, it was probably me holding back as I was afraid of upsetting the apple cart. Here I was in love with a new woman who had shown love, acceptance and understanding of me, and in many ways, I thought it was all too good to be true. But after she had taken the lead one evening when I had dropped her off at her house and she had invited me in, it all developed from there.

The subject of moving in together was actually brought up in conversation by me. Yet again it was the New Me showing that I wasn't prepared to dilly-dally about things. I just came out with it when we were watching tv one evening.

'You seem to be around here a lot, Ann,' I began.

'What do you think of the idea of us moving in together?' I ventured.

She seemed taken aback by my suggestion, but as she usually did, she was chewing the question over in her mind.

'You mean me move in here?' she queried.

'Not necessarily,' I answered. 'There's always your place?'

'I'm really not sure,' she replied. 'We both like our independence.'

She paused.

'But we are madly in love,' I ventured. 'Something which I thought would never happen to me after my divorce.'

Clearly, she was confused.

'I'm sorry if I threw you there, Ann. It's just a thought that I had.'

'No Gary. Don't be sorry. It's lovely being here with you and your house is much bigger than mine.'

She seemed to be coming round.

Then she hung back a little.

'Perhaps if I sleep on it?' she suggested. 'We've known each other for less than six months. But it does seem like I've known you for years. I suppose living with someone on a permanent basis will bring to light any issues we may have. Let me think about it.'

And with that the conversation was changed and we went back to watching the TV programme.

I didn't want to bring up the conversation again, in case she thought I was pressurising her, so I kept quiet. After all, the ball was in her court.

About a week later, when we hadn't slept at each other's houses for a couple of days due her being away in London visiting her son, the topic came up.

'Gary. You know you said about us moving in together?'

'Yes....?' I replied.

'Well maybe I would like to try it, say for a month and see how we get on.'

'Wow. That's a turn up for the books,' I answered, trying hard to hide my delight.

'Any particular reason?' I ventured.

'Well actually there is. A few weeks ago, a new family moved in a few doors down and they've just got a dog. It keeps barking when it's out in the garden and it is driving me mad! I'm trying to sleep, and it wakes me up and then if I'm painting and want some peace and quiet, I'm not getting it. It's not all the time, but it is starting to get to me.'

'So, it's a dog that's made you change your mind?' I half joked.

I must admit that I hadn't actually noticed it when I'd been round her place the past few times, but maybe it was just quiet then.

'OK, so you're ready to move in here then?' I asked.

'Yes,' she replied. 'As soon as!'

Over the next few days, Ann started to bring across some of her stuff to mine. It was mainly clothes, which went in the spare wardrobe, but also her painting equipment, DVD's and CD's and her laptop.

It didn't make that much difference with the extra stuff in my house, but it did seem funny that whenever I went out, say on my homeless volunteering, Ann would be waiting for me when I got in. Life had come full circle for me once again and I was feeling the happiest I had been since I had lived at Chorlton.

It was as though my life was just starting over again.

* * *

There was one more thing from my past that needed closure and that was Tracy. She had been the one who had affected me the most over the past few years, not the lottery. I wasn't really looking to see her again, but it was through Jon that I finally met up with Tracy after all the years not seeing her. If he'd asked me six months earlier, I would have definitely said, "No", but since the New Me had surfaced I knew it was something that I needed to do.

I was careful to make sure that the meeting took place at a neutral venue; something that wasn't too public just in case it became a slanging match. So, I hired a room at a hotel near Stockport where we wouldn't be disturbed, and I insisted that Tracy would be there first as I didn't fancy the idea of being stood up. In fact, Jon agreed to be there, not necessarily as a referee, but more of a peacemaker if needed.

The whole thing was like a scene from the TV show, *Long Lost Relative*, only this time it wasn't about sons or daughters that were meeting their mothers or fathers from years ago. It was really just to clear up some odds and ends and hopefully to come out as friends and not enemies.

As soon as I got the text from Jon, I got out of my car and made my way into the hotel where Jon was waiting. He led me to the room and there was Tracy sitting with her back to the door. When she turned round, she looked so much older, as though the weight of the world was on her shoulders. She had grey streaks in her hair and her face was a lot more wrinkled than when I last saw her.

She broke the ice with a 'Hello Gary' and then continued with, 'You're looking well'. Perhaps she was shocked to see a newer fitter me, after the reports from Jon about how I looked when he'd last met me.

'How are you?' I ventured.

'Not too bad,' she replied with a slight frown, indicating that she wasn't 100% telling me the truth. Then she blurted out with, 'Look Gary. I never meant for all this to happen. I'm sorry that I hurt you like I did.'

I was silent.

'If it's any comfort to you, Howard finished with me after six months and taught me a very hard lesson that the grass isn't always greener and all that.'

There were tears in her eye, but I wasn't going to be taken in by it all. Too much water had gone under the bridge by now and I knew that I would never go back to her. She was part of my old life, and I wasn't going to go back there. Not in a million years.

I tried to be diplomatic, but all sorts of emotions were going on inside me.

'Have you found someone else?' I ventured.

'No.' was her reply. 'I'm not sure if I will ever find love again', she said as more tears fell down her cheeks.

I didn't reply but waited for her to compose herself.

'How about you?', she ventured.

'Yes. I've been in a relationship for the past six months, and it seems to be going OK.' I was being honest with her; though I knew what I said hurt her.

'It's taken me a long time to get over what you did to me, but I've moved on from that and I forgive you Tracy.'

I couldn't believe what I was saying, but I knew that was the best way to get closure from all that I had gone through because of her. It only made her cry even more, though I suppose this was inevitable.

Instinctively I put my arms out to comfort her and she moved forward to receive my embrace; though as soon as we touched, I knew that I didn't have any romantic feelings for her. It was just one human being comforting another human being. Nothing more than that.

'Don't cry Tracy,' I said. 'I'm sure you'll get through this, just as I have. Besides, we've got two wonderful children that we both created.'

This made her cry even more, though I realised that she needed to go through this as part of her healing process, just as much as I did.

There were so many questions that I wanted to ask her, such as, Why did you leave me? Was it the house move? Was it me? Why did you cut yourself off from me? Why didn't you come to Lesley's wedding? Yet I felt quite strongly that now was not the best time to ask them. There would be another time in the future. The important thing was that we had "made up" so to speak. We were speaking with each other once again and had started building bridges between the two of us.

We did talk some more though. Mainly about the children and how they were getting on. Plus, we did agree to see each other again sometime. I really wasn't sure about giving her my mobile number, which had obviously changed since 2013, but I said that my e mail address was the same, so if she wanted to contact me that way, she could do so.

As I drove away, my feelings were quite mixed. I felt relieved more than anything else. Thanks to Jon, we had been reunited. We had verbally told each other that we forgave the other, which was possibly the most important thing to come out of the meeting. And we had become friends again, so I suppose it wasn't a bad result.

It was a huge weight off my shoulders as I didn't want to live the rest of my life not knowing if I could face Tracy again. This meeting had proved that we could finally get on with our lives and put the past behind us. It had been one hell of a ride!

When I got home and Ann was waiting for me, I knew that I could never go back to Tracy. This was my life now and I was so glad that Ann had come into my life.

The final piece in the jigsaw of my new life was the news that Lesley was expecting a baby. At twenty five she was the perfect age to have a baby and it was due in September next year. I was overjoyed by the news, finding it hard to take in that I was going to be a grandfather.

Nowadays from the scans that they do in the early days of a pregnancy, it is possible to know what sex the baby is going to be. Whilst some couples do not want to know the sex, Lesley and Mike did. So, I was told by Lesley that it would be a boy. Her pregnancy went fine and on 6th September 2016 Leo Gareth Johnson was born. The Whitemore family line would continue for a few years more yet. embrace every new thing that occurred in my life. Things were finally looking up.

11 NEW LIFE

In the second week of September Ann and I drove down to Bath to see the new baby. The moment I first saw baby Leo Gareth, I was almost in tears again, yet I managed to hold my composure this time. To think that he was a part of me from a family line that went back to God knows when, was quite beyond words. As soon as I held him for the first time, I felt a great sense of pride that I was now a grandfather at the age of only forty nine; yet I didn't care about that. Here in my arms was my own flesh and blood, ready to carry on the next generation of my family.

Although he wasn't a Whitemore, he was still a part of me and for that I was extremely proud. Ann had knitted him some blue baby clothes which Lesley and Mike were extremely grateful for. They appreciated the effort that had gone into creating them and thanked Ann profusely for them. In a way Ann saw in Leo her own grandchild and we were all happy for her to see him that way.

We stayed for about an hour, watching Lesley feed him herself – she wasn't in the least bit bothered – and change his nappy before she put him down for a nap. It all brought back memories of when Lesley was just a tiny baby. I never forget how wonderful a new life is; all helpless and needy. Yet that tiny baby will eventually grow up into a man who will take his place in the world and hopefully be a force for good.

A few years ago, I dreaded going to family get togethers; whether it was a wedding, someone's special birthday, or an anniversary get together. I would be in fear of Tracy appearing and then losing it with me, as I really didn't want to cause a scene, or be caught up in one.

Nowadays, we have both settled down into our new lives. She is partly just somebody that I used to know, but she is partly the mother of our two children and the grandmother of our grandchild, and any future grandchildren for that matter. So, there is still a need to take care not to rock the boat. We both know that enough water has passed under the bridge for us to have forgiven each other the past.

* * *

One of the results of becoming a grandfather was that it started me thinking about my roots and where I came from. I'd heard tales from both my mum and dad about my grandparents and great grandparents. In fact, I could remember three of them from my childhood, but they had all died by the time I reached my twenties, mainly as a result of the poor childhoods they had, with lack of both basic health facilities and poor education.

I decided that I would like to find out as much about my ancestors as possible so that I could tell my grandson and any others that would come after him about his family history. I'd watched the TV programme *Who Do You Think You Are* lots of times and had found the stories of the celebrities featured on it fascinating, so it spurred me on to find out all about my family on both my father's and mother's sides.

One day I met up with my sister who had an old brown suitcase stuffed full of old photographs and papers which gave up a wealth of information on both sides of the family. Obviously, with the Whitemore side it was easier as there were more documents available such as my father's railway paperwork and army records. On my mum's side, the Daley's it was harder, especially as her grandfather had come over from Ireland during the Great Famine there. I began to look things up on the internet through the many websites that offered you access to all the birth, death, and marriage records – for a price.

In fact, the hobby of genealogy became an avid interest of mine. I loved going back in each family line, finding out the names of my various ancestors. But I also enjoyed trying to find out the details of their lives, such as what job they had, where they lived and what happy or sad events happened in their lives.

It was as a result of all the family history research that I was doing that I went over to Ireland to meet some of the relatives on my mother's side. Ann came with me and really enjoyed the trip. We found the Irish people that we met so welcoming and friendly that we said we should return again for a holiday sometime.

The main reason for going was that through my research I had found out that I had several distant cousins living in the centre of Ireland, mainly in the towns of Kildare and Tullamore. They were descendants of my great great grandfather, Patrick Daley who'd had three sons and two daughters. My great grandfather and his wife Megan, along with one of his sisters, Mary had come over to escape the famine and poverty that was so destructive in the Ireland of the 1840's. Of the children that stayed behind, two of them died whilst the third son survived and it from his line that I found several relatives, still living in Ireland today.

Another interest or hobby (if you can call it that), that I have started to do recently is to collect autographs. It all started when I decided to see if I could find the Manchester City signed picture that my dad had that my sister got rid of. It took a lot of time with several dealers looking out for it, but it did come up at auction last year and I successfully bid on it for the price of £535. It made me so happy to be reunited with that particular piece of memorabilia.

Since then, I have amassed a few more sets of autographs and posters as I soon caught the collecting bug. You have to be very careful as to whether they're genuine or not. I would never buy from one of those autograph and memorabilia shops you find in large shopping centres.

I usually buy from UK auction houses, but once in a while I might go for a US or a Japanese auction online. In these cases, it's important to make sure exactly what the exchange rate is and what that comes to in increments of thousands of pounds. These autographs aren't cheap, but I see them as a safe investment, seeing as once an artist or film star has passed away the demand for something connected with them will get greater as time goes on.

I am lucky enough to have bought a set of Beatles autographs, and also those of Jimi Hendrix, James Dean and Errol Flynn. I would love to get hold of an Elvis Presley autograph one day, but that is like finding the Holy Grail. With someone as big as him there are loads of fakes around and a possible genuine one would even be too much for my wallet.

Some experts reckon that the most sought after autographs can easily double their value in three to five years. That's a great return for your initial investment. I guess that some of you may be wondering why I haven't gone for pieces of art or antiques. The simple reason is that they just don't do it for me. I think if you want to go into the antiques market as an investor, you really need to know your stuff. Besides what would I do if I bought a Ming vase and then one day, I accidentally knocked it over!

I reckon that autographs are much easier to look after. Mind you, I don't have them on display in my house, as you never know who might pass on the information to someone else, who then passes it onto a burglar. You have to be so careful in my situation not to flaunt your wealth, as I learnt quite early on in this process.

* * *

I suppose some of you may be thinking with all that money in the bank, why did I never give any of it away to charity? Well yes, I did, and I still do. In the early days I was quite happy to give some of my lottery winnings away to charity, seeing as I had all that money that I didn't really need.

Most of the charities I gave to were the well-known ones who you might see advertising on television or in the newspapers. I deliberately didn't give them large amounts like thousands of pounds, but it kept it down to the hundreds. This was not because I was being mean, but rather the old chestnut of me not wanting to be found out as a lottery winner was the thing that influenced my donations. I preferred to spread out my donations over lots of different charities rather than just a few specific ones. With this method I felt that it was better that more charities and good causes would benefit from my giving, rather than just a few.

The problem though was that each time you made a donation they wanted your details, which I did guessing that I would be seen as just another donor rather than some rich millionaire. It did mean though that I soon got the inevitable letters and emails from them begging for more money, which I didn't like. So, like most members of the public, it put me off giving to them again.

Then I found out that some of these large, well known charities employed various staff, not just to fund raise, but also to run their operations. When I investigated this in more detail, I found out just how much some of their directors and chief executives earned and I was appalled. Surely if you work for a charity, you should be working not for peanuts of course, but not for six figure sums either. It was taking the piss I reckoned.

Nowadays, I tend to prefer to give donations to local charities that are doing lots of good at a local level, such as my homeless charity in Stockport. I am a big fan of the Channel 4 Programme *The Secret Millionaire* where a millionaire goes and lives in a particular town for a week or so and pretends to be doing a documentary on some local charity and then gives them some money at the end. I don't think it's on television anymore, but I would love to be on it. The only problem would be that everyone would know who I was, and my cover would be blown.

Taking a leaf from their book, I have started my own charity. My financial advisor knows all about it and although he is not that keen on me giving my money away, he has helped me set it up. The idea of it is to help local charities who are struggling to survive in the work they are doing at a local level.

It's called "Local Action and Development Support", or LADS for short. I am the founder and overseer, whilst the charity is run by my old school friend Jim McKeith, who employs a staff of five who go out all over the country checking out local charities and groups who need financial help to keep going. Naturally, we have been inundated with requests for help and Jim checks through each one individually and then one of the five staff that we employ will go and check out these groups to see what they're doing in practice and if they're genuine or not. When the staff are not visiting the local charities, they are involved in fundraising for the charity, as I am keen that it is not just reliant on my money per se. Otherwise, it would flounder and die when my money runs out.

So, in a way this new venture is keeping me busy and active, both in mind and body. More importantly though, it is helping me to repay back some of the money that I was given in the lottery win. It shows that it is not all spent by me on luxury items, but it is being used in a positive way to help those who are less fortunate than me.

* * *

One thing winning the lottery has given me the freedom to do so, is to travel anywhere I want to. More recently, I have started to go less far afield and have started to explore Britain more. After all, there is so much on our doorstep that we often take for granted, and rather than spend money and time travelling miles to a far off country I have found pleasure in visiting several places in Britain.

For instance, on one journey that Ann and I made, we drove down to Dorset, a county I had never been to before, seeing as it's only two hundred and fifty miles away from Manchester. Rather than driving there in one go, we stopped off on the way at Stratford-Upon-Avon, a place I last visited in my student days. We were able to see a performance of Shakespeare's *Coriolanus* at the Royal Shakespeare Theatre performed by some of the best actors I have ever seen. Ann was blown away. We also visited Shakespeare's birthplace and Anne Hathaway's Cottage, which she found delightful.

Then we drove onto Bournemouth where we stayed a few days, visiting such places as Poole, Dorchester, Salisbury, and Weymouth. We had a wonderful time and grew even closer than we were before we went away. So much so that we talked about the idea of getting married and before I knew it, I had proposed as we looked out onto Swanage Bay! On the way home, we called in to see Lesley and Mike and share the good news.

Lesley was fine about it and said, 'Dad. After all that you've been through, you deserve some happiness in your life. I truly hope you will both be very happy.'

If that's not a blessing, I don't know what is.

Jon, on the other hand was not so accepting. I realise that he sided more with Tracy when we split up and although we had gradually got closer together since then, there was still a gap between us. Maybe, being the youngest and a male, he was less accepting of Ann, hoping that there might be reconciliation between Tracy and me one day. I know that time is great healer and hope that he will finally accept Ann one day.

In Jan 2017 Ann and I went down to London for the weekend, partly to see a show in the West End and partly for me to meet her son, Harry for the first time. She had shown me pictures of him, and he certainly had his mother's looks. He worked in a theatre as part of the backstage crew and was pretty busy from four o'clock onwards each night, so we met him for lunch in a quiet restaurant away from the centre of town. He was very welcoming of me and brought his partner along, a guy called Josh who seemed a little shy and didn't join in the conversation much. I was fine with the fact that Harry was gay, though I suppose that some of my family might not be so open minded. I think it was important to meet Harry, as in a way Ann wanted to get his blessing and not see me as a threat. She hadn't told him of my lottery winnings just yet but had told him that I wasn't too short of a penny.

The other most important person in Ann's family after her son was her mother, who was now in her eighties. She lived in Derby, near to Ann's sister, Gemma who seemed to have taken on the role of looking after her. Like my mother, she was now in a nursing home and seemed to be quite settled there. One Sunday soon after we got back from Dorset, we drove over to Derby to see her. It was a pleasant drive through the Peak District via Buxton and only took us just over an hour.

We went to her sister's house first and unlike my old relationship with my sister, Ann's relationship with Gemma was one of mutual respect. She was very friendly and welcoming to me and said straight away, 'I've heard a lot about you Gary!' with a twinkle in her eye.

'All good, I hope?' was my immediate reply.

That seemed to break the ice and we chatted about the journey and the weather, before I asked her about her mother.

She warned me that she might be a bit reserved with me at first, but that was because she hardly knew me. I asked her if she had any particular interest and she said, 'Cliff Richard', so I made a mental note to check up some facts on the internet about him before we met.

Gemma drove us to the home which was about ten minutes' drive away.

When I actually came face to face with her, Gladys seemed a lot frailer than I expected, but still had the light shining in her eyes.

She was fine with me, and we seemed to hit it off straight away. Like me, she had been born in the North West, in Chester, so there was a common link straight away. Ann was relieved that she gave us her blessing and although she was too frail to attend our wedding later in the year, she still took an interest in all the preparations.

* * *

They say, "Life begins at Forty", but I would argue that "Life actually begins at Fifty!" In fact, as far as I am concerned Fifty is the new Forty! By that I mean that most people are younger both in mind and in body than their parents, and their parents in turn, were at the same age. With better health and education for most people nowadays, we seem to be ageing much slower than our parents did, and we seem more younger than our ancestors were at the same age. I mean who would have put money on the Rolling Stones still touring in their seventies?

For me becoming fifty was not something that scared me; something I didn't want to face; but rather a new chapter in my life. I know things had been up and down in my life for the past five years, but gradually I was sorting myself out again. What with the breakup of my marriage and the various addictions I had gone through, life should be a lot easier now?

I was eternally grateful to Richard for "sorting me out" and helping me to overcome all the fear and guilt that had been a part of my life ever since I had won the lottery. I now felt calmer and more focused, and I had direction in what I wanted to do with my life. My family had become important to me once again and now that I had found a new partner, life sure was rosy

The day of my second wedding will count as one of the happiest days of my life. I know that I said that my first wedding day was one of the happiest days of my life, but……. Well, that was true for the time; before things started going wrong. This time round I was so much more mature. I knew all the pros and cons of marriage and I knew the importance of being ready to compromise. I was determined it would last and all being well, will be for life.

We chose Saturday 17th June as the day. The significance of that was that it was my 50th birthday and I had been thinking of having a big party to celebrate that fact. Well why not have a double whammy and get married on the same day?!!

As both of us were divorced, we had the choice of a register office wedding or hiring a hotel somewhere. There was no question of it being the latter. We looked at several possible places first on the internet and then went and viewed ones that really appealed to us. We eventually settled on a hotel in the Lake District. We had actually stayed there on one of our jaunts around Britain and loved the setting, with gorgeous views across Lake Windermere to the fells beyond. Although it wasn't Manchester, it was still in the North West and for those who wished, we paid for them to stay at the hotel both before and after the wedding ceremony.

Luckily, the gods were kind to us as it was a glorious sunny day after six days solid of wet weather. Ann looked beautiful, dressed in a pale pink silk outfit, as she walked down the aisle of chairs to be next to me. She was given away by Harry, who shed a tear or two during the ceremony. I'm pleased to say that Jon was present along with his new girlfriend, as were Lesley and Mike along with my grandson, Leo who behaved impeccably. It was great that Richard was able to come along as well. It was testament to his care and advice that I was able to achieve such a momentous landmark in my life. Other friends included Jim McKeith, Tom Webster and some of my old school colleagues and university friends.

The reception was held in a marquee in the hotel grounds which had its own private beach by the lakeside and the party went on well into the small hours, with an eighties covers band playing some of both mine and Ann's favourite tunes.

I didn't invite Tracy though; not because I still wasn't having anything to do with her - the meeting a few months earlier had changed all that. It was more to be respectful to Ann. I'm sure she wouldn't have been happy having her new husband's ex-wife present! Tracy did know about it though, as we were talking to each other via email every so often.

Our honeymoon was just wonderful. Ann had always wanted to visit Venice and although I had been there on a school trip back in the 90's, I thought it was the perfect destination for us to spend our honeymoon in. We both had never been on a sleeper train before, so I agreed to us taking the luxury "Orient Express" train from London Victoria.

Both of us enjoyed the trip tremendously, leaving London Victoria just before 11 o'clock in the morning, going as far as Folkestone, where we got onto a coach. This took us to the Euro tunnel terminal where we got onto a Eurostar train to take us under the Channel to Calais, which was an experience in itself. Then we got back onto the coach which took us to Calais Ville station where we got onto the authentic 1920's carriages for a through journey all the way to Venice. We stopped at Paris, Innsbruck, and Verona on the way, before arriving in Venice shortly before half past six the next evening. Passing through the Alps on a train was a highlight in itself.

We then had three whole days in Venice taking in the sites like St Mark's Square, Doge's Palace and taking a trip on a gondola. The weather was hot as you would expect, but not stifling.

Coming back, we took a conventional train to Turin where we stayed overnight, before getting a High Speed train back to Paris. We then changed onto a Eurostar train taking us back to London St Pancras. Finally, we spent a couple of days in London, seeing Josh, as well as visiting some of London's sights which we had never visited before like Greenwich and Richmond. All in all, it was a delightful experience.

By now life for me had begun to be actually enjoyable once more, what with Ann in my life, all the broken relations "healed" - to a certain extent I suppose, and all the travelling we were doing. There was one other thing travel wise that I wanted to do which I'd never done in my life before, and that was to go on a cruise.

My sole experience of travelling by ship had been limited to a cross channel ferry. So, when Ann was suggesting places that we could visit in the future, the idea of taking a cruise to one of these places was mooted. At first, I wasn't that interested, but when we put our toe in the water by going on a mini-cruise to Bruges and Amsterdam for four days, our appetites were whetted.

We chose a Baltic Cruise as a way of celebrating our 50th birthdays as Ann was a little less than a year younger than me. The cruise took in the Scandinavian countries of Denmark, Sweden, and Finland, before reaching Russia and the city of St Petersburg. Here we would spend two days before returning via Poland and Norway. Neither of us had ever been to any of these countries before, so it would be great to see some places which not everyone goes to on their holidays. Plus, in St Petersburg we would have the opportunity of going to see Tchaikovsky's *Swan Lake* ballet performed in his home city.

So that's what we did in September, soon after baby Leo's first birthday party. We had possibly the best holiday I have ever had. I was relaxed and happy, as was Ann. The feeling of happiness that I now had was a state I hadn't really been in since my youth. Since then, there were always things going on in my life that made me anxious or unhappy.

Now I really didn't have any worries. My life had settled down again. I was now married to someone who I consider to be the love of my life. More importantly I was with someone I knew I could trust. This trust had been broken by Tracy in such a dramatic way that I never thought I could ever trust a woman again. Yet through all the experiences I have had since then, plus the wonderful counselling of Richard, coupled with me learning about mindfulness, I have come through to a more peaceful and relaxed life and lifestyle.

Another thing that happened on the cruise that halfway in I decided to put pen to paper so to speak and started writing this book. Richard had said that sometimes the best therapy for anyone who had gone through what I had is to write it all down and then forget about it.

So, in a way I suppose this book is me getting all that drama that I went through off my chest. It's been pretty painful at times writing this book, yet through it all I have learnt so much about life, about how people tick and most importantly of all, who I am and who I am not.

As I come to the end of this book and I look back at my life both before and after I won the lottery, I would say that it has certainly been an up and down ride. If I think of my life before winning the lottery, it was like going on an old fashioned roller coaster with a few ups and downs - nothing very extreme or scary. Then if I look back on my life since winning the lottery, I would liken it to going on a modern roller coaster super-scary ride with not just the very fast ups and downs, but also the fast twists and turns! Something I would never have expected as I got onto the ride.

I suppose my life could be split into three parts. The first part was my life before winning the lottery. The second part is my life since winning the lottery and the third part is the section yet to be written or should I say lived. I am definitely going to make sure that this third part will be nice and smooth, like a leisurely sail on a boating lake and not a voyage over a wild ocean!

Having spent the first fifty years of my life learning all that life has to throw at me, I am determined that the last twenty, thirty or even forty years are ones that I am going to enjoy and cherish.

I have my children who are now growing into responsible adults (I hope!); my grandchildren to cherish and guide as they grow older, and finally my new wife to love and appreciate. I will try to make sure that I don't make the same mistakes that I made with my first marriage.

For me, a good marriage is where you learn to give and take. You have to compromise at times if you are to stay together. You must have an open mind, plenty of patience, be prepared to forgive and forget, and always try to stay in love. You also need to give your partner their space to do their own things, just as you would expect them to do the same for you. That I believe is what makes for a good, lasting marriage, or should I say relationship. I didn't have to get married, but we both felt for us at least that was the best thing for us to do.

* * *

After all that I have been through, you might think that I am quite bitter about winning the lottery, seeing as it caused the breakup of my marriage, nearly killed me, and led me to becoming addicted to drink and drugs and turned me into something that I wasn't.

On the contrary, I have learnt through all these experiences that "Life is what you make it". If it wasn't for the help and guidance I received from Richard, I don't think I would be here today. He helped me to go inside myself and find "the real me" if you like, not the person who I thought I should be or who I wished I could be.

He showed me that essentially, we are all human beings with our strengths and our weaknesses, our good points, and our bad points. In a way there is a constant battle going on inside us as to who will win. He also taught me that we are all souls on a journey here on Earth, each having experiences which are teaching us "life's lessons" that are there to make us a better human being in the end.

These experiences that we all have could be called 'good' or 'bad', yet perhaps might be better thought of as 'positive' or 'negative'. We can't have one without the other; otherwise, we wouldn't have anything to compare them with. Plus, we would never make progress on this journey and would get stuck somewhere, as many people do who become addicted to all sorts of human behaviours.

In other words, it is what we experience in life that makes us the person we are. Having experienced both loss and gain in my life, I would hope that I have finally balanced out everything and am now leading a happy yet controlled and fulfilled life.

I no longer look back on my life and think, "If only I did this or that", or "I wish I hadn't done that". I now accept the past and move on. I don't focus on what might have happened. Instead, I am now looking to the future. In a way, the future is all that there is.

I admit that I'm still finding my way in life. Aren't we all when push comes to shove?

We, as human beings, are constantly striving to make our lives easier, or better, or nicer in some way and for many, no matter how hard we work, there is very little reward. We have this eternal hope that one day things will get better for us

As my dear father always used to say, "Count your blessings. You never know what you've really got until it's gone."

So, learn to be grateful for what you have got. Things like having a roof over your head, food on the table, clothes on your body and peace in your country. We may not have as much money as we want, but it is important to learn that money isn't everything. I should know.

It's having people in your life that really matters I would say. Having lots of money doesn't necessarily make you happier. It can make life easier, but at the same time it can bring lots of other problems that you don't expect. Again, I should know.

So, my final words after sharing this part of my life's journey with you are:

"Be careful what you wish for."

Printed in Great Britain
by Amazon